PRAISE FOR THOMAS LIGOTTI

'Thomas Ligotti is an absolute master of supernatural horror and weird fiction, and is a true original. He pursues his unique vision with admirable honesty and rigorousness and conveys it in prose as powerfully evocative as any writer in the field. I'd say he might just be a genius.' Ramsey Campbell

'Ligotti is wonderfully original; he has a dark vision of a new and special kind, a vision that no one had before him.' *Interzone*

'[Ligotti's] is a unique voice, which speaks with a profound elegance – and a precious seriousness – of matters which few other literary voices have ever touched – Ligotti is old-fashioned in the very best sense of the term and there is nothing dated about his work, which is unmistakably contemporary.' Brian Stableford in *Horror, Ghost & Gothic Writers*

'Ligotti gave me the first genuine frisson – in the literal sense of the term – that I had received in years. His work made me realize why I had become a student of weird fiction to begin with – it was to experience that indescribable sensation of being *unnerved*.' S. T. Joshi, author of *The Modern Weird Tale*, in *Horror: Another 100 Best Books*

'Ligotti is arguably the pre-eminent living writer of horror fiction.' Matt Cardin (in *The Thomas Ligotti Reader*)

'*Songs of a Dead Dreamer* is full of inexplicable and alarming delights . . . Put this volume on the shelf right between H. P. Lovecraft and Edgar Allan Poe. Where it belongs.' Michael Swanwick, *The Washington Post*

'*Grimscribe* confirms [Ligotti] as an accomplished conjuror of nightmares in the tradition of H. P. Lovecraft.' *The Times*

'In *Grimscribe* Ligotti manages to write that secret book, presenting us with stories that are paradoxically beautiful and horrific.' *San Francisco Chronicle*

'The most disturbing terror comes from within, springs unexpectedly from bland or half-formed memories of the past. This is the terror that Ligotti cultivates in the richly evocative tales of *Noctuary*.' *Booklist*

'*My Work Is Not Yet Done* displays a Thomas Ligotti at the height of his form – in imaginative range, in verve of style and precision of language, and in cumulative power and intensity.' S. T. Joshi, *Necrofile*

ABOUT THE AUTHOR

Thomas Ligotti was born in Detroit in 1953 and grew up in the nearby suburb of Grosse Pointe Woods. He graduated from Wayne State University in 1978. From 1979 to 2001, Ligotti worked for a reference book publisher in the Detroit area, serving as an editor on such titles as *Twentieth-Century Literary Criticism* and *Contemporary Authors*. His first collection of stories, *Songs of a Dead Dreamer*, was published in 1986, with an expanded version issued three years later. Other collections include *Grimscribe* (1991), *Noctuary* (1994), and *My Work Is Not Yet Done* (2002).

Ligotti is the recipient of several awards, including the Horror Writers Association Bram Stoker award for his omnibus collection *The Nightmare Factory* (1996) and short novel *My Work Is Not Yet Done*. He has also written a nonfiction book, *The Conspiracy Against the Human Race: A Short Life of Horror*, which comprises an excursion through the darker byways of literature, philosophy and psychology. A short film of Ligotti's story *The Frolic* was completed in 2006 and is scheduled to appear as a DVD. In addition, through an agreement with Fox Studios' subsidiary Fox Atomic, a graphic novel based on his works was released in 2007. For more information visit: http://www.ligotti.net

TEATRO GROTTESCO

Thomas Ligotti

PENGUIN BOOKS

This paperback edition first published in Great Britain in
2008 by
Virgin Books Ltd
Thames Wharf Studios
Rainville Road
London
W6 9HA

First published in hardback in the US in 2006 by Durtro.

A catalogue record for this book is available from the British
Library.

ISBN 978 0 7535 13743 UK

Distributed in the USA by MacMillan, LLC,
175 Fifth Avenue, New York, NY 10010, USA

Typeset by TW Typesetting, Plymouth, Devon

Printed and bound in Great Britain by Clays Ltd, Elcograf S.p.A.

CONTENTS

CONTENTS

DERANGEMENTS

PURITY

We were living in a rented house, neither the first nor the last of a long succession of such places that the family inhabited throughout my childhood years. It was shortly after we had moved into this particular house that my father preached to us his philosophy of 'rented living.' He explained that it was not possible to live in any other way and that attempting to do so was the worst form of delusion. 'We must actively embrace the reality of *non-ownership*,' he told my mother, my sister and me, towering over us and gesturing with his heavy arms as we sat together on a rented sofa in our rented house. 'Nothing belongs to us. Everything is something that is rented out. Our very heads are filled with rented ideas passed on from one generation to the next. Wherever your thoughts finally settle is the same place that the thoughts of countless other persons have settled and have left their impression, just as the backsides of other persons have left their impression on that sofa where you are now sitting. We live in a world where every surface, every opinion or passion, everything altogether is tainted by the bodies and minds of strangers. Cooties – intellectual cooties and physical cooties from other people – are crawling all around us and all over us at all times. There is no escaping this fact.'

Nevertheless, it was precisely this fact that my father seemed most intent on escaping during the time we spent in that house. It was an especially cootie-ridden residence in a bad neighborhood that bordered on an even worse neighborhood. The place was also slightly haunted, which was more or less the norm for the habitations my father chose to rent. Several times a year, in fact, we packed up at one place and settled into another, always keeping a considerable distance between our locations, or relocations. And every time we entered one of our newly rented houses for the first time, my father would declaim that this was a place where he could 'really get something accomplished.' Soon afterward, he would begin spending more and more time in the basement of the house, sometimes living down there for weeks on end. The rest of us were banned from any intrusion on my father's lower territories unless we had been explicitly invited to participate in some project of his. Most of the time I was the only available subject, since my mother and sister were often away on one of their 'trips,' the nature of which I was never informed of and seldom heard anything about upon their return. My father referred to these absences on the part of my mother and sister as 'unknown sabbaticals' by way of disguising his ignorance or complete lack of interest in their jaunts. None of this is to protest that I minded being left so much to myself. (Least of all did I miss my mother and her European cigarettes fouling the atmosphere around the house.) Like the rest of the family, I was adept at finding ways to occupy myself in some wholly passionate direction, never mind whether or not my passion was a rented one.

One evening in late autumn I was upstairs in my bedroom preparing myself for just such an escapade when the doorbell rang. This was, to say the least, an uncommon event for our household. At the time, my mother and sister were away on one of their sabbaticals, and my father had not emerged from his basement for many days. Thus, it seemed up to me to answer the startling sound of the doorbell, which I had not heard since we had moved into the house and could not remember hearing in any of the other rented houses in which I spent my childhood. (For some reason I had always believed that my father disconnected all the doorbells as soon as we relocated to a newly rented house.) I moved hesitantly, hoping the intruder or intruders would be gone by the time I arrived at the door. The doorbell rang again. Fortunately, and incredibly, my father had come up from the basement. I was standing in the shadows at the top of the stairs when I saw his massive form moving across the living room, stripping himself of a dirty lab coat and throwing it into a corner before he reached the front door. Naturally I thought that my father was expecting this visitor, who perhaps had something to do with his work in the basement. However, this was obviously not the case, at least as far as I could tell from my eavesdropping at the top of the stairs.

By the sound of his voice, the visitor was a young man. My father invited him into the house, speaking in a straightforward and amiable fashion that I knew was entirely forced. I wondered how long he would be able to maintain this uncharacteristic tone in conversation, for he bid the young man to have a seat in the living room where the two of them could talk 'at leisure,' a locution that sounded absolutely bizarre as spoken by my father.

'As I said at the door, sir,' the young man said, 'I'm going around the neighborhood telling people about a very worthy organization.'

'Citizens for Faith,' my father cut in.

'You've heard of our group?'

'I can read the button pinned to the lapel of your jacket. This is sufficient to allow me to comprehend your general principles.'

'Then perhaps you might be interested in making a donation,' said the young man.

'I would indeed.'

'That's wonderful, sir.'

'But only on the condition that you allow me to *challenge* these absurd principles of yours – to really put them to the test. I've actually been hoping that you, or someone like you, would come along. It's almost as if a fortuitous element of intervention brought you to this house, if I were to believe in something so preposterous.'

So ended my father's short-lived capitulation to straightforwardness and amiability.

'Sir?' said the young man, his brow creasing a bit with incomprehension.

'I will explain. You have these two principles in your head, and possibly they are the only principles that are holding your head together. The *first* is the principle of nations, countries, the whole hullabaloo of mother lands and father lands. The *second* is the principle of deities. Neither of these principles has anything real about them. They are merely impurities poisoning your head. In a single phrase – Citizens for Faith – you have incorporated two of the *three* major principles – or impurities – that must be eliminated, completely eradicated, before our species can begin an approach to a pure conception of existence. Without pure conception, or something approaching pure conception, everything is a disaster and will continue to be a disaster.'

'I understand if you're not interested in making a donation, sir,' said the young man, at which point my father dug his hand into the right pocket of his trousers and pulled out a wad of cash that was rolled into a tube and secured with a thick rubber band. He held it up before the young man's eyes.

'This is for you, but only if you will give me a chance to take those heinous principles of yours and clean them out of your head.'

'I don't believe my faith to be something that's just in my head.'

Until this point, I thought that my father was taunting the young man for pure diversion, perhaps as a means of distracting himself from the labors in which he had been engaged so intensely over the past few days. Then I heard what to my ears was an ominous shift in my father's words, signifying his movement from the old-school iconoclast he had been playing to something desperate and unprincipled with respect to the young man.

'Please forgive me. I didn't mean to suggest that anything like that was *only* in your head. How could such a thing be true when I know quite well that something of the kind inhabits this very house?'

'He is in every house,' said the young man. 'He is in all places.'

'Indeed, indeed. But something like that is very much in this particular house.'

My suspicion was now that my father made reference to the haunted condition – although it barely deserved the description – of our rented house. I myself had already assisted him in a small project relevant to this condition and what its actual meaning might be, at least insofar as my father chose to explain such things. He even allowed me to keep a memento of this 'phase-one experiment,' as he called it. I was all but sure that this was the case when my father alluded to his basement.

'Basement?' said the young man.

'Yes,' said my father. 'I could show you.'

'Not in my head but in your basement,' said the young man as he attempted to clarify what my father was claiming.

'Yes, yes. Let me show you. And afterward I will make a generous donation to your group. What do you say?'

The young man did not immediately say anything, and perhaps this was the reason that my father quickly shouted out my name. I backed up a few steps and waited, then descended the stairway as if I had not been eavesdropping all along.

'This is my son,' my father said to the young man, who stood up to shake my hand. He was thin and wore a second-hand suit, just as I imagined him while I was eavesdropping at the top of the stairs. 'Daniel, this gentleman and I have some business to conduct. I want you to see that we're not disturbed.' I simply stood there as if I had every intention of obediently following these instructions. My father then turned to the young man, indicating the way to the basement. 'We won't be long.'

No doubt my presence – that is, the *normality* of my presence – was a factor in the young man's decision to go into the basement. My father would have known that. He would not know, nor would he have cared, that I quietly left the house as soon as he had closed the basement door behind him and his guest. I did consider lingering for a time at the house, if only to gain some idea of what phase my father's experimentation had now entered, given that I was a participant in its early stages. However, that night I was eager to see a friend of mine who lived in the neighborhood.

To be precise, my friend did not live in the *bad* neighborhood where my family had rented a house but in the *worse* neighborhood nearby. It was only a few streets away, but this was the difference between a neighborhood where some of the houses had bars across their doors and windows and one in which there was nothing left to protect or to save or to care about in any way. It was another world altogether ... a twisted paradise of danger and derangement ... of crumbling houses packed extremely close together ... of burned-out houses leaning toward utter extinction ... of houses with black openings where once there had been doors and windows ... and of empty fields over which shone a moon that was somehow different from the one seen elsewhere on this earth.

Sometimes there would be an isolated house hanging onto the edge of an open field of shadows and shattered glass.

And the house would be so contorted by ruin that the possibility of its being inhabited sent the imagination swirling into a pit of black mysteries. Upon closer approach, one might observe thin, tattered bedsheets in place of curtains. Finally, after prolonged contemplation, the miracle of a soft and wavering glow would be revealed inside the house.

Not long after my family moved into a vicinity where such places were not uncommon, I found one particular house that was nothing less than the ideal of the type of residence, so to speak, I have just described. My eyes became fixed upon it, held as if they were witnessing some miraculous vision. Then one of the bedsheets that covered the front window moved slightly, and the voice of a woman called out to me as I stood teetering on the broken remnants of a sidewalk.

'Hey, you. Hey, boy. You got any money on you?'

'Some,' I replied to that powerful voice.

'Then would you do something for me?'

'What?' I asked.

'Would you go up to the store and get me some salami sticks? The long ones, not those little ones. I'll pay you when you come back.'

When I returned from the store, the woman again called out to me through the glowing bedsheets. 'Step careful on those porch stairs,' she said. 'The door's open.'

The only light inside the house emanated from a small television on a metal stand. The television faced a sofa that seemed to be occupied from end to end by a black woman of indefinite age. In her left hand was a jar of mayonnaise, and in her right hand was an uncooked hot dog, the last one from an empty package lying on the bare floor of the house. She submerged the hot dog into the mayonnaise, then pulled it out and finished it off without taking her eyes from the television. After licking away some mayonnaise from her fingers, she screwed the lid back on the jar and set it to one side on the sofa, which appeared to be the only piece of furniture in the room. I held out the salami sticks to her, and she put some money in my hand. It was the exact amount I had paid, plus one dollar.

I could hardly believe that I was actually standing inside one of the houses I had been admiring since my family moved into the neighborhood. It was a cold night, and the house was unheated. The television must have operated on batteries, because it had no electrical cord trailing behind it. I felt as if I had crossed a great barrier to enter an outpost that had been long abandoned by the world, a place cut off from reality itself. I wanted to ask the woman if I might be allowed to curl up in some corner of that house and never again leave it. Instead, I asked if I could use the bathroom.

She stared at me silently for a moment and then reached down behind the cushions of the sofa. What she brought forth was a flashlight. She handed it to me and said, 'Use this and watch yourself. It's the second door down that hall. Not the first door – the second door. And don't fall in.'

As I walked down the hall I kept the flashlight focused on the gouged and filthy wooden floor just a few feet ahead of me. I opened the second door, not the first, then closed it behind me. The room in which I found myself was not a toilet but a large closet. Toward the back of the closet there was a hole in the floor. I shone the flashlight into the hole and saw that it led straight into the basement of the house. Down there were the pieces of a porcelain sink and commode, which must have fallen through the floor of the bathroom that was once behind the first door I had passed in the hallway. Because it was a cold night, and the house was unheated, the smell was not terribly strong. I knelt at the edge of the hole and shone the flashlight into it as far its thin beam would reach. But the only other objects I could see were some broken bottles stuck within the strata of human waste. I thought about what other things might be in that basement . . . and I became lost in those thoughts.

'Hey, boy,' I heard the woman call out. 'Are you all right?'

When I returned to the front of the house, I saw that the woman had other visitors. When they held up their hands in front of their faces, I realized that I still had the shining flashlight in my hand. I switched it off and handed it back to the woman on the sofa.

'Thank you,' I said as I maneuvered my way past the others and toward the front door. Before leaving I turned to the woman and asked if I might come back to the house.

'If you like,' she said. 'Just make sure you bring me some of those salami sticks.'

That was how I came to know my friend Candy, whose house I visited many times since our first meeting on that thrilling night. On some visits, which were not always at night, she would be occupied with her business, and I would keep out of her way as a steady succession of people young and old, black and white, came and went. Other times, when Candy was not so busy, I squeezed next to her on the sofa, and we watched television together. Occasionally we talked, although our conversations were usually fairly brief and superficial, stalling out as soon as we arrived at some chasm that divided our respective lives and could not be bridged by either of us. When I told her about my mother's putrid European cigarettes, for instance, Candy had a difficult time with the idea of 'European,' or perhaps with the very word itself. Similarly, I would often be unable to supply a context from my own life that would allow me to comprehend something that Candy would casually interject as we sat watching television together. I had been visiting her house for at least a month when, out of nowhere, Candy said to me, 'You know, I had a little boy that was just about your age.'

'What happened to him?' I asked.

'Oh, he got killed,' she said, as if such an answer explained itself and warranted no further elaboration. I never urged Candy to expand upon this subject, but neither could I forget her words or the resigned and distant voice in which she had spoken them.

Later I found out that quite a few children had been killed in Candy's neighborhood, some of whom appeared to have been the victims of a child-murderer who had been active throughout the worst neighborhoods of the city for a number of years before my family moved there. (It was, in fact, my mother who, with outrageous insincerity, warned me about 'some dangerous pervert' stealthily engaged in cutting kids' throats right and left in what she called 'that terrible neighborhood where your friend lives.') On the night that I left our rented house after my father had gone into the basement with the young man who was wearing a second-hand suit, I thought about this child-murderer as I walked the streets leading to Candy's house. These streets gained a more intense hold upon me after I learned about the child killings, like a nightmare that exercises a hypnotic power forcing your mind to review its images and events over and over no matter how much you want to forget them. While I was not interested in actually falling victim to a child-murderer, the threat of such a thing happening to me only deepened my fascination with those crowded houses and the narrow spaces between them, casting another shadow over the ones in which that neighborhood was already enveloped.

As I walked toward Candy's house, I kept one of my hands in the pocket of my coat where I carried something that my father had constructed to be used in the event that, to paraphrase my irrepressibly inventive parent, anyone ever tried to inflict personal harm upon me. My sister was given an identical gadget, which looked something like a fountain pen. (Father told us not to say anything about these devices to anyone, including my mother, who for her part had long ago equipped herself with self-protection in the form of a small-caliber automatic pistol.) On several occasions I had been tempted to show this instrument to Candy, but ultimately I did not break the vow of secrecy on which my father had insisted. Nevertheless, there was something else my father had given me, which I carried in a small paper bag swinging at my side, that I was excited to show Candy that night. No restrictions had been placed on disclosing this to anyone, although it probably never occurred to my father that I would ever desire to do so.

What I carried with me, contained in a squat little jar inside the paper bag, was a by-product, one might say, of the first-phase experiment in which I had assisted my father not long after we moved into our rented house. I have already mentioned that, like so many of the houses where my family lived during my childhood years, our current residence was imbued with a certain haunted aspect, however mild it may have been in this instance. Specifically, this haunting was manifested in a definite presence I sensed in the attic of the house, where I spent a great deal of time before I became a regular visitant at Candy's. As such things go, in my experience, there was nothing especially noteworthy about this presence. It seemed to be concentrated near the wooden beams which crossed the length of the attic and from which, I imagined, some former inhabitant of the house may once have committed suicide by hanging. Such speculation, however, was of no interest to my father, who strongly objected to the possibility of spooks or spirits of any kind or even the use of these terms. 'There is nothing in the attic,' he explained to me. 'It's only the way that your head is interacting with the space of that attic. There are certain fields of forces that are everywhere. And these forces, for reasons unknown to me as yet, are potentiated in some places more than others. Do you understand? The attic is not haunting your head – your head is haunting the attic. Some heads are more haunted than others, whether they are haunted by ghosts or by gods or by creatures from outer space. These are not real things. Nonetheless, they are *indicative* of real forces, animating and even creative forces, which your head only conceives to be some kind of spook or who knows what. You are going to help me prove this by allowing me to use my apparatus in the basement to siphon from your head that thing which you believe is haunting the attic. This siphoning will take place in a very tiny part of your head, because if I siphoned your whole head . . . well, never mind about that. Believe me, you won't feel a thing.'

After it was over, I no longer sensed the presence in the attic. My father had siphoned it away and contained it in a small jar, which he gave to me once he was through with it as an object of research, his first phase of experimentation in a field in which, unknown to other scientists who have since performed similar work, my father was the true Copernicus or Galileo or whomever one might care to name. However, as may be obvious by now, I did not share my father's scientific temperament. And although I no longer felt the presence in the attic, I was entirely resistant to abandoning the image of someone hanging himself from the wooden beams crossing the length of a lonely attic and leaving behind him an unseen guideline to another world. Therefore, I was delighted to find that the sense of this presence was restored to me in the portable form of a small jar, which, when I cupped it tightly in my hands, conveyed into my system an even more potent sense of the supernatural than I had previously experienced in the attic. This was what I was bringing to Candy on that night in late autumn.

When I entered Candy's house, there was no business going on that might distract us from what I had to show her. There were in fact two figures slumped against the wall on the opposite side of the front room of the house, but they seemed inattentive, if not completely oblivious, to what was happening around them.

'What did you bring for Candy?' she said, looking at the paper bag I held in my hand. I sat down on the sofa beside her, and she leaned close to me.

'This is something . . .' I started to say as I removed the jar from the bag, holding it by its lid. Then I realized that I had no way to communicate to her what it was I had brought. It was not my intention to distress her in any way, but there was nothing I could say to prepare her. 'Now don't open it,' I said. 'Just hold it.'

'It looks like jelly,' she said as I placed the jar in her meaty hands.

Fortunately, the contents of the jar presented no disturbing images, and in the glowing light of the television they took on a rather soothing appearance. She gently closed her grip on the little glass container as if she were aware of the precious nature of what was inside. She seemed completely unafraid, even relaxed. I had no idea what her reaction would be. I knew only that I wanted to share with her something that she could not otherwise have known in this life, just as she had shared the wonders of her house with me.

'Oh my God,' she softly exclaimed. 'I knew it. I knew that he wasn't gone from me. I knew that I wasn't alone.'

Afterward, it occurred to me that what I had witnessed was in accord with my father's assertions. Just as my head had been haunting the attic with the presence of someone who had hanged himself, Candy's head was now haunting the jar with a presence of her own design, one which was wholly unlike my own. It seemed that she wished to hold on to that jar forever. Typically, forever was about to end. A nondescript car had just pulled up and stopped in front of Candy's house. The driver quickly exited the vehicle and slammed its door behind him.

'Candy,' I said, 'There's some business coming.'

I had to tug at the jar to free it from her grasp, but she finally let it go and turned toward the door. As usual, I wandered off to one of the back rooms of the house, an empty bedroom where I liked to huddle in a corner and think about all the sleeping bodies that had dreamed there throughout innumerable nights. But on this occasion I did not huddle in a corner. Instead, I kept watch on what was happening in the front room of the house. The car outside had come to a stop too aggressively, too conspicuously, and the man in the long coat who walked toward the house moved in a way that was also too aggressive, too conspicuous. He pushed open the door of Candy's house and left it open after he stepped inside.

'Where's the white kid?' said the man in the long coat.

'No white people in here,' said Candy, who held her eyes on the television. 'Not including you.'

The man walked over to the two figures across the room and gave each of them a nudge with his foot.

'If you didn't know, I'm the one who lets you do business.'

'I know who you are, Mr Police Detective. You're the one who took my boy. You took other ones too, I know that.'

'Shut up, fat lady. I'm here for the white kid.'

I took the pen out of my pocket and pulled off the top, revealing a short, thick needle like the point of a pushpin. Holding the pen at my side and out of sight, I walked back down the hallway.

'What do you want?' I said to the man in the long coat.

'I'm here to take you home, kid.'

If there was anything I had ever known in my life as a cold, abstract certainty, it was this: if I went with this man, I would not be going home.

'Catch,' I said as I threw the little jar at him.

He caught the jar with both hands, and for a moment his face flashed a smile. I have never seen a smile die so quickly or so completely. If I had blinked, I would have missed the distressed transition. The jar then seemed to jump out of his hands and onto the floor. Recovering himself, he took a step forward and grabbed me. I have no reason to think that Candy or the others in the room saw me jab the pen into his leg. What they saw was the man in the long coat releasing me and then crumbling into a motionless pile. Evidently the effect was immediate. One of the two figures stepped out of the shadows and gave the fallen man the same kind of contemptuous nudge that had been given to him.

'He's dead, Candy,' said the one figure.

'You sure?'

The other figure rose to his feet and mule-kicked the head of the man on the floor. 'Seems so,' he said.

'I'll be damned,' said Candy, looking my way. 'He's all yours. I don't want no part of him.'

I found the jar, which fortunately was unbroken, and went to sit on the sofa next to Candy. In a matter of minutes, the two figures had stripped the other man down to his boxer shorts. Then one of them pulled off the boxer shorts, saying, 'They look practically new.' However, he stopped pulling soon enough when he saw what was under them. We all saw what was there, no doubt about that. But I wondered if the others were as confused by it as I was. I had always thought about such things in an ideal sense, a mythic conception handed down over the centuries. But it was nothing like that.

'Put him in the hole!' shouted Candy, who had stood up from the sofa and was pointing toward the hallway. 'Put him in the goddamn hole!'

They dragged the body into the closet and dropped it into the basement. There was a slapping sound made by the unclothed form as it hit the floor down there. When the two figures came out of the closet, Candy said, 'Now get rid of the rest of this stuff and get rid of the car and get rid of yourselves.'

Before exiting the house, one of the figures turned back. 'There's a big hunk of cash here, Candy. You're going to need some traveling money. You can't stay here.'

To my relief, Candy took part of the money. I got up from the sofa and set the jar on the cushion beside my friend.

'Where will you go?' I asked.

'There are plenty of places like this one in the city. No heat, no electricity, no plumbing. And no rent. I'll be all right.'

'I won't say anything.'

'I know you won't. Good-bye, boy.'

I said good-bye and wandered slowly home, dreaming all the while about what was now in Candy's basement.

By the time I arrived at the house it was after midnight. My mother and sister must have also returned because I could smell the stench from my mother's European cigarettes as soon as I took two steps inside. My father was lying on the living-room sofa, clearly exhausted after so many days of working in the basement. He also seemed quite agitated, his eyes wide open and staring upward, his head moving back and forth in disgust or negation or both, and his voice repeatedly chanting, 'Hopeless impurities, hopeless impurities.' Hearing these words helped to release my thoughts from what I had seen at Candy's. They also reminded me that I wanted to ask my father about something he had said to the young man in the second-hand suit who had visited the house earlier that night. But my father's condition at the moment did not appear to lend itself to such talk. In fact, he betrayed no awareness whatever of my presence. Since I did not yet feel up to confronting my mother and sister, who I could now hear were moving about upstairs (probably still unpacking from their trip), I decided to take this opportunity to violate my father's sanctions against entering the basement without his explicit authorization. This, I believed, would provide me with something to take my mind off the troubling events of that night.

However, as I descended the stairs into my father's basement, I felt my mind and senses being pulled back into the dark region of Candy's basement. Even before I reached the bottom of the stairs, that underground place imposed upon me its atmosphere of ruin and wreckage and of an abysmal chaos that, I was thankful to discover, I still found captivating. And when I saw the state of things down there, I was overcome with a trembling awe that I had never experienced before.

Everything around me was in pieces. It looked as if my father had taken an ax and hacked up the whole apparatus on which he had once placed all his hopes of accomplishing some task that only he cared to envision. Wires and cords hung from the ceiling, all of them chopped through and dangling like vines in a jungle. A greasy, greenish liquid was running across the floor and sluicing into the basement drain. I waded through an undergrowth of broken glass and torn papers. I reached down and picked up some of the pages savagely ripped from my father's voluminous note-books. Meticulous diagrams and graphs were obscured by words and phrases written with a thick, black marker. Page after page had the word 'IMPURE' scrawled over them like graffiti on the walls of a public toilet. Other recurring exclamations were: 'NOTHING BUT IMPURITIES,' 'IM-PURE HEADS,' 'NOTHING REVEALED,' 'NO PURE CONCEPTION,' 'IMPOSSIBLE IMPURITIES,' and, finally, 'THE FORCES OF AN IMPURE UNIVERSE.'

At the far end of the basement I saw a hybrid contraption that looked as if it were a cross between a monarch's throne and an electric chair. Bound to this device by straps confining his arms and legs and head was the young man in a second-hand suit. His eyes were open, but they had no focus in them. I noticed that the greasy, greenish liquid had its source in a container the size of a water-cooler bottle that was upended next to the big chair. There was a label on the container, written on masking tape, that read SIPHONAGE. Whatever spooks or spirits or other entities had inhabited the young man's head – and my father appeared to have drained off a sizeable quantity of this stuff – were now making their way into the sewer system. They must have lost something, perhaps grown stale, once released from their container, because I felt no aura of the spectral – either malignant or benign – emanating from this residual sub-stance. I was unable to tell if the young man was still alive in any conventional sense of the word. He may have been. In any case, his condition was such that my family would once again need to find another house in which in live.

'What happened down here?' said my sister from the other side of the basement. She was sitting on the stairs. 'Looks like another one of dad's projects took a bad turn.'

'That's the way it looks,' I said, walking back toward the stairs.

'Do you think that guy was carrying much money on him?'

'I don't know. Probably. He was here collecting for some kind of organization.'

'Good, because mom and I came back broke. And it's not as if we spent all that much.'

'Where did you go?' I said, taking a seat beside my sister.

'You know I can't talk about that.'

'I had to ask.'

After a pause, my sister whispered, 'Daniel, do you know what a hermaphrodite is?'

I tried my best to conceal any reaction to my sister's question, even though it had caused a cyclone of images and emotions to arise within me. That was what had confused me about the police detective's body. In my imagination, I had always pictured a neat separation of parts. But it was nothing like that, as I have already pointed out. Everything was all mixed together. Thank you, Elisa. Despite her adherence to my mother's strict rule of silence, my sister always managed to give away something of what they had been up to.

'Why do ask that?' I said, also whispering. 'Did you meet someone like that when you were with mom?'

'Absolutely not,' she said.

'You have to tell me, Elisa. Did mom ... did she talk about me ... did she talk about me to this person?'

'I wouldn't know. I really wouldn't,' said Elisa as she rose to her feet and walked back upstairs. When she reached the top step, she turned around and said, 'How's this thing between you and mom going to end? Every time I mention your name, she just clams up. It doesn't make any sense.'

'The forces of an impure universe,' I said rhetorically.

'What?' said my sister.

'Nothing that drives anybody makes any sense, if you haven't noticed that by now. It's just our heads, like dad's always saying.'

'Whatever that means. Anyway, you better keep your mouth shut about what I said. I'm never telling you anything ever again,' she finished and then went upstairs.

I followed my sister into the living room. My father was now sitting up on the sofa next to my mother, who was opening boxes and pulling things out of bags, presumably showing what she had bought on her latest trip with Elisa. I sat down in a chair across from them.

'Hi, baby,' said my mother.

'Hi, Mom,' I said, then turned to my father. 'Hey, Dad, can I ask you something?' He still seemed a bit delirious. 'Dad?'

'Your father's very tired, honey.'

'I know. I'm sorry. I just want to ask him one thing. Dad, when you were talking to that guy, you said something about three . . . you called them principles.'

'Countries, deities,' said my father from a deep well of depression. 'Obstacles to pure conception.'

'Yeah, but what was the *third* principle? You never said anything about that.'

But my father had faded out and was now gazing disconsolately at the floor. My mother, however, was smiling. No doubt she had heard all of my father's talk many times over.

'The third principle?' she said, blowing a cloud of cigarette smoke in my direction. 'Why, it's families, sweetheart.'

THE TOWN MANAGER

O ne gray morning not long before the onset of winter, some troubling news swiftly travelled among us: the town manager was not in his office and seemed nowhere to be found. We allowed this situation, or apparent situation, to remain tentative for as long as we could. This was simply how we had handled such developments in the past.

It was Carnes, the man who operated the trolley which ran up and down Main Street, who initially recognized the possibility that the town manager was no longer with us. He was the first one who noticed, as he was walking from his house at one end of town to the trolley station at the other end, that the dim lamp which had always remained switched on inside the town manager's office was now off.

Of course, it was not beyond all credibility that the lightbulb in the lamp that stood in the corner of the town manager's desk had simply burned out or that there had been a short circuit in the electrical system of the small office on Main Street. There might even have been a more extensive power failure that also affected the rooms above the office, where the town manager resided since he had first arrived among us to assume his duties. Certainly we all knew the town manager as someone who was in no way vigilant regarding the state of either his public office or his private living quarters.

Consequently, those of us in the crowd that had gathered outside the town manager's office, and his home, considered both the theory of an expired lightbulb and that of an electrical short circuit at some length. Yet all the while, our agitation only increased. Carnes was the one whose anxiety over this matter was the most severe, for the present state of affairs had afflicted him longer than anyone else, if only by a few minutes. As I have already indicated, this was not the first time that we had been faced with such a development. So when Carnes finally called for action, the rest of us soon abandoned our refuge in the theoretical. 'It's time to do something,' said the trolley driver. 'We have to know.'

Ritter, who ran the local hardware store, jimmied open the door to the town manager's office, and several of us were soon searching around inside. The place was fairly neat, if only by virtue of being practically unfurnished. There was simply a chair, a desk, and the lamp on top of the desk. The rest of it was just empty floor space and bare walls. Even the drawers of the desk, as some of the more curious members of our search party discovered, were all empty. Ritter was checking the wall socket into which the lamp's cord was plugged, and someone else was inspecting the fuse box at the back of the office. But these were merely stall tactics. No one wanted to reach under the lampshade and click the switch to find out whether the bulb had merely burned out or, more ominously, the place had been given over to darkness by design. The latter action, as all of us were aware, signaled that the tenure of any given town manager was no longer in effect.

At one time, our nexus of public services and functions was a traditional town hall rising up at the south end of Main Street. Rather than a small lamp clinging to the edge of a time-worn desk, that impressive structure was outfitted with a great chandelier. This dazzling fixture served as a beacon assuring us that the town's chief official was still with us. When the town hall fell into decay and finally had to be abandoned, other buildings gave out their illumination – from the upper floors of the old opera house (also vacated in the course of time) to the present storefront office that had more recently served as the center of the town's civic administration. But there always came a day when, without notice to anyone in the town, the light went out.

'He's not upstairs,' Carnes yelled down to us from the town manager's private rooms. At that precise moment, I had taken it upon myself to try the light switch. The bulb lit up, and everyone in the room went mute. After a time, somebody – to this day I cannot recall who it was – stated in a resigned voice, 'He has left us.'

Those were the words that passed through the crowd outside the town manager's office . . . until everyone knew the truth. No one even speculated that this development might have been caused by mischief or a mistake. The only conclusion was that the old town manager was no longer in control and that a new appointment would be made, if in fact this had not already been done.

Nonetheless, we still had to go through the motions. Throughout the rest of that gray morning and into the afternoon, a search was conducted. Over the course of my life, these searches were performed with increasingly greater speed and efficiency whenever one town manager turned up missing as the prelude to the installation of another. The buildings and houses comprising our town were now far fewer than in my childhood and youth. Whole sections that had once been districts of prolific activity had been transformed by a remarkable corrosion into empty lots where only a few bricks and some broken glass indicated that anything besides weeds and desiccated earth had ever existed there. During my years of youthful ambition, I had determined that one day I would have a house in a grand neighborhood known as The Hill. This area was still known as such, a designation bitterly retained even though the real estate in question – now a rough and empty stretch of ground – no longer rose to a higher elevation than the land surrounding it.

After satisfying ourselves that the town manager was nowhere to be found within the town, we moved out into the countryside. Just as we were going through the motions when we searched inside the town limits, we continued going through the motions as we tramped through the landscape beyond them. As previously stated, the time of year was close to the onset of winter, and there were only a few bare trees to obstruct our view in any direction as we wandered over the hardening earth. We kept our eyes open, but we could not pretend to be meticulous searchers.

In the past, no town manager had ever been found, either alive or dead, once he had gone missing and the light in his office had been turned off. Our only concern was to act in such a way that would allow us to report to the new town manager, when he appeared, that we had made an effort to discover the whereabouts of his predecessor. Yet this ritual seemed to matter less and less to each successive town manager, the most recent of whom barely acknowledged our attempts to locate the dead or living body of the previous administrator. 'What?' he said after he finally emerged from dozing behind the desk in his office.

'We did the best we could,' repeated one of us who had led the search, which on that occasion had taken place in early spring. 'It stormed the entire time,' said another.

After hearing our report, the town manager merely replied, 'Oh, I see. Yes, well done.' Then he dismissed us and returned to his nap.

'Why do we even bother?' said Leeman the barber when we were outside the town manager's office. 'We never find anything.'

I referred him and the others to the section of the town charter, a brief document to be sure, that required 'a fair search of the town and its environs' whenever a town manager went missing. This was part of an arrangement that had been made by the founders and that had been upheld throughout succeeding generations. Unfortunately, nothing in the records that had come to be stored in the new opera house, and were subsequently lost to the same fire that destroyed this shoddily constructed building some years before, had ever overtly stated with whom this arrangement had been made. (The town charter itself was now only a few poorly phrased notes assembled from recollections and lore, although the specifics of this rudimentary document were seldom disputed.) At the time, no doubt, the founders had taken what seemed the best course for the survival and prosperity of the town, and they forged an arrangement that committed their descendants to this same course. There was nothing extraordinary about such actions and agreements.

'But that was years ago,' said Leeman on that rainy spring afternoon. 'I for one think that it's time to find out just who we're dealing with.'

Others agreed with him. I myself did not disagree. Nonetheless, we never did manage to broach the subject with the old town manager. But as we walked across the countryside on that day so close to the onset of winter, we talked among ourselves and vowed that we would pose certain questions to the new town manager, who usually arrived not long after the disappearance or abdication of the previous administrator, sometimes on the very same day.

The first matter we wished to take up was the reason we were required to conduct a futile search for missing town managers. Some of us believed that these searches were merely a way of distracting us, so that the new town manager could take office before anyone had a chance to observe by what means he arrived or from what direction he came. Others were of the opinion that these expeditions did in fact serve some purpose, although what that may have been was beyond our understanding. Either way, we were all agreed that it was time for the town – that is, what there was left of it – to enter a new and more enlightened era in its history. However, by the time we reached the ruined farmhouse, all our resolutions dissolved into the grayness in which that day had been enveloped.

Traditionally, the ruined farmhouse, along with the wooden shed that stood nearby, marked the point at which we ended our search and returned to town. It was now close to sundown, which would give us just enough time to be back in our homes before dark once we had made a perfunctory inspection of the farmhouse and its shed. But we never made it that far. This time we kept our distance from that farmhouse, which was no more than a jagged and tilting outline against the gray sky, as well as from the shed, a narrow structure of thin wooden planks that someone had hammered together long ago. There was something written across those weathered boards, markings that none of us had ever seen before. They were scored into the wood, as if with a sharp blade. Some of the letters were either missing or unreadable in the places where they were gouged into planks that had separated from one another. Carnes the trolley man was standing at my side.

'Does that say what I think it says?' he said to me, almost in a whisper.

'I think so.'

'And the light inside?'

'Like smoldering embers,' I said concerning the reddish glow that was shining through the wooden slats of the shed.

Having recognized the arrival of the new town manager – from whatever direction and by whatever means he may have come – we all turned away and walked silently toward town, pacing slowly through the gray countryside that day by day was being seized by the coming winter.

Despite what we had come across during our search, we soon reconciled ourselves to it, or at least we had reached a point where we no longer openly expressed our anxiety. Did it really matter if, rather than occupying a building on Main Street with a sign that read TOWN MANAGER over the door, the one who now held this position chose to occupy a shed whose rotting wooden planks had roughly the same words inscribed upon them with a sharp blade? Things had always been moving in that direction. At one time the town manager conducted business from a suite of offices in the town hall and lived in a fine house in The Hill district of town. Now this official would be working out of a weather-beaten shed next to a ruined farmhouse. Nothing remained the same for very long. Change was the very essence of our lives.

My own situation was typical. As previously mentioned, I had ambitions of owning a residence in The Hill district. For a time I operated a delivery business that almost certainly would have led to my attaining this goal. However, by the time the old town manager arrived, I was sweeping the floors at Leeman's barbershop and taking whatever odd jobs came along. In any case, my drive to build up a successful delivery business was all but extinguished once The Hill district had eroded away to nothing.

Perhaps the general decline in the conditions of the town, as well as the circumstances of its residents, could be attributed to poor officiating on the part of our town managers, who in many ways seemed to be less and less able in their duties as one succeeded another over the years. Whatever apprehensions we had about the new town manager, it could not be said that the old town manager had been a model administrator. For some time before his term came to an end, he had spent the whole of each working day asleep behind his desk.

On the other hand, every town manager could be credited with introducing some element of change, some official project of one kind or another, that was difficult to condemn as wholly detrimental. Even if the new opera house had never been anything but a shoddily constructed firetrap, it nonetheless represented an effort at civic rehabilitation, or at least gave this impression. For his part, the old manager had been responsible for the trolley which ran up and down Main Street. In the early days of his administration, he had brought in workers from outside the town to construct this monument to his spirit of innovation. Not that there had ever been a great outcry for such a conveyance in our town, which could easily be traversed from one end to the other either on foot or by bicycle without causing the least exertion to those of us who were in reasonably good health. Nevertheless, once the trolley had been built, most of us rode the thing at one time or another, if only for the novelty of it. Some people, for whatever reason, made regular use of this new means of transportation and even seemed to depend on it to carry them the distance of only a few blocks. If nothing else, the trolley provided Carnes with regular employment, which he had not formerly enjoyed.

In brief, we had always managed to adapt to the ways of each town manager who had been sent to us. The difficult part was waiting for new administrators to reveal the nature of their plans for the town and then adjusting ourselves to whatever form they might take. This was the system in which we had functioned for generations. This was the order of things into which we had been born and to which we had committed ourselves by compliance. The risk of opposing this order, of plunging into the unknown, was simply too much for us to contemplate for very long. But we did not foresee, despite having witnessed the spectacle of the shed beside the ruined farmhouse, that the town was about to enter a radically new epoch in its history.

The first directive from the new town manager was communicated to us by a torn piece of paper that came skipping down the sidewalk of Main Street one day and was picked up by an old woman, who showed it to the rest of us. The paper was made from a pulpy stock and was brownish in color. The writing on the paper looked as if it had been made with charred wood and resembled the same hand that had written those words across the old boards of the town manager's shed. The message was this: DUSTROY TROLY.

While the literal sense of these words was apparent enough, we were reluctant to act upon a demand that was so obscure in its point and purpose. It was not unprecedented for a new town manager to obliterate some structure or symbol that marked the administration of the one who had come before him, so that the way might be cleared for him to erect a defining structure or symbol of his own, or simply to efface any prominent sign of the previous order and thereby display the presence of a new one. But usually some reason was offered, some excuse was made, for taking this action. This obviously was not the case with the town manager's instruction to destroy the trolley. So we decided to do nothing until we received some enhancement regarding this matter. Ritter suggested that we might consider composing a note of our own to request further instructions. This note could be left outside the door of the town manager's shed. Not surprisingly, there were no volunteers for this mission. And until we received a more detailed notice, the trolley would remain intact.

The following morning the trolley came tooting down Main Street for its first run of the day. However, it made no stops for those waiting along the sidewalk. 'Look at this,' Leeman said to me as he stared out the front window of his barbershop. Then he went outside. I set my broom against a wall and joined him. Others were already standing on the street, watching the trolley until it finally came to rest at the other end of town. 'There was no one at the switch,' said Leeman, an observation that a number of persons echoed. When it seemed that the trolley was not going to make a return trip, several of us walked down the street to investigate. When we entered the vehicle, we found the naked body of Carnes the trolley driver lying on the floor. He had been severely mutilated and was dead. Burned into his chest were the words: DUSTROY TROLY.

We spent the next few days doing exactly that. We also pulled up the tracks that ran the length of the town and tore down the electrical system that had powered the trolley. Just as we were completing these labors, someone spotted another piece of that torn, brownish paper. It was being pushed about by the wind in the sky above us, jerking about like a kite. Eventually it descended into our midst. Standing in a circle around the piece of paper, we read the scrawled words of the message. 'GUD,' it said. 'NXT YUR JBS WULL CHNG.'

Not only did our jobs change, but so did the entire face of the town. Once again, workmen came from outside with orders to perform various kinds of construction, demolition, and decoration that began along Main Street and ultimately extended into the outlying neighborhoods. We had been instructed by the usual means not to interfere with them. Throughout the deep gray winter, they worked on the interiors of the town's buildings. With the coming of spring, they finished off the exteriors and were gone. What they left behind them was a place that did not resemble a town as much as it did a carnival funhouse. And those of us who lived there functioned as sideshow freaks once we had been notified, by the usual method, of exactly how our jobs had changed.

For example, Ritter's Hardware had been emptied of its traditional merchandise and restructured as an elaborate maze of lavatories. Upon entering the front door you immediately found yourself standing between a toilet and a sink. Built into one of the walls of this small room was another door that opened upon another lavatory that was somewhat larger in dimensions. This room had two doors that led to further lavatories, some of which could be reached only by ascending a spiral staircase or walking down a long, narrow corridor. Each lavatory differed somewhat in size and décor. None of the lavatories was functional. The exterior of Ritter's Hardware was given a new façade constructed of large stone blocks and a pair of fake towers standing on either side of the building and rising some distance above it. A sign above the front door designated the former hardware store COMFORT CASTLE.

Ritter's new job was to sit in a chair on the sidewalk outside his former place of business wearing a simple uniform with the word ATTENDANT displayed in sewn lettering below the left shoulder.

Leeman the barber was even less fortunate in the new career that had been assigned to him. His shop, renamed 'Baby Town,' had been refurbished into a gigantic playpen. Amid stuffed animals and an array of toys, Leeman was required to languish in infants' clothing sized for an adult.

All of the businesses along Main Street had been transformed in some manner, although their tone was not always as whimsical as Ritter's Comfort Castle or Leeman's Baby Town. A number of the buildings appeared simply as abandoned storefronts – until one explored the interior and discovered that the back room was actually a miniature movie theater where foreign cartoons were projected upon a bare wall or that hidden in the basement was an art gallery filled entirely with paintings and sketches of questionable taste. Sometimes these abandoned storefronts were precisely what they appeared to be, except you would find yourself locked inside once the door had closed, forcing you to exit out the back.

Behind the stores of Main Street was a world of alleys where it was perpetually night, an effect created by tunnel-like arcades enclosing this vast area. Dim lamps were strategically placed so that no stretch of alley was entirely in darkness as you wandered between high wooden fences or brick walls. Many of the alleys ended up in someone's kitchen or living room, allowing an escape back into the town. Some of them kept growing more and more narrow until no further progress was possible and every step leading to this point needed to be retraced. Other alleys gradually altered as one walked along their length, eventually presenting a complete change of scene from that of a small town to one of a big city where screams and sirens could be heard in the distance, although these sounds were only recordings piped in through hidden speakers. It was in just such a vicinity, where painted theatrical backdrops of tall tenement buildings with zig-zagging fire escapes rose up on every side, that I worked at my own new job.

At the terminus of an obscure alley where steam was pumped through the holes of a false sewer grating, I had been stationed in a kiosk where I sold soup in paper cups. To be more accurate, it was not actually soup that I was given to sell but something more like bouillon. Behind the counter that fronted my kiosk there was a thin mattress on the floor where I could sleep at night, or whenever I felt like sleeping, since it seemed unlikely that any customers would venture through that labyrinth of alleys so that I might serve them. I subsisted on my own bouillon and the water I used to concoct this desolate repast. It seemed to me that the new town manager would finally succeed in the task which his predecessors had but lazily pursued over the years: that of thoroughly bleeding the town of the few resources that had been left to it. I could not have been more wrong in this assessment.

Within a matter of weeks, I had a steady stream of customers lined up outside my bouillon concession who were willing to pay an outrageous price for my watery, yellowish liquid. These were not my fellow citizens but people from outside. I noticed that nearly all of them carried folded brochures which either extruded from their pockets or were grasped in their hands. One of these was left behind on the counter that fronted my kiosk, and I read it as soon as business slowed down. The cover of the brochure bore the words HAVE A FUN TIME IN FUNNY TOWN. Inside were several captioned photographs of the various 'attractions' that our town had to offer to the curious tourist. I was in awe of the town manager's scheme. Not only had this faceless person taken our last penny to finance the most extensive construction project the town had ever seen, from which there was no doubt a considerable amount of kickback involved, but this ingenious boondoggle had additionally brought an unprecedented flood of revenue into our town.

Yet the only one who truly prospered was the town manager. Daily, sometimes hourly, collections were made at each of the town's attractions and concessions. These were carried out by solemn-faced strangers who were visibly armed with an array of weapons. In addition, I noticed that spies had been integrated among the tourists, just to insure that none of us withheld more than a meager allotment of the profits that derived from the town's new enterprise. Nonetheless, whereas we had once had reason to expect nothing less than total impoverishment under the governance of the town manager, it now appeared that we would at least survive.

One day, however, the crowds of tourists began to thin out. In short order, the town's new business dwindled to nothing. The solemn-faced men no longer bothered to make their collections, and we began to fear the worst. Hesitantly, we started to emerge from our places and gathered together on Main Street under a sagging banner that read WELCOME TO FUNNY TOWN.

'I think that's it,' said Ritter, who was still wearing his bathroom attendant's uniform.

'Only one way to be sure,' said Leeman, now back in adult clothes.

Once again we tramped out to the countryside under a gray sky some weeks before the onset of winter. It was approaching dusk, and long before we reached the town manager's shed we could see that no reddish light glowed inside. Nevertheless, we searched the shed. Then we searched the farmhouse. There was no town manager. There was no money. There was nothing.

When the rest of them turned away and began to head back to town, I stayed behind. Another town manager would arrive before long, and I did not wish to see what form the new administration would take. This was the way it had always been – one town manager succeeding another, each of them exhibiting signs of greater degeneracy, as if they were festering away into who knows what. And there was no telling where it would all end. How many others would come and go, taking with them more and more of the place where I had been born and was beginning to grow old? I thought about how different that place had been when I was a child. I thought about my youthful dream of having a home in The Hill district. I thought about my old delivery business.

Then I walked in the opposite direction from the town. I walked until I came to a road. And I walked down that road until I came to another town. I passed through many towns, as well as large cities, doing clean-up work and odd jobs to keep myself going. All of them were managed according to the same principles as my old home town, although I came upon none that had reached such an advanced stage of degeneracy. I had fled that place in hopes of finding another that had been founded upon different principles and operated under a different order. But there was no such place, or none that I could find. It seemed the only course of action left to me was to make an end of it.

Not long after realizing the aforementioned facts of my existence, I was sitting at the counter of a crummy little coffee shop. It was late at night, and I was eating soup. I was also thinking about how I might make an end of it. The coffee shop may have been in a small town or a large city. Now that I think of it, the place stood beneath a highway overpass, so it must have been the latter. The only other customer in the place was a well-dressed man sitting at the other end of the counter. He was drinking a cup of coffee and, I noted, directing a sidelong glance at me every so often. I turned my head toward him and gave him a protracted stare. He smiled and asked if he could join me at my end of the counter.

'You can do whatever you like. I'm leaving.'

'Not just yet,' he said as he sat down at the counter stool next to mine. 'What business are you in?'

'None in particular. Why?'

'I don't know. You just seem like someone who knows his way around. You've been some places, am I right?'

'I suppose so,' I said.

'I thought as much. Look, I'm not just interested in chit-chat here. I work on commission finding people like you. And I think you've got what it takes.'

'For what?' I asked.

'Town management,' he replied.

I finished off the last few spoonfuls of my soup. I wiped my mouth with a paper napkin. 'Tell me more,' I said.

It was either that or make an end of it.

SIDESHOW, AND OTHER STORIES

FOREWORD

At the time I met the man who authored the stories that follow, I had reached a crisis point in my own work as a writer of fiction. This gentleman, who was considerably older than I, was several steps ahead of me along the same path. 'I have always desired to escape,' he said, 'from *the grip of show business.*' He said these words to me across the table in a corner booth of the coffee shop where all our meetings took place in the late hours of the night.

We had been first introduced by a waitress working the night shift who noticed we were both insomniacs who came into the coffee shop and sat for many hours smoking cigarettes (the same brand), drinking the terrible decaffeinated coffee they served in that place, and every so often jotting something in the respective notebooks which we both kept at hand. 'All of the myths of mankind are nothing but show business,' the other man said to me during our initial meeting. 'Everything that we supposedly live by and supposedly die by – whether it's religious scriptures or makeshift slogans – all of it is show business. The rise and fall of empires – show business. Science, philosophy, all of the disciplines under the sun, and even the sun itself, as well as all those other clumps of matter wobbling about in the blackness up there –' he said to me, pointing out the window beside the coffee-shop booth in which we sat, 'show business, show business, show business.' 'And what about dreams?' I asked, thinking I might have hit upon an exception to his dogmatic view, or at least one that he would accept as such. 'You mean the dreams of the sort we are having at this moment or the ones we have when we're fortunate enough to sleep?' I told him his point was well taken and withdrew my challenge, having only half-heartedly advanced it in the first place. The conversation nevertheless proceeded along the same course – he submitting one example after another of *show business phenomena*; I attempting to propose plausible exceptions to the idiosyncratic doctrine with which he seemed hopelessly obsessed – until we went our separate ways just before dawn.

That first meeting set the tone and fixed the subject matter of my subsequent encounters in the coffee shop with the gentleman I would come to regard as my lost literary father. I should say that I deliberately encouraged the gentleman's mania and did all I could to keep our conversations focused on it, since I felt that his show-business obsession related in the most intimate way with my own quandary, or crisis, as a writer of fiction. What exactly did he mean by 'show business'? Why did he find the 'essentially show-business nature' of all phenomena to be problematic? How did his work as an author coincide with, or perhaps oppose, what he called the 'show-business world'?

'I make no claims for my writing, nor have any hopes for it as a means for escaping the grip of show business,' he said. 'Writing is simply another action I perform *on cue*. I order this terrible coffee because I'm in a second-rate coffee shop. I smoke another cigarette because my body tells me it's time to do so. Likewise, I write because I'm *prompted* to write, nothing more.'

Seeing an entrance to a matter more closely related to my own immediate interest, or quandary or crisis, I asked him about his writing and specifically about what focus it might be said to have, what 'center of interest,' as I put it.

'My focus, or center of interest,' he said, 'has always been the wretched show business of my own life – an autobiographical wretchedness that is not even first-rate show business but more like a series of sideshows, senseless episodes without continuity or coherence except that which, by virtue of my being the ringmaster of this miserable circus of sideshows, I *assign* to it in the most bogus and show-businesslike fashion, which of course fails to maintain any genuine effect of continuity or coherence, inevitably so. But this, I've found, is the very essence of show business, all of which in fact is no more than *sideshow* business. The unexpected mutations, the sheer baselessness of beings, the volatility of things ... By necessity we live in a world, a sideshow world, where everything is ultimately peculiar and ultimately ridiculous.'

'By what standard?' I interjected before his words – which had arrived at the very heart of the crisis, quandary, and suffocating cul-de-sac of my existence as a writer of fiction – veered away. 'I said by what standard,' I repeated, 'do you consider everything peculiar and ridiculous?'

After staring at me in a way that suggested he was not only considering my question, but was also evaluating me and my entire world, he replied: 'By the standard of that unnameable, unknowable, and no doubt nonexistent order that is *not* show business.'

Without speaking another word he slid out of the corner booth, paid his check at the counter cash register, and walked out of the coffee shop.

That was the last occasion on which I spoke with this gentleman and fellow writer. The next time I visited the coffee shop and sat in the corner booth, the waitress who worked the night shift presented me with a small sheaf of pages. 'He said to give these to you and that he wouldn't be back for them.'

'That's all he said?' I asked.

'That's all,' she answered.

I thanked her, ordered a decaffeinated coffee, lit a cigarette, and began to read the tales that follow.

I. THE MALIGNANT MATRIX

For years I had been privileged to receive frequent and detailed communications regarding the most advanced scientific and metaphysical studies. This information was of a highly specialized nature that seemed to be unknown to the common run of scientists and metaphysicians, yet was nevertheless attainable by such avid non-specialists as myself, providing of course that one possessed a receptive temperament and willingly opened oneself to certain channels of thought and experience.

One day I received a very special communication whereby I learned that an astounding and quite unexpected breakthrough had been achieved – the culmination, it appeared, of many years of intense scientific and metaphysical study. This breakthrough, the communication informed me, concerned nothing less than the discovery of the true origins of all existential phenomena, both physical and metaphysical – the very source, as I understood the claims being made, of existence in the broadest possible sense. This special communication also told me that I had been selected to be among those who would be allowed a privileged view of everything involved in this startling breakthrough discovery, and therefore would be guaranteed a rare insight into the true origins of all existential phenomena. Since I was an individual who was highly receptive in temperament to the matter at hand, I need only present myself at the particular location where this incredible advance in scientific and metaphysical knowledge had occurred.

Scrupulously I followed the directions communicated to me, even though, for reasons that were not explained, I was not fully apprised of the specifics of my actual destination. Nevertheless, I could not help imagining that I would ultimately find myself a visitor at a sophisticated research facility of some kind, a shining labyrinth of the most innovative devices and apparatus of extraordinary complexity. The place where I finally arrived, however, in no way conformed to my simple-minded and deplorably conventional expectations. This scientific and metaphysical installation, as I thought of it, was located in a large building, but one that was very old. I entered it, according to my instructions, through a small door that I found at the end of a dark and narrow alley that ran along the side of the old building. I opened the door and stepped inside, barely able to see two paces in front of me, for by now it was the middle of the night. There was a faint click as the door closed behind my back, and all I could do was wait for my eyesight to adjust to the darkness.

Moonlight shone down through a window somewhere above me and spread dimly across a dirty concrete floor. I could see that I was standing at the bottom of an empty stairwell. I heard faint sounds of something dragging itself directly toward me. Then I saw what it was that emerged from a shadowy area of that empty stairwell. It was a head supported by a short length of neck on which it pulled itself along like a snail, moving by inches upon the concrete floor. Its features were indistinct yet nonetheless seemed deformed or mutilated, and it was making sounds whose meaning I could not comprehend, its angular jaw opening and closing mechanically. Before the head moved very close to me I noticed there was something else in another, even more shadowy corner of that bleak, moonlit stairwell. Not much larger than the head that was approaching me across the floor, this other object was to my eyes an almost wholly shapeless mass, quite pale, which I was able to identify as *animated tissue* only because, every so often, it opened itself up like a giant bivalved mollusk found at great suboceanic depths. And it made the same sound as the crawling head was making, both of them crying out at the bottom of that dim and empty stairwell, the place, I had been informed, where I might confront the source of all existential phenomena.

I thought that I might have been misled, as I stood there listening to the cries of those creatures at the bottom of that empty stairwell, and I left that place through the door by which I had entered it. But just as that door was closing behind me I realized how much those sounds I heard reminded me of the tiny voices of things which, however imperfect their form, have been newly thrust into the world of phenomenal existence.

II. PREMATURE COMMUNICATION

Early one winter morning during my childhood, while I was still lying in bed upstairs, watching a few snowflakes floating outside my bedroom window, I heard a voice from downstairs say these words: 'The ice is breaking up on the river.' This voice was like no other that was familiar to me. It was very harsh and yet very quiet at the same time, as though a heap of rusted machinery had whispered something from the shadows of an old factory. Nothing else was said by this voice.

When I left my room and went downstairs, I found my parents in the kitchen as they usually were at that time on winter mornings, my father reading the newspaper and my mother preparing breakfast while the same snowflakes which were floating outside the window of my room upstairs were now floating so slowly outside the kitchen window. Before I could say anything to either of my parents, my mother suddenly told me that I would have to stay inside the house for the rest of the day, offering no reason for making this demand. In reaction I asked, in the words of a child, if my confinement to the house that day had anything to do with the words that the voice had spoken, that 'the ice was breaking up on the river.' From across the kitchen my father looked up at my mother, neither of them saying a word. In that moment I realized for the first time how many things in the world were entirely unknown to me, how reticent, often wholly silent, were the people and places of my small childhood world.

I have no memory of the explanation my mother or my father might have offered me as the reason why I had to stay in the house the rest of that day. Actually I had no desire to go outdoors that winter morning, not while that voice, whose mystery remained undispelled by my mother or my father, continued to speak to me in its harsh and quietly distant tone from all the dim corners of the house, as the snowflakes floated outside every window, repeating over and over that the ice was breaking up on the river.

It was not many days afterward that my parents placed me in a hospital where I was administered several potent medications and other forms of treatment. On the way to the hospital my father restrained me in the back seat of the car while my mother served as driver, and I calmed down only during those brief moments when we passed across an old bridge that was built over a fairly wide river which I had never before seen.

During my stay in the hospital I found that it was the medications I was given, rather than the other forms of treatment, that allowed me to grasp the nature of the voice which I had heard on a particular winter morning. I knew that my parents would be crossing that old bridge whenever they came to visit me at the hospital, so on the day when my doctor and a close relative of mine appeared in my room to explain to me the details of a certain 'tragic event,' I was the first one to speak. Before they could tell me of my mother and father's fate, and the way in which it had all happened, I said to them: 'The ice has broken up on the river.'

And the voice speaking these words was not the voice of a child but a harsh yet whispery voice emanating from the depths of that great and ancient machinery which powered, according to its own faulty and unknown mechanisms, the most infinitesimal movements of the world as I knew it. Thus, as my doctor and a close relative of mine explained further what had happened to my parents, I only stared out the window, watching the machinery (into which I had now been assimilated) as it produced each snowflake that fell one by one outside the window of my hospital room.

III. THE ASTRONOMIC BLUR

Along a street of very old houses there was a building that was not a house at all but a little store which kept itself open for business at all hours of the day and night, every single day of the year. At first the store appeared to me as merely primitive, a throwback to some earlier time when a place of business might be allowed to operate in an otherwise residential district, however decayed the houses of the neighborhood may have been. But it was much more than primitive in the usual sense, for the little store declared no name for itself, offered no outward sign to give an indication of its place in the world around it. It was only the local residents who called it 'the little store,' when they spoke of it at all.

There was a small window beside the dark wooden door of the building, but if one tried to peer through the foggy glass of this window, nothing recognizable could ever be seen – only a swirling blur of indefinite shapes. And although the building's interior lights were always left on, even in the middle of the night, it was not the bright steady illumination of electricity that seemed to shine through the window of the place but a dim, vaguely flickering glow. Neither was anyone spied who might have been regarded as the proprietor of the little store, and no one was ever seen either going into or coming out of it, least of all the people in the surrounding neighborhood. Even if a passing car stopped in front and someone got out of the vehicle with the apparent intention of entering the store, they would never get farther than the sidewalk before turning around, getting back inside their car, and driving away. The children in the area always crossed to the opposite side of the street when walking by the little store.

Of course I was curious about this building from the time I first moved into one of the old houses in the neighborhood. I immediately noticed what I then considered the primitive, virtually primal nature of the little store, and I would at great length observe this darkly luminous structure whenever I went out walking, as I often did, in the late hours of the night. I followed this practice for some time, never noticing any change in the little store, never seeing anything that I had not seen the first night I began observing the place.

Then one night something did change in the little store, and something also changed in the neighborhood around it. It was only for a moment that the dim glow burning within the little store seemed to flare up before returning to its usual state of a dull, smoldering flicker. This was all that I saw. Nevertheless, that night I did not return to my home, because it was now glowing with the same primordial light as that within the little store. All the old houses in the neighborhood were lit up in the same way, all of their little windows glowing dimly at that late hour. *No one will ever again emerge from those houses*, I thought as I abandoned the streets of that neighborhood. *Nor will anyone ever desire to enter them*.

Perhaps I had seen too deeply into the nature of the little store, and it was simply warning me to look no further. On the other hand, perhaps I had been an accidental witness to something else altogether, some plan or process whose ultimate stage is impossible to foresee, although there still comes to me, on certain nights, the dream or mental image of a dark sky in which the stars themselves burn low with a dim, flickering light that illuminates an indefinite swirling blur wherein it is not possible to observe any definite shapes or signs.

IV. THE ABYSS OF ORGANIC FORMS

For years I lived with my half-brother, who had been confined to a wheelchair since childhood due to a congenital disease of the spine. Although placid much of the time, my brother, or rather half-brother, would frequently gaze upon me with a bitter and somehow brutish stare. His eyes were such a strange shade of gray, so pale and yet so luminous, that they were the first thing one noticed upon approaching him, and the fact that he inhabited a wheelchair always took second place to the unusual, the truly demonic character of his eyes, in which there was something that I could never bring myself to name.

It was only on rare occasions that my half-brother left the house in which he and I lived together, and these were almost exclusively those times when, at his insistence, I took him to a local racecourse where horses ran most afternoons during the racing season. There we watched the animals come parading out onto the track and run every race from first to last on a given day, never placing a single wager on any of them, although we always brought home a racing program which contained the names and performance statistics relating to all the horses we had seen. For years I observed my brother, as he sat in his wheelchair just behind the fence that bordered the racetrack, and I noticed how intensely he gazed upon those horses, his gray eyes displaying a different aspect altogether from the bitter and brutish quality they always assumed when we were at home. On days when we did not visit the racecourse, he would pore over the old racing programs containing the names of countless horses and the complex statistics relating to their competitive performance, as well as information regarding their physical nature, including the age of the horses and their various colors, whether brown or bay, roan or gray.

One day I returned to the house where I had lived for many years with my half-brother and found his wheelchair empty in the middle of our living room. Surrounding it in a circle were pieces of paper torn from the old racing programs that my brother collected. A rather considerable mound of these scraps of paper were heaped around my brother's, my half-brother's, wheelchair, and on each of them was printed the name of one of the many horses we had seen on our visits to the racecourse. I myself was quite familiar with these names: Avatara, Royal Troubadour, Hallview Spirit, Mechanical Harry T, and so on. Then I noticed that there was a trail of these torn pieces of paper which seemed to lead away from the wheelchair and toward the front door. I followed them outside the house, where I found a few more fragments of old racing programs out on the porch. But the trail ended even before I reached the sidewalk, the small scraps of paper having been dispersed by the brisk winds of a cold September day. After investigating for some time, I could find nothing to indicate what had become of my brother – that is, my half-brother – and nor could anyone else. No explanation by any agency or person ever sufficiently illuminated the reason for or method of his disappearance.

It was not long after this incident that, for the first time in my life, I went alone to the racecourse which my brother and I had visited together on so many previous occasions. There I watched the horses come parading out onto the track for each race from first to last.

Following the final race of the day, as the horses were leaving the track to return to the area where they were kept in barns, I saw that one of these animals, a roan stallion, had eyes that were the palest and most peculiar shade of gray. When this particular horse passed the spot where I was standing, these eyes turned upon me, staring directly into my own eyes in a way that seemed bitter and thoroughly brutish and which conveyed to me the sense of something unusual, something truly demonic that I could never bring myself to name.

V. THE PHENOMENAL FRENZY

For a time I had been looking to buy a house in which, barring unforeseen developments, I was planning to live out the rest of my life. During this period of house-searching, I found myself considering properties that were increasingly distant from those nearest to them, until ultimately my search for a house in which to live out the rest of my life took place entirely in remote areas miles from the most out-of-the-way towns. I myself was sometimes surprised at the backroad landscapes in which I ventured to investigate some old place where a real estate agent had sent me or upon which I simply happened in the course of wandering farther and farther from any kind of developed region, or even one that had the least proximity to other houses.

It was while driving my car through one of these backroad landscapes, on a windy November afternoon, that I discovered the sort of isolated house which at that point was the only conceivable place where I could live out the rest of my life with any chance of being at peace in the world. Although this two-story frame structure stood in a relatively level and austere backroad landscape, with a few bare trees and a ruined water tower intervening between it and the dull autumnal horizon, I did not become aware of its presence until I had nearly passed it by. There was no sign of landscaping immediately surrounding the house, only the same grayish scrub grass that covered the ground everywhere else in the area as far as the eye could see. Yet the house itself seemed relatively new in its construction, and was not exactly the type of run-down place in which I expected to live out the rest of my life in decayed seclusion.

I have already mentioned that it was a windy day, and, as I stood contemplating that spectacularly isolated house, the atmosphere of that vast backroad landscape became almost cyclonic. Furthermore, the sky was beginning to darken at the edges of the horizon, even though there were no clouds to be seen and several hours remained until the approach of twilight. As the force of the winds grew stronger, the only other features in that backroad landscape – the few bare trees and the ruined water tower – seemed to be receding into the distance away from me, while the house before which I stood appeared to loom closer and closer. In a thoughtless moment of panic I ran back to my car, struggling to open the door as the wind pounded against it. As soon as I was inside the car, I started the engine and drove as fast as conditions would allow. Nevertheless, it seemed that I was making no progress along the route by which I had come to that region: the horizon was still darkening and receding ahead of me while the house in my rear-view mirror remained constant in its looming perspective. Eventually, however, things began to change and that backroad landscape, along with the isolated two-story house, diminished behind me.

Only later did I ask myself where I would live out the rest of my life if not in that backroad landscape, that remote paradise in which a house had been erected that seemed perfectly designed for me. But this same place, a true resting place in which I should have been able to live out the rest of my life in some kind of peace, was now only one more thing that I had to fear.

AFTERWORD

In addition to the five stories presented here, I also found notes, mostly in the form of unconnected phrases, for a sixth story with the apparent working title of 'Sideshow.' Following the manner of the other pieces, this story similarly seemed destined to be no more than a dreamlike vignette, an episode of 'peculiar and ridiculous show business,' to quote from the author's notes. There were other unique phrases or ideas that appeared in these notes which had also emerged in my conversations with the author as we sat in the corner booth of that coffee shop throughout the course of several nights. For example, such phrases as 'the volatility of things' and 'unexpected muta-tions' appeared repeatedly, as if these were to serve as the guiding principles of this presumably abandoned narrative.

I suppose I should not have been surprised to find that the author of the aborted narrative had made references to myself, since he had clearly characterized his work to me as 'autobiographical wretchedness.' In these notes I am fairly designated as the 'other man in the coffee shop' and as a 'pitiful insomniac who manufactures artistic conundrums for himself in order to distract his mind from the sideshow town in which he has spent his life.' The words 'sideshow town' appear earlier in what seems to be the intended opening sentence of the aborted, or perhaps deliberately abandoned, story. This particular sentence is interesting in that it directly suggests a continuity with one of the other stories, something that, in my notice, is otherwise absent among these feverish, apparently deranged fragments. 'After failing to find a house in which I might live out the rest of my life,' the sentence begins, 'I began to travel frantically from one sideshow town to another, each of them descend-ing further than the one before it into the depths of a show-business world.'

Given the incomplete nature of the notes for the story called 'Sideshow,' not to mention the highly elliptical quality that was conspicuous even in the author's completed works which I had read, I did not search very long for the modicum of 'coherence and continuity' that he claimed to assign to the 'senseless episodes' forming the fundamental stratum of both his writings and his experience of the world. And at some point these notes ceased to resemble a rough outline for a work-in-progress and took on the tone of a journal or private confession. 'Told X [a reference to myself, I assumed] that I wrote when I was *prompted*,' he wrote.

'Didn't mention what might constitue such a prompt, and he didn't ask. Very strange, since he seemed to display all the subtle qualities of a highly receptive temperament, not to mention those far less subtle traits which were evident from our first meeting. Like gazing into a funhouse mirror: the glaring likeness of our literary pursuits, our shared insomnia, even the brand of cigarette which we both smoked, often lighting up at the same time. *I* wasn't going to draw attention to these details, but why didn't *he*?'

I recalled that one night I had questioned the meaning of my companion's statement that everything (in a 'sideshow world,' that is) was 'ultimately peculiar and ultimately ridiculous.' In his notes, or confession, he wrote: 'No standard exists for the peculiarity and ridiculousness of things, not even one that is unspeakable or unknowable, words which are merely a front or a subterfuge. These qualities – the peculiar and the ridiculous – are immanent and absolute in all existence and would be in any conceivable existent order . . .' This last sentence is transcribed thus from the author's notes, truncated by ellipsis so that he could immediately jump to his next thought, which was written on the same line. 'Why didn't X challenge *this* assertion? Why did he allow so many things to remain on the surface that might easily have gone so much deeper?' And on the line directly below that, he wrote: 'Some peculiar and ridiculous fate in a sideshow town.'

After I finished reading the five completed stories and the notes-cum-journal or confession relating to a sixth tale, I left the coffee shop, eager not to allow even the faintest touch of the approaching dawn to catch me sitting in that corner booth, a circumstance that I always found intensely depressing for some reason. I followed my usual course of backstreets and alleys home, pausing every so often to admire the suggestive glow in the window of a little store or the network of sagging wires that was everywhere strung above me, the power surging within them seeming to pull me along and put each of my steps in place. This was indeed a sideshow town in every way, peculiar and ridiculous in its essence, though no more so than any other place. I think that my coffee-shop companion might at one time have had a profound appreciation for this state of affairs but had somehow lost it. In the end it seemed that he could not attain even an attitude of resignation, let alone the strength to let himself be carried along by the immanent and absolute realities, the great inescapable matters which he had been privileged to glimpse, so to speak, at the bottom of a dim and empty stairwell.

I was almost home when I heard a commotion in a pile of debris beneath the silvery-blue luminescence of a street-light in an alley. Looking deep into the mound of empty paint cans, bicycle wheels stripped of their tires, rusty curtain rods, and the like, I saw the little creature. It was something that might have come from a jar in a museum exhibit or a carnival sideshow. What I most clearly remember is the impression made on me by its pale gray eyes, which I had already guessed were a family trait and which had looked at me numerous times from the other side of a corner booth in a coffee shop. These eyes now stared at me accusingly over a bundled stack of old newspapers, those heaping chronicles of the sideshow world. As I began to walk away, the shrunken creature tried to call out to me, but the only sound it managed to make was a coarse raspy noise that briefly echoed down the alley. 'No,' he had written in his notes to the unfinished sixth story. 'I refuse to be a scribe for this show-business phenomenon any longer.' I, on the other hand, had triumphed over my literary crisis and wanted nothing more than to get back to my desk, my brain practically vibrating with an unwonted energy in spite of passing another night without any sleep.

THE CLOWN PUPPET

It has always seemed to me that my existence consisted purely and exclusively of nothing but the most outrageous nonsense. As long as I can remember, every incident and every impulse of my existence has served only to perpetrate one episode after another of conspicuous nonsense, each completely outrageous in its nonsensicality. Considered from whatever point of view – intimately close, infinitely remote, or any position in between – the whole thing has always seemed to be nothing more than some freak accident occurring at a painfully slow rate of speed. At times I have been rendered breathless by the impeccable chaoticism, the absolutely perfect nonsense of some spectacle taking place outside myself, or, on the other hand, some spectacle of equally senseless outrageousness taking place within me. Images of densely twisted shapes and lines arise in my brain. *Scribbles of a mentally deranged epileptic*, I have often said to myself. If I may allow any exception to the outrageously nonsensical condition I have described – and I will allow *none* – this single exception would involve those *visits* which I experienced at scattered intervals throughout my existence, and especially one particular visit that took place in Mr Vizniak's medicine shop.

I was stationed behind the counter at Mr Vizniak's modest establishment very late one night. At that hour there was practically no business at all, none really, given the backstreet location of the shop and its closet-like dimensions, as well as the fact that I kept the place in almost complete darkness both outside and inside. Mr Vizniak lived in a small apartment above the medicine shop, and he gave me permission to keep the place open or close it up as I liked after a certain hour. It seemed that he knew that being stationed behind the counter of his medicine shop at all hours of the night, and in almost complete darkness except for a few lighting fixtures on the walls, provided my mind with some distraction from the outrageous nonsense which might otherwise occupy it. Later events more or less proved that Mr Vizniak indeed possessed a special knowledge and that there existed, in fact, a peculiar sympathy between the old man and myself. Since Mr Vizniak's shop was located on an obscure backstreet, the neighborhood outside was profoundly inactive during the later hours of the night. And since most of the streetlamps in the neighborhood were either broken or defective in some way, the only thing I could see through the small front window of the shop was the neon lettering in the window of the meat store directly across the street. These pale neon letters remained lit throughout the night in the window of the meat store, spelling out three words: BEEF, PORK, GOAT. Sometimes I would stare at these words and contemplate them until my head became so full of meat nonsense, of beef and pork and goat nonsense, that I had to turn away and find something to occupy myself in the back room of the medicine shop, where there were no windows and thus no possibility of meat-store visions. But once I was in the back room I would become preoccupied with all the medicines which were stored there, all the bottles and jars and boxes upon boxes stacked from floor to ceiling in an extremely cramped area. I had learned quite a bit about these medicines from Mr Vizniak, although I did not have a license to prepare and dispense them to customers without his supervision. I knew which medicines could be used to most easily cause death in someone who had ingested them in the proper amount and proper manner. Thus, whenever I went into the back room to relieve my mind from the meat nonsense brought on by excessive contemplation of the beef-pork-and-goat store, I almost immediately became preoccupied with fatal medicines; in other words, I would then become obsessed with death nonsense, which is one of the worst and most outrageous forms of all nonsense. Usually I would end up retreating to the small lavatory in the back room, where I could collect myself and clear my head before returning to my station behind the counter of Mr Vizniak's medicine shop.

It was there – behind the medicine shop counter, that is – that I experienced one of those *visits*, which I might have allowed as the sole exception to the intensely outrageous nonsense of my existence, but which in fact, I must say, were the nadir of the nonsensical. This was my *medicine-shop visit*, so called because I have always experienced only a single visitation in any given place – after which I begin looking for a new situation, however similar it may actually be to my old one. Each of my situations prior to Mr Vizniak's medicine shop was essentially a medicine-shop situation, whether it was a situation working as a night watchman who patrolled some desolate property, or a situation as a groundskeeper for a cemetery in some remote town, or a situation in which I spent endless gray afternoons sitting in a useless library or shuffling up and down the cloisters of a useless monastery. All of them were essentially medicine-shop situations, and each of them sooner or later involved a *visit* – either a monastery visit or a library visit, a cemetery visit or a visit while I was delivering packages from one part of town to another in the dead of the night.

At the same time there were certain aspects to the medicine-shop visit that were unlike any of the other visits, certain new and unprecedented elements which made this visit unique.

It began with an already familiar routine of nonsense. Gradually, as I stood behind the counter late one night at the medicine shop, the light radiated by the fixtures along the walls changed from a dim yellow to a rich reddish-gold. I have never developed an intuition that would allow me to anticipate when this is going to happen, so that I might say to myself: 'This will be the night when the light changes to reddish-gold. This will be the night of another visit.' In the new light (the rich reddish-gold illumination) the interior of the medicine shop took on the strange opulence of an old oil painting; everything became transformed beneath a thick veneer of gleaming obscurity. And I have always wondered how my own face appears in this new light, but at the time I can never think about such things because I know what is about to happen, and all I can do is hope that it will soon be over.

After the business with the tinted illumination, only a few moments pass before there is an appearance, which means that the visit itself has begun. First the light changes to reddish-gold, then the visit begins. I have never been able to figure out the reason for this sequence, as if there might be a reason for such nonsense as these visits or any particular phase of these visits. Certainly when the light changes to a reddish-gold tint I am being forewarned that an appearance is about to occur, but this has never enabled me to witness the *actual manifestation*, and I had given up trying by the time of the medicine-shop visit. I knew that if I looked to my left, the appearance would take place in the field of vision to my right; conversely, if I focused on the field of vision to my right, the appearance would take place, in no time at all, on my left. And of course if I simply gazed straight ahead, the appearance would take place just beyond the edges of my left or right fields of vision, silently and instantaneously. Only after it had appeared would it begin to make any sound, clattering as it moved directly in front of my eyes, and then, as always happened, I would be looking at a creature that I might say had all the appearances of an antiquated marionette, a puppet figure of some archaic type.

It was almost life-sized and hovered just far enough above the floor of the medicine shop that its face was at the same level as my own. I am describing the puppet creature as it appeared during the medicine-shop visit, but it always took the form of the same antiquated marionette hovering before me in a reddish-gold haze. Its design was that of a clown puppet in pale pantaloons overdraped by a kind of pale smock, thin and pale hands emerging from the ruffled cuffs of its sleeves, and a powder-pale head rising above a ruffled collar. I always found it difficult at first to look directly at the face of the puppet creature whenever it appeared, because the expression which had been created for that face was so simple and bland, yet at the same time so intensely evil and perverse. In the observation of at least one commentator on puppet theater, the expressiveness of a puppet or marionette resides in its arms, hands, and legs, never in its face or head, as is the case with a human actor. But in the case of the puppet thing hovering before me in the medicine shop, this was not true. Its expressiveness was all in that face with its pale and pitted complexion, its slightly pointed nose and delicate lips, and its dead puppet eyes – eyes that did not seem able to fix or focus themselves upon anything but only gazed with an unchanging expression of dreamy malignance, an utterly nonsensical expression of stupefied viciousness and cruelty. So whenever this puppet creature first appeared I avoided looking at its face and instead looked at its tiny feet which were covered by a pair of pale slippers and dangled just above the floor. Then I always looked at the wires which were attached to the body of the puppet thing, and I tried to follow those wires to see where they led. But at some point my vision failed me; I could visually trace the wires only so far along their neat vertical path ... and then they became lost in a thick blur, a ceiling of distorted light and shadow that always formed some distance above the puppet creature's head – and my own – beyond which my eyes could perceive no clear image, nothing at all except a vague sluggish movement, like a layer of dense clouds seen from far away through a gloomy reddish-gold twilight. This phenomenon of the wires disappearing into a blur supported my observation over the years that the puppet thing did not have a life of its own. It was solely by means of these wires, in my view, that the creature was able to proceed through its familiar motions. (The term 'motions,' as I bothered myself to discover in the course of my useless research into the subject, was commonly employed at one time, long ago, to refer to various types of puppets, as in the statement: 'The motions recently viewed at St Bartholomew's Fair were engaged in antics of a questionable probity before an audience which might have better profited by deep contemplation of the fragile and uncertain destiny of their immortal souls.') The puppet swung forward toward the counter of the medicine shop behind which I stood. Its body parts rattled loosely and noisily in the late-night quiet before coming to rest. One of its hands was held out to me, its fingers barely grasping a crumpled slip of paper.

Of course I took the tiny page, which appeared to have been torn from an old pad used for writing pharmaceutical prescriptions. I had learned through the years to follow the puppet creature's cues obediently. At one time, years before the visit at the medicine shop, I was crazy or foolish enough to call the puppet and its visits exactly what they were – outrageous nonsense. Right to the face of that clown puppet I said, 'Take your nonsense somewhere else,' or possibly, 'I'm sick of this contemptible and disgusting nonsense.' But this outburst counted for nothing. The puppet simply waited until my foolhardy craziness had passed and then continued through the motions which had been prepared for that particular visit. So I examined the prescription form the creature had passed across the counter to me, and I noticed immediately that what was written upon it was nothing but a chaos of scrawls and scribbles, which was precisely the sort of nonsense I should have expected during the medicine-shop visit. I knew that it was my part to play along with the clown puppet, although I was never precisely certain what was expected of me. From previous experience I had learned that it was futile to guess what would eventually transpire during a particular visit, because the puppet creature was capable of almost anything. For example, once it visited me when I was working through the night at a skid-row pawn shop. I told the thing that it was wasting my time unless it could produce an exquisitely cut diamond the size of a yo-yo. Then it reached under its pale smocklike garment and rummaged about, its hand seeking deep within its pantaloons. 'Well, let's see it,' I shouted at the clown puppet. 'As big as a yo-yo,' I repeated. Not only did it come up with an exquisitely cut diamond that was, generally speaking, as large as a yo-yo, but the object that the puppet thing flashed before my eyes – brilliant in the pawn-shop dimness – was also made in the *form* of a yo-yo . . . and the creature began to lazily play with the yo-yo diamond right in front of me, spinning it slowly on the string that was looped about one of those pale puppet-fingers, throwing it down and pulling it up over and over while the facets of that exquisitely cut diamond cast a pyrotechnic brilliance into every corner of the pawn shop.

Now, as I stood behind the counter of the medicine shop staring at the scrawls and scribbles on that page torn from an old prescription pad, I knew that it was pointless to test the clown puppet in any way or to attempt to guess what would occur during this particular visit, which would be unlike previous visits in several significant ways. Thus I tried only to play my part, my medicine-shop part, as close as possible to the script that I imagined had already been written, though by whom or what I could have no idea.

'Could you please show me some proper identification?' I asked the creature, while at the same time looking away from its pale and pasty clown face and its dead puppet eyes, gazing instead through the medicine-shop window and focusing on the sign in the window of the meat store across the street. Over and over I read the words BEEF-PORK-GOAT, BEEF-PORK-GOAT, filling my head with meat nonsense, which was infinitely less outrageous than the puppet nonsense with which I was now confronted. 'I cannot dispense this prescription,' I said while staring out the medicine-shop window. 'Not unless you can produce proper identification.' And all the time I had no idea what to do once the puppet thing reached into its pantaloons and came up with what I requested.

I continued to stare out the medicine-shop window and think about the meat nonsense, but I could still see the clown puppet gyrating in the reddish-gold light, and I could hear its wooden parts clacking against one other as it struggled to pull up something that was cached away inside its pantaloons. With stiff but unerring fingers the creature was now holding what looked like a slim booklet of some kind, waving it before me until I turned and accepted the object. When I opened the booklet and looked inside I saw that it was an old passport, a foreign passport with no words that I recognized save those of its rightful owner: Ivan Vizniak. The address below Mr Vizniak's name was a very old address, because I knew that many years had passed since Mr Vizniak had emigrated from his homeland, opened the medicine shop, and moved into the rooms directly above it. I also noticed that the photograph had been torn away from its designated place in the document belonging to Mr Vizniak.

Nothing like this had ever occurred during one of these puppet visits: no one else had ever been involved in any of the encounters I had had over the years with the clown puppet, and I was now at a loss for my next move. The only thing that occupied my mind was the fact that Mr Vizniak lived in the rooms above the medicine shop, and here in my hands was his passport, which the puppet creature had given me when I asked it to provide some identification so that I could fill the prescription it had given me, or rather, go through the motions of filling such a prescription, since I had no hope of deciphering the scrawls and scribbles on that old prescription form. And all of this was nothing but the most outrageous nonsense, as I well knew from past experience. I was actually on the verge of committing some explosive action, some display of violent hysterics by which I might bring about an end, however unpleasant, to this intolerable situation. The eyes of the puppet creature were so dark and so dead in the reddish-gold light that suffused the medicine shop; its head was bobbing slightly and also quivering in a way that caused my thought processes to race out of control, becoming all tangled in a black confusion. But exactly at the moment when I approached my breaking point, the head of the puppet thing turned away from me and its eyes seemed to be looking toward the curtained doorway that led to the back room of the medicine shop. Then it began to move in the direction of the curtained doorway, its limbs swinging freely with the sort of spastic and utterly mindless gestures of playfulness that only puppets can make. Nothing like this had ever happened before in the course of the creature's previous visits: it had never left my presence in this manner. And as soon as it disappeared entirely behind the curtain of the doorway leading to the back room, I heard a voice calling to me from the street outside the medicine shop. It was Mr Vizniak. 'Open the door,' he said. 'Something has happened.'

I could see him through the paned windows of the front door, the eyes of his thin face squinting into the dimness of the medicine shop. With his right hand he kept beckoning, as if this incessant gesturing alone could bring me to open the door for him. *Another person is about to enter the place where one of these visits is occurring*, I thought to myself. But there seemed to be nothing I could do, nothing I could say, not with the clown puppet only a few feet away in the back room. I stepped around the counter of the medicine shop, unlocked the front door, and let Mr Vizniak inside. As the old man shuffled in I could see that he was wearing an old robe with torn pockets and a pair of old slippers.

'Everything is all right,' I whispered to him. And then I pleaded: 'Go back to bed. We can talk about it in the morning.'

But Mr Vizniak seemed to have heard nothing that I said to him. From the moment he entered the medicine shop he appeared to be in some unusual state of mind. His whole manner had lost the vital urgency he displayed when he was rapping at the door and beckoning to me. He pointed one of his pale, crooked fingers upward and slowly gazed around the shop. 'The light . . . the light,' he said as the reddish-gold illumination shone on his thin, wrinkled face, making it look as if he were wearing a mask that had been hammered out of some strange metal, some ancient mask behind which his old eyes were wide and bright with fear.

'Tell me what happened,' I said, trying to distract him. I had to repeat myself several times before he finally responded. 'I thought I heard someone in my room upstairs,' he said in a completely toneless voice. 'They were going through my things. I thought I might have been dreaming, but I was awake when I heard something going down the stairs. Not footsteps,' he said. 'Just something quietly brushing against the stairs. I wasn't sure. I didn't come down right away.'

'I didn't hear anyone come down the stairs,' I said to Mr Vizniak, who now seemed lost in a long pause of contemplation. 'I didn't see anyone on the street outside. You were probably just dreaming. Why don't you go back to bed and forget about everything,' I said. But Mr Vizniak no longer seemed to be listening to me. He was staring at the curtained doorway leading to the back room of the medicine shop.

'I have to use the toilet,' he said while continuing to stare at the curtained doorway.

'You can go back to your room upstairs,' I suggested.

'No,' he said. 'Back there. I have to use the toilet.' Then he began shuffling toward the back room, his old slippers lightly brushing against the floor of the medicine shop. I called to him, very quietly, a number of times, but he continued to move steadily toward the back room, as if he were in a trance. In a few moments he had disappeared behind the curtain.

I thought that Mr Vizniak might not find anything in the back room of the medicine shop. I thought that he might see only the bottles and jars and boxes upon boxes of medicines. *Perhaps the visit has already ended*, I thought. It occurred to me that the visit could have ended the moment the puppet creature went behind the curtain of the doorway leading to the back room. I thought that Mr Vizniak might return from the back room, after having used the toilet, and go upstairs again to his rooms above the medicine shop. I thought all kinds of nonsense in the last few moments of that particular visit from the clown puppet.

But in a number of its significant aspects this was unlike any of the previous puppet visits I had experienced. I might even claim that I was not the one whom the puppet creature was visiting on this occasion, or at least not exclusively so. Even though I had always felt that my encounters with the clown puppet were nothing but the most outrageous nonsense, the very nadir of the nonsensical, as I have said, I nonetheless always had the haunting sense of being singled out in some way from all others of my kind, of being *cultivated* for some special fate. But after Mr Vizniak disappeared behind the curtained doorway I discovered how wrong I had been. Who knows how many others there were who might say that their existence consisted of nothing but the most outrageous nonsense, a nonsense that had nothing unique about it at all and that had nothing behind it or beyond it except more and more nonsense – a new order of nonsense, perhaps an utterly unknown nonsense, but all of it nonsense and nothing but nonsense.

Every place I had been in my life was only a place for puppet nonsense. The medicine shop was only a puppet place like all the others. I came there to work behind the counter and wait for my visit, but I had no idea until that night that Mr Vizniak was also waiting for his. Upon reflection, it seemed that he knew what was behind the curtained doorway leading to the back room of the medicine shop, and that he also knew that there was no longer any place to go except behind that curtain, since any place he went in his life would only be another puppet place. Yet it still seemed he was surprised by what he found back there. And this is the most outrageously nonsensical thing of all – that he should have stepped behind the curtain and cried out with such profound surprise as he did. *You*, he said, or rather cried out. *Get away from me*. These were the last words that I heard clearly before Mr Vizniak's voice faded quickly out of earshot, as though he were being carried away at incredible velocity toward some great height. *Now he would see*, I thought during that brief moment. *Mr Vizniak would see what controlled the strings of the clown puppet.*

When morning finally came, and I looked behind the curtain, there was no one there. I told myself, as if for the sake of reassurance, that I would not be so surprised when my time came. No doubt Mr Vizniak had told himself, at some point in his life, the same, utterly nonsensical thing.

THE RED TOWER

The ruined factory stood three stories high in an other-wise featureless landscape. Although somewhat imposing on its own terms, it occupied only the most unobtrusive place within the gray emptiness of its surroundings, its presence serving as a mere accent upon a desolate horizon. No road led to the factory, nor were there any traces of one that might have led to it at some time in the distant past. If there had ever been such a road it would have been rendered useless as soon as it arrived at one of the four, red-bricked sides of the factory, even in the days when the facility was in full operation. The reason for this was simple: no doors had been built into the factory; no loading docks or entranceways allowed penetration of the outer walls of the structure, which was solid brick on all four sides without even a single window below the level of the second floor. The phenomenon of a large factory so closed off from the outside world was a point of extreme fascination to me. It was almost with regret that I ultimately learned about the factory's subterranean access. But of course that revelation in its turn also became a source for my truly degenerate sense of amazement, my decayed fascination.

The factory had long been in ruins, its innumerable bricks worn and crumbling, its many windows shattered. Each of the three enormous stories that stood above the ground level was vacant of all but dust and silence. The machinery, which had densely occupied the three floors of the factory as well as considerable space beneath it, is said to have evaporated – I repeat, *evaporated* – soon after the factory ceased operation, leaving behind only a few spectral outlines of deep vats and tanks, twisting tubes and funnels, harshly grinding gears and levers, giant belts and wheels that could be most clearly seen at twilight – and later, not at all. According to these strictly hallucinatory accounts, the whole of the Red Tower, as the factory was known, had always been subject to *fadings* at certain times. This phenomenon, in the delirious or dying words of several witnesses, was due to a profound hostility between the noisy and malodorous operations of the factory and the desolate purity of the landscape surrounding it, the conflict occasionally resulting in temporary erasures, or fadings, of the former by the latter.

Despite their ostensibly mad or credulous origins, these testimonies, it seemed to me, deserved more than a cursory hearing. The legendary conflict between the factory and the grayish territory surrounding it may very well have been a fabrication of individuals who were lost in the advanced stages of either physical or psychic deterioration. Nonetheless, it was my theory, and remains so, that the Red Tower was not always that peculiar color for which it ultimately earned its fame. Thus the *encrimsoning* of the factory was a betrayal, a breaking-off, for it is my postulation that this ancient structure was in long-forgotten days the same pale hue as the world which encompassed it. Furthermore, with an insight born of dispassion to the point of total despair, I envisioned that the Red Tower was never solely devoted to the lowly functions of an ordinary factory.

Beneath the three soaring stories of the Red Tower were two, possibly three, other levels. The one immediately below the first floor of the factory was the nexus of a unique distribution system for the goods which were manufactured on all three of the floors above. This first subterranean level in many ways resembled, and functioned in the manner of, an old-fashioned underground mine. Elevator compartments enclosed by a heavy wire mesh, twisted and corroded, descended far below the surface into an expansive chamber which had been crudely dug out of the rocky earth and was haphazardly perpetuated by a dense structure of supports, a criss-crossing network of posts and pillars, beams and rafters, that included a variety of materials – wood, metal, concrete, bone, and a fine sinewy webbing that was fibrous and quite firm. From this central chamber radiated a system of tunnels that honeycombed the land beneath the gray and desolate country surrounding the Red Tower. Through these tunnels the goods manufactured by the factory could be carried, sometimes literally by hand, but more often by means of small wagons and carts, reaching near and far into the most obscure and unlikely delivery points.

The trade that was originally produced by the Red Tower was in some sense remarkable, but not, at first, of an extraordinary or especially ambitious nature.

This was a gruesome array of goods that could perhaps best be described as novelty items. In the beginning there was a chaotic quality to the objects and constructions produced by the machinery at the Red Tower, a randomness that yielded formless things of no consistent shape or size or apparent design. Occasionally there might appear a peculiar ashen lump that betrayed some semblance of a face or clawing fingers, or perhaps an assemblage that looked like a casket with tiny irregular wheels, but for the most part the early productions seemed relatively innocuous. After a time, however, things began to fall into place, as they always do, rejecting a harmless and uninteresting disorder – never an enduring state of affairs – and taking on the more usual plans and purposes of a viciously intent creation.

So it was that the Red Tower put into production its new, more terrible and perplexing, line of unique novelty items. Among the objects and constructions now manufactured were several of an almost innocent nature. These included tiny, delicate cameos that were heavier than their size would suggest, far heavier, and lockets whose shiny outer surface flipped open to reveal a black reverberant abyss inside, a deep blackness roaring with echoes. Along the same lines was a series of lifelike replicas of internal organs and physiological structures, many of them evidencing an advanced stage of disease and all of them displeasingly warm and soft to the touch. There was a fake disembodied hand on which fingernails would grow several inches overnight and insistently grew back should one attempt to clip them. Numerous natural objects, mostly bulbous gourds, were designed to produce a long, deafening scream whenever they were picked up or otherwise disturbed in their vegetable stillness. Less scrutable were such things as hardened globs of lava into whose rough, igneous forms were set a pair of rheumy eyes that perpetually shifted their gaze from side to side like a relentless pendulum. And there was also a humble piece of cement, a fragment broken away from any street or sidewalk, that left a most intractable stain, greasy and green, on whatever surface it was placed. But such fairly simple items were eventually followed, and ultimately replaced, by more articulated objects and constructions. One example of this complex type of novelty item was an ornate music box that, when opened, emitted a brief gurgling or sucking sound in emulation of a dying individual's death rattle. Another product manufactured in great quantity at the Red Tower was a pocket watch in a gold casing which opened to reveal a curious timepiece whose numerals were represented by tiny quivering insects while the circling 'hands' were reptilian tongues, slender and pink. But these examples hardly begin to hint at the range of goods that came from the factory during its novelty phase of production. I should at least mention the exotic carpets woven with intricate abstract patterns that, when focused upon for a certain length of time, composed themselves into fleeting phantasmagoric scenes of a kind which might pass through a fever-stricken or even permanently damaged brain.

As it was revealed to me, and as I have already revealed to you, the means of distributing the novelty goods fabricated at the Red Tower was a system of tunnels located on the first level, not the second (or, possibly, third), that had been excavated below the three-story factory building itself. It seems that these subterranean levels were not necessarily the foundation of the original plan of the factory but were in fact a perverse and unlikely development that might have occurred only as the structure known as the Red Tower underwent, over time, its own mutation from some prior state until it finally became a lowly site for manufacturing. This mutation apparently demanded the excavation – whether from above or below I cannot say – of a system of tunnels as a means for distributing the novelty goods which, for a time, the factory produced.

As the unique inventions of the Red Tower achieved their final forms, they seemed to be assigned specific locations to which they were destined to be delivered, either by hand or by small wagons or carts pulled over sometimes great distances through the system of underground tunnels. Where they might ultimately pop up was anybody's guess. It might be in the back of a dark closet, buried under a pile of undistinguished junk, where some item of the highest and most extreme novelty would lie for quite some time before it was encountered by sheer accident or misfortune. Conversely, the same invention, or an entirely different one, might be placed on the night-table beside someone's bed for near-immediate discovery. Any delivery point was possible; none was out of the reach of the Red Tower. There has even been testimony, either intensely hysterical or semi-conscious, of items from the factory being uncovered within the shelter of a living body, or one not long deceased. I know that such an achievement was within the factory's powers, given its later production history. But my own degenerate imagination is most fully captured by the thought of how many of those monstrous novelty goods produced at the Red Tower had been scrupulously and devoutly delivered – solely by way of those endless underground tunnels – to daringly remote places where they would never be found, nor ever could be. Truly, the Red Tower worked in mysterious ways.

Just as a system of distribution tunnels had been created by the factory when it developed into a manufacturer of novelty goods, an expansion of this system was required as an entirely new phase of production gradually evolved. Inside the wire-mesh elevator compartment that provided access between the upper region of the factory and the underground tunnels, there was now a special lever installed which, when pulled back, or possibly pushed forward (I do not know such details), enabled one to descend to a second subterranean level. This latterly excavated area was much smaller, far more intimate, than the one directly above it, as could be observed the instant the elevator compartment came to a stop and a full view of things was attained. The scene which now confronted the uncertain minds of witnesses was in many ways like that of a secluded graveyard, surrounded by a rather crooked fence of widely spaced pickets held together by rusty wire. The headstones inside the fence all closely pressed against one another and were quite common, though somewhat antiquated, in their design. However, there were no names or dates inscribed on these monuments – nothing at all, in fact, with the exception of some rudimentary and abstract ornamentation. This could be verified only when the subterranean graveyard was closely approached, for the lighting at this level was dim and unorthodox, provided exclusively by the glowing stone walls enclosing the area. These walls seemed to have been covered with phosphorescent paint which bathed the graveyard in a cloudy, grayish haze. For the longest time – how long I cannot say – my morbid reveries were focused on this murky vision of a graveyard beneath the factory, a subterranean graveyard surrounded by a crooked picket fence and suffused by the highly defective illumination given off by phosphorescent paint applied to stone walls. For the moment I must emphasize the vision itself, without any consideration paid to the utilitarian purposes of this place, that is, the function it served in relation to the factory above it.

The truth is that at some point all of the factory's functions were driven underground to this graveyard level. Long before the complete *evaporation* of machinery in the Red Tower, something happened to require the shut-down of all operations in the three floors of the factory which were above ground level. The reasons for this action are deeply obscure, a matter for contemplation only when a state of hopeless and devouring curiosity has reached its height, when the burning light of speculation becomes so intense that it threatens to incinerate everything on which it shines. To my own mind it seems entirely valid to reiterate at this juncture the longstanding tensions that existed between the Red Tower, which I believe was not always stigmatized by such a hue and such a title, and the grayish landscape of utter desolation that surrounded this structure on all sides, looming around and above it for quite incalculable distances. But below the ground level of the factory was another matter: it was here that its operations at some point retreated; it was here, specifically at this graveyard level, that they continued.

Clearly the Red Tower had committed some violation or offense, its clamoring activities and unorthodox products – perhaps its very existence – constituting an affront to the changeless quietude of the world around it. In my personal judgment there had been a betrayal involved, a treacherous breaking of a bond. I can certainly picture a time before the existence of the factory, before any of its features blemished the featureless country that extended so gray and so desolate on every side. Dreaming upon the grayish desolation of that landscape, I also find it quite easy to imagine that there might have occurred a lapse in the monumental tedium, a spontaneous and inexplicable impulse to deviate from a dreary perfection, perhaps even an unconquerable desire to risk a move toward a tempting defectiveness. As a concession to this impulse or desire *out of nowhere*, as a minimal surrender, a creation took place and a structure took form where there had been nothing of its kind before. I picture it, at its inception, as a barely discernable irruption in the landscape, a mere sketch of an edifice, possibly translucent when making its first appearance, a gray density rising in the grayness, embossed upon it in a most tasteful and harmonious design. But such structures or creations have their own desires, their own destinies to fulfill, their own mysteries and mechanisms which they must follow at whatever risk.

From a gray and desolate and utterly featureless landscape a dull edifice had been produced, a pale, possibly translucent tower which, over time, began to develop into a factory and to issue, as if in the spirit of the most grotesque belligerence, a line of quite morbid, quite wonderfully disgusting novelty goods. In an expression of defiance, at some point, it reddened with an enigmatic passion for betrayal and perversity. On the surface the Red Tower might have seemed a splendid complement to the grayish desolation of its surroundings, making a unique, picturesque composition that served to define the glorious essence of each of them. But in fact there existed between them a profound and ineffable hostility. An attempt was made to reclaim the Red Tower, or at least to draw it back toward the formless origins of its being. I am referring, of course, to that show of force which resulted in the *evaporation* of the factory's dense arsenal of machinery. Each of the three stories of the Red Tower had been cleaned out, purged of its offending means of manufacturing novelty items, and the part of the factory that rose above the ground was left to fall into ruins.

Had the machinery in the Red Tower *not* been evaporated, I believe that the subterranean graveyard, or something very much like it, would nonetheless have come into existence at some point or another. This was the direction in which the factory had been moving, a fact suggested by some of its later models of novelty items. Machines were becoming obsolete as the diseased mania of the Red Tower intensified and evolved into more experimental, even visionary projects. I have previously reported that the headstones in the factory's subterranean graveyard were absent of any names of the interred and were without dates of birth and death. This truth has been confirmed by numerous accounts rendered in borderline gibberish. The reason for these blank headstones is entirely evident as one gazes upon them standing crooked and closely packed together in the phosphorescent haze given off by the stone walls covered with luminous paint. None of these graves, in point of fact, could be said to have anyone buried in them whose names and dates of birth and death would require inscription on the headstones. These were not what might be called *burying graves*. This is to say that these were in no sense graves for burying the dead. Quite the contrary: these were graves of a highly experimental design from which the newest productions of the Red Tower were to be born.

From its beginnings as a manufacturer of novelty items of an extravagant nature, the factory had now gone into the business of creating what came to be known as 'hyper-organisms.' These new productions were also of a fundamentally extreme nature, representing an even greater divergence on the part of the Red Tower from the bland and gray desolation in the midst of which it stood. As implied by their designation as *hyper-organisms*, this line of goods displayed the most essential qualities of their organic nature, which meant, of course, that they were wildly conflicted in their two basic features. On the one hand, they manifested an intense *vitality* in all aspects of their form and function; on the other hand, and simultaneously, they manifested an ineluctable element of *decay* in these same areas. To state this matter in the most lucid terms: each of these hyper-organisms, even as they scintillated with an obscene degree of vital impulses, also, and at the same time, had degeneracy and death written deeply upon them. In accord with a tradition of dumbstruck insanity, it seems the less said about these offspring of the *birthing graves*, or any similar creations, the better. I myself have been almost entirely restricted to a state of seething speculation concerning the luscious particularities of all hyper-organic phenomena produced in the subterranean graveyard of the Red Tower. Although we may reasonably assume that such creations were not to be called beautiful, we cannot know for ourselves the mysteries and mechanisms of, for instance, how these creations moved throughout the hazy luminescence of that underground world; what creaky or spasmic gestures they might have been capable of executing, if any; what sounds they might have made or the organs used for making them; how they might have appeared when awkwardly emerging from deep shadows or squatting against those nameless headstones; what trembling stages of mutation they almost certainly would have undergone following the generation of their larvae upon the barren earth of the graveyard; what their bodies might have produced or emitted in the way of fluids and secretions; how they might have responded to the mutilation of their forms for reasons of an experimental or entirely savage nature. Often I picture to myself what frantically clawing efforts these creations probably made to deliver themselves from that confining environment which their malformed or nonexistent brains could not begin to understand. They could not have comprehended, any more than can I, for what purpose they were bred from those graves, those incubators of hyper-organisms, minute factories of flesh that existed wholly within and far below the greater factory of the Red Tower.

It was no surprise, of course, that the production of hyper-organisms was not allowed to continue for very long before a second wave of destruction was visited upon the factory. This time it was not merely the *fading* and ultimate *evaporation* of machinery that took place; this time it was something far more brutal. Once again, forces of ruination were directed at the factory, specifically the subterranean graveyard located at its second underground level, its three-story structure that stood above ground having already been rendered an echoing ruin. Information on what remained of the graveyard, and of its cleverly blasphemous works, is available to my own awareness only in the form of shuddering and badly garbled whispers of mayhem and devastation and wholesale sundering of the most unspeakable sort. These same sources also seem to regard this incident as the culmination, if not the conclusion, of the longstanding hostilities between the Red Tower and that grayish halo of desolation that hovered around it on all sides. Such a shattering episode would appear to have terminated the career of the Red Tower.

Nevertheless, there are indications that, appearances to the contrary, the factory continues to be active despite its status as a silent ruin. After all, the evaporation of the machinery which turned out countless novelty items in the three-story red-brick factory proper, and the ensuing obsolescence of its sophisticated system of tunnels at the first underground level, did not prevent the factory from pursuing its business by other and more devious means. The work at the second underground level (the graveyard level) went very well for a time. Following the vicious decimation of those ingenious and fertile graves, along with the merchandise they produced, it may have seemed that the manufacturing history of the Red Tower had been brought to a close. Yet there are indications that below the three-story above-ground factory, below the first and the second

75

underground levels, there exists a *third* level of subterranean activity. Perhaps it is only a desire for symmetry, a hunger for compositional balance in things, that has led to a series of the most vaporous rumors anent this third underground level, in order to provide a kind of complementary proportion to the three stories of the factory that rise into the gray and featureless landscape above ground. At this third level, these rumors maintain, the factory's schedule of production is being carried out in some new and strange manner, representing its most ambitious venture in the output of putrid creations, ultimately consummating its tradition of degeneracy, reaching toward a perfection of defect and disorder, according to every polluted and foggy rumor concerned with this issue.

Perhaps it seems that I have said too much about the Red Tower, and perhaps it has sounded far too strange. Do not think that I am unaware of such things. But as I have noted throughout this document, I am only repeating what I have heard. I myself have never seen the Red Tower – no one ever has, and possibly no one ever will. And yet wherever I go, people are talking about it. In one way or another they are talking about the nightmarish novelty items or about the mysterious and revolting hyper-organisms, as well as babbling endlessly about the subterranean system of tunnels and the secluded graveyard whose headstones display no names and no dates designating either birth or death. Everything they are saying is about the Red Tower, in one way or another, and about nothing else but the Red Tower. We are all talking and thinking about the Red Tower in our own degenerate way. I have only recorded what everyone is saying (though they may not know they are saying it), and sometimes what they have seen (though they may not know they have seen it). But still they are always talking, in one deranged way or another, about the Red Tower. I hear them talk of it every day of my life. Unless, of course, they begin to speak about that gray and desolate landscape, that hazy void in which the Red Tower – the great and industrious

Red Tower – is so precariously nestled. Then the voices grow quiet until I can barely hear them as they attempt to communicate with me in choking scraps of post-nightmare trauma. Now is just such a time when I must strain to hear the voices. I wait for them to reveal to me the new ventures of the Red Tower as it proceeds into even more corrupt phases of production, including the creations being turned out by the shadowy workshop of its third subterranean level. I must keep still and listen for the voices; I must remain quiet for a terrifying moment. Then I will hear the news of the factory starting up its operations once more. Then I will be able to speak again of the Red Tower.

DEFORMATIONS

MY CASE FOR RETRIBUTIVE ACTION

It was my first day working as a processor of forms in a storefront office. As soon as I entered the place – before I had a chance to close the door behind me or take a single step inside – this rachitic individual wearing mismatched clothes and eyeglasses with frames far too small for his balding head came hopping around his desk to greet me. He spoke excitedly, his words tumbling over themselves, saying, 'Welcome, welcome. I'm Ribello. Allow me, if you will, to help you get your bearings around here. Sorry there's no coat rack or anything. You can just use that empty desk.'

Now, I think you've known me long enough, my friend, to realize that I'm anything but a snob or someone who by temperament carries around a superior attitude toward others, if for no other reason than that I simply lack the surplus energy required for that sort of behavior. So I smiled and tried to introduce myself. But Ribello continued to inundate me with his patter. 'Did you bring what they told you?' he asked, glancing down at the briefcase hanging from my right hand. 'We have to provide our own supplies around here, I'm sure you were told that much,' he continued before I could get a word in. Then he turned his head slightly to sneak a glance around the storefront office, which consisted of eight desks, only half of them occupied, surrounded by towering rows of filing cabinets that came within a few feet of the ceiling. 'And don't make any plans for lunch,' he said. 'I'm going to take you someplace. There are some things you might want to know. Information, anecdotes. There's one particular anecdote . . . but we'll let that wait. You'll need to get your bearings around here.'

Ribello then made sure I knew which desk I'd been assigned, pointing out the one closest to the window of the storefront office. 'That used to be my desk. Now that you're with us I can move to one of the desks farther back.' Anticipating Ribello's next query, I told him that I had already received instructions regarding my tasks, which consisted entirely of processing various forms for the Quine Organization, a company whose interests and activities penetrate into every enterprise, both public and private, on this side of the border. Its headquarters are located far from the town where I secured a job working for them, a drab outpost, one might call it, that's even quite distant from any of the company's regional centers of operation. In such a place, and many others like it, the Quine Organization also maintains offices, even if they are just dingy storefront affairs permeated by a sour, briny odor. This smell could not be ignored and led me to speculate that before this building had been taken over as a facility for processing various forms relating to the monopolist Q. Org, as it is often called for shorthand, it had long been occupied by a pickle shop. You might be interested to know that this speculation was later confirmed by Ribello, who had taken it upon himself to help me get my bearings in my new job, which was also my first job since arriving in this little two-street town.

As I sat down at my desk, where a lofty stack of forms stood waiting to be processed, I tried to put my encounter with Ribello out of my head. I was very much on edge for reasons that you well know (my nervous condition and so forth), but in addition I was suffering from a lack of proper rest. A large part of the blame for my deprivation of sleep could be attributed to the woman who ran the apartment house where I lived in a single room on the top floor. For weeks I'd been pleading with her to do something about the noises that came from the space underneath the roof of the building, which was directly above the ceiling of my room. This was a quite small room made that much smaller because one side of it was steeply slanted in parallel to the slanted roof above. I didn't want to come out and say to the woman that there were mice or some other kind of vermin living under the roof of the building which she ran, but that was my implication when I told her about the 'noises.' In fact, these noises suggested something far more sizeable, and somehow less identifiable, than a pack of run-of-the-mill vermin. She kept telling me that the problem would be seen to, although it never was. Finally, on the morning which was supposed to be the first day of my new job – after several weeks of struggling with inadequate sleep in addition to the agitations deriving from my nervous condition – I thought I would just make an end of it right there in that one-room apartment on the top floor of a building in a two-street town on the opposite side of the border from the place where I had lived my whole life and to where it seemed I would never be able to return. For the longest time I sat on the edge of my bed holding a bottle of nerve medicine, shifting it from one hand to the other and thinking, 'When I stop shifting this bottle back and forth – an action that seemed to be occurring without the intervention or control of my own mind – if I find myself holding it in my left hand I'll swallow the entire contents and make an end of it, and if I find myself holding it in my right hand I'll go and start working in a storefront office for the Quine Organization.'

I don't actually recall in which hand the bottle ended up, or whether I dropped it on the floor in passing it from hand to hand, or what in the world happened. All I know is that I turned up at that storefront office, and, as soon as I stepped inside, Ribello was all over me with his nonsense about how he would help me get my bearings. And now, while I was processing forms one after another like a machine, I also had to anticipate going to lunch with this individual. None of the other three persons in the office – two middle-aged men and an elderly woman who sat in the far corner – had exercised the least presumption toward me, as had Ribello, whom I already regarded as an unendurable person. I credited the others for their consideration and sensitivity, but of course there might have been any number of reasons why they left me alone that morning. I remember that the doctor who was treating both you and me, and whom I take it you are still seeing, was fond of saying, as if in wise counsel, 'However much you may believe otherwise, nothing in this world is unendurable – nothing.' If he hadn't gotten me to believe that, I might have been more circumspect about him and wouldn't be in the position I am today, exiled on this side of the border where fogs configure themselves with an astonishing regularity. These fogs are thick and gray; they crawl down my throat and all but cut off my breathing.

Throughout that morning I tried to process as many forms as possible, if only to keep my mind off the whole state of affairs that made up my existence, added to which was having to go to lunch with Ribello. I had brought along something to eat, something that would keep in my briefcase without going rotten too soon. And for some hours the need to consume these few items I had stored in my briefcase was acutely affecting me, yet Ribello gave no sign that he was ready to take me to this eating place he had in mind. I didn't know exactly what time it was, since there wasn't a clock in the office and none of the others seemed to have taken a break for lunch, or anything else for that matter. But I was beginning to feel light-headed and anxious. Even more than food, I needed the medication that I had left behind in my one-room apartment.

Outside the front window I couldn't see what was going on in the street due to an especially dense fog that formed sometime around mid-morning and hung about the town for the rest of the day. I had almost finished processing all the forms that were on my desk, which was far more work than I had initially calculated I would be able to accomplish in a single day. When there were only a few forms left, the elderly woman who sat in the corner shuffled over to me with a new stack that was twice the size of the first, letting them fall on my desk with a thump. I watched her limp back to her place in the corner, her breath now audibly labored from the effort of carrying such a weighty pile of forms. While I was turned in my seat, I saw Ribello smiling and nodding at me as he pointed at his wristwatch. Then he pulled out a coat from underneath his desk. It seemed that it was finally time for us to go to lunch, although none of the others budged or blinked as we walked past them and left the office through a back door that Ribello pointed me toward.

Outside was a narrow alley which ran behind the storefront office and adjacent structures. As soon as we were out of the building I asked Ribello the time, but his only reply was, 'We'll have to hurry if we want to get there before closing.' Eventually I found that it was almost the end of the working day, or what I would have considered to be such. 'The hours are irregular,' Ribello informed me as we rushed down the alley. There the back walls of various structures stood on one side and high wooden fences on the other, the fog hugging close to both of them.

'What do you mean, irregular?' I said.

'Did I say irregular? I meant to say *indefinite*,' he replied. 'There's always a great deal of work to be done. I'm sure the others were as glad to see you arrive this morning as I was, even if they didn't show it. We're perpetually short-handed. All right, here we are,' said Ribello as he guided me toward an alley door with a light dimly glowing above it.

It was a small place, not much larger than my apartment, with only a few tables. There were no customers other than ourselves, and most of the lights had been turned off. 'You're still open, aren't you?' said Ribello to a man in a dirty apron who looked as if he hadn't shaved for several days.

'Soon we close,' the man said. 'You sit there.'

We sat where we were told to sit, and in short order a woman brought two cups of coffee, slamming them in front of us on the table. I looked at Ribello and saw him pulling a sandwich wrapped in wax paper out of his coat pocket. 'Didn't you bring your lunch?' he said. I told him that I thought we were going to a place that served food. 'No, it's just a coffeehouse,' Ribello said as he bit into his sandwich. 'But that's all right. The coffee here is very strong. After drinking a cup you won't have any appetite at all. And you'll be ready to face all those forms that Erma hauled over to your desk. I thought she was going to drop dead for sure.'

'I don't drink coffee,' I said. 'It makes me –' I didn't want to say that coffee made me terribly nervous, you understand. So I just said that it didn't agree with me.

Ribello set down his sandwich for a moment and stared at me. 'Oh dear,' he said, running a hand over his balding head.

'What's wrong?'

'Hatcher didn't drink coffee.'

'Who is Hatcher?'

Taking up his sandwich once again, Ribello continued eating while he spoke. 'Hatcher was the employee you were hired to replace. That's the anecdote I wanted to relate to you in private. About him. Now it seems I might be doing more harm than good. I really did want to help you get your bearings.'

'Nevertheless,' I said as I watched Ribello finish off his sandwich.

Ribello wiped his hands together to shake free the crumbs clinging to them. He adjusted the undersized eyeglasses which seemed as if they might slip off his face at any moment. Then he took out a pack of cigarettes. Although he didn't offer me any of his sandwich, he did offer me a cigarette.

'I don't smoke,' I told him.

'You should, especially if you don't drink coffee. Hatcher smoked, but his brand of cigarettes was very mild. I don't suppose it really matters, your not being a smoker, since they don't allow us to smoke in the office anymore. We received a memo from headquarters. They said that the smoke got into the forms. I don't know why that should make any difference.'

'What about the pickle smell?' I said.

'For some reason they don't mind that.'

'Why don't you just go out into the alley to smoke?'

'Too much work to do. Every minute counts. We're short-handed as it is. We've always been short-handed, but the work still has to get done. They never explained to you about the working hours?'

I was hesitant to reveal that I had gotten my position not by applying to the company, but through the influence of my doctor, who is the only doctor in this two-street town. He wrote down the address of the storefront office for me on his prescription pad, as if the job with Q. Org were another type of medication he was using to treat me. I was suspicious, especially after what happened with the doctor who treated us both for so long. *His* therapy, as you know from my previous correspondence, was to put me on a train that traveled clear across the country and over the border. This was supposed to help me overcome my dread of straying too far from my own home, and perhaps effect a breakthrough with all the other fears accompanying my nervous condition. I told him that I couldn't possibly endure such a venture, but he only repeated his ridiculous maxim that nothing in the world is unendurable. To make things worse, he wouldn't allow me to bring along any medication, although of course I did. But this didn't help me in the least, not when I was traveling through the mountains with only bottomless gorges on either side of the train tracks and an infinite sky above. In those moments, which were eternal I assure you, I had no location in the universe, nothing to grasp for that minimum of security which every creature needs merely to exist without suffering from the sensation that everything is spinning ever faster on a cosmic carousel with only endless blackness at the edge of that wheeling ride. I know that your condition differs from mine, and therefore you have no means by which to fully comprehend my ordeals, just as I cannot fully comprehend yours. But I do acknowledge that both our conditions are unendurable, despite the doctor's second-hand platitude that nothing in this world is unendurable. I've even come to believe that the world itself, by its very nature, is unendurable. It's only our responses to this fact that deviate: mine being predominantly a response of passive terror approaching absolute panic; yours being predominantly a response of gruesome obsessions that you fear you might act upon. When the train that the doctor put me on finally made its first stop outside of this two-street town across the border, I swore that I would kill myself rather than make the return trip. Fortunately, or so it seemed at the time, I soon found a doctor who treated my state of severe disorientation and acute panic. He also assisted me in attaining a visa and working papers. Thus, after considering the matter, I ultimately told Ribello that my reference for the position in the storefront office had in fact come from my doctor.

'That explains it, then,' he said.

'Explains what?'

'All doctors work for the Quine Organization. Sooner or later he would have brought you in. That's how Hatcher was brought in. But he couldn't persevere. He couldn't take the fact that we were short-handed and that we would always be short-handed. And when he found out about the indefinite hours . . . well, he exploded right in the office.'

'He had a breakdown?' I said.

'I suppose you could call it that. One day he just jumped up from his desk and started ranting about how we were always short-handed . . . and the indefinite hours. Then he became violent, turning over several of the empty desks in the office and shouting, "We won't be needing these." He also pulled out some file drawers, throwing their contents all over the place. Finally he started tearing up the forms, ones that hadn't yet been processed. That's when Pilsen intervened.'

'Which one is he?'

'The large man with the mustache who sits at the back of the office. Pilsen grabbed Hatcher and tossed him into the street. That was it for Hatcher. Within a few days he was officially dismissed from the company. I processed the form myself. There was no going back for him. He was completely ruined,' said Ribello as he took a sip of coffee and then lit another cigarette.

'I don't understand. How was he ruined?' I said.

'It didn't happen all at once,' explained Ribello. 'These things never do. I told you that Hatcher was a cigarette smoker. Very mild cigarettes that he special-ordered. Well, one day he went to the store where he purchased his cigarettes and was told that the particular brand he used, which was the only brand he could tolerate, was no longer available.'

'Not exactly the end of the world,' I said.

'No, not in itself,' said Ribello. 'But that was just the beginning. The same thing that happened with his cigarettes was repeated when he tried to acquire certain foods he needed for his special diet. Those were also no longer available. Worst of all, none of his medications were in stock anywhere in town, or so he was told. Hatcher required a whole shelf of pharmaceuticals to keep him going, far more than anyone else I've ever known. Most important to him were the medications he took to control his phobias. He especially suffered from a severe case of arachnophobia. I remember one day in the office when he noticed a spider making its way across the ceiling. He was always on the lookout for even the tiniest of spiders. He practically became hysterical, insisting that one of us exterminate the spider or he would stop processing forms. He had us crawling around on top of the filing cabinets trying to get at the little creature. After Pilsen finally caught the thing and killed it, Hatcher demanded to see its dead body and to have it thrown out into the street. We even had to call in exterminators, at the company's expense, before Hatcher would return to work. But after he was dismissed from the company, Hatcher was unable to procure any of the old medications that had allowed him to keep his phobias relatively in check. Of course the doctor was no help to him, since all doctors are also employees of Q. Org.'

'What about doctors on the other side of the border?' I said. 'Do they also work for the company?'

'I'm not sure,' said Ribello. 'It could be. In any case, I saw Hatcher while I was on my way to the office one day. I asked him how he was getting along, even though he was obviously a complete wreck, almost totally ruined. He did say that he was receiving some kind of treatment for his phobias from an old woman who lived at the edge of town. He didn't specify the nature of this treatment, and since I was in a hurry to get to the office I didn't inquire about it. Later I heard that the old woman, who was known to make concoctions out of various herbs and plants, was treating Hatcher's arachnophobia with a medicine of sorts which she distilled from spider venom.'

'A homeopathic remedy of sorts,' I said.

'Perhaps,' said Ribello in a distant tone of voice.

At this point the unshaven man came over to the table and told us that he was closing for the day. Since Ribello had invited me to lunch, such as it was, I assumed that he would pay for the coffee, especially since I hadn't taken a sip of mine. But I noted that he put down on the table only enough money for himself, and so I was forced to do the same. Then, just before we turned to leave, he reached for my untouched cup and quickly gulped down its contents. 'No sense in it going to waste,' he said.

Walking back to the office through the narrow, fog-strewn alley, I prompted Ribello for whatever else he could tell me about the man whose position in the storefront office I had been hired to fill. His response, however, was less than enlightening and seemed to wander into realms of hearsay and rumor. Ribello himself never saw Hatcher again after their meeting in the street. In fact, it was around this time that Hatcher seemed to disappear entirely – the culmination, in Ribello's view, of the man's ruin. Afterward a number of stories circulated around town that seemed relevant to Hatcher's case, however bizarre they may have been. No doubt others aside from Ribello were aware of the treatments Hatcher had been taking from the old woman living on the edge of town. This seemed to provide the basis for the strange anecdotes which were being spread about, most of them originating among children and given little credence by the average citizen. Prevalent among these anecdotes were sightings of a 'spider thing' about the size of a cat. This fabulous creature was purportedly seen by numerous children as they played in the streets and back alleys of the town. They called it the 'nobby monster,' the source of this childish phrase being that, added to the creature's resemblance to a monstrous spider, it also displayed a knob-like protrusion from its body that looked very much like a human head. This aspect of the story was confirmed by a few older persons whose testimony was invariably dismissed as the product of the medications that had been prescribed for them, even though practically everyone in town could be discredited for the same reason, since they were all – that is, *we* were all – taking one kind of drug or another in order to keep functioning in a normal manner. There came a time, however, when sightings of the so-called nobby monster ceased altogether, both among children and older, heavily medicated persons. Nor was Hatcher ever again seen around town.

'He just abandoned his apartment, taking nothing with him,' said Ribello just as we reached the alley door of the office. 'I believe he lived somewhere near you, perhaps even in the same building. I hear that the woman who ran the apartment house wasn't put out at all by Hatcher's disappearance, since he was always demanding that she accommodate his phobias by bringing in exterminators at least once a week.'

I held the door open for Ribello but he didn't take a step toward the building. 'Oh no,' he said. 'My work's done for the day. I'm going home to get some sleep. We have to rest sometime if we're to process the company's forms at an efficient pace. But I'll be seeing you soon.'

After a few moments Ribello could no longer be seen at all through the fog. I went back inside the office, my mind fixed on only one thing: the items of food stashed within my briefcase. But I wasn't two steps inside when I was cornered by Pilsen near the lavatory. 'What did Ribello say to you?' he said. 'It was about the Hatcher business, wasn't it?'

'We just went out for a cup of coffee,' I said, for some reason concerned to keep Ribello's confidence.

'But you didn't bring your lunch. You've been working all day, and you haven't had anything to eat. It's practically dark now, your first day on the job. And Ribello doesn't make sure you take your lunch?'

'How do you know we didn't go somewhere to eat?'

'Ribello only goes to that one place,' Pilsen said. 'And it doesn't serve food.'

'Well, I admit it. We went to the place that doesn't serve food, and now I'm famished. So if I could just return to my desk . . .'

But Pilsen, a large man with a large mustache, grabbed the collar of my coat and pulled me back toward the lavatory.

'What did Ribello say about the Hatcher business?'

'Why don't you ask him?'

'Because he's a congenital liar. It's a sickness with him – one of many. You see how he dresses, how he looks. He's a lunatic, even if he is a very good worker. But whatever he told you about Hatcher is completely false.'

'Some of it did sound far-fetched,' I said, now caught between the confidences of Ribello, who may have been no more than a congenital liar, and Pilsen, who was a large man and probably someone I didn't want to offend.

'Far-fetched is right,' said Pilsen. 'The fact is that Hatcher was promoted to work in one of the company's regional centers. He may even have moved on to company head-quarters by now. He was very ambitious.'

'Then there's nothing to say. I appreciate your straightening me out concerning this Hatcher business. Now, if you don't mind, I'd like to go back to my desk. I'm really very hungry.'

Pilsen didn't say another word, but he watched me as I walked to my desk. And I felt that he continued to watch me from his place at the back of the office. As I ate the few items of food I kept in my briefcase, I also made it quite conspicuous that I was processing forms at the same time, not lagging behind in my work. Nevertheless, I wasn't sure that this ferocious display of form processing was even necessary, as Ribello had implied was the case, due to the monumental quantity of work we needed to accomplish with a perpetually short-handed staff. I wondered if Pilsen wasn't right about Ribello. Specifically, I wondered if Ribello's assertion that our working schedule was 'indefinite' had any truth to it. Yet several more hours passed and still no one, except Ribello, had gone home since I arrived at the office early that morning. Finally I heard one of the three persons sitting behind me stand up from his, or possibly her, desk. Moments later, Pilsen walked past me wearing his coat. He was also carrying a large briefcase, so I surmised that he was leaving for the day – it was now evening – when he exited the office through the front door. After waiting a short while, I did the same.

I had walked only a block or so from the storefront office when I saw Ribello heading toward me. He was now wearing a different set of mismatched clothes. 'You're leaving already?' he said when he stopped in front of me on the sidewalk.

'I thought you were going home to get some sleep,' I said.

'I did go home, and I did get some sleep. Now I'm going back to work.'

'I talked to Pilsen, or rather he talked to me.'

'I see,' said Ribello. 'I see very well. And I suppose he asked what I might have said about Hatcher.'

'In fact he did,' I said.

'He told you that everything I said was just nonsense, that I was some kind of confirmed malcontent who made up stories that showed the company in a bad light.'

'Something along those lines,' I said.

'That's just what he would say.'

'Why is that?'

'Because he's a company spy. He doesn't want you hearing what's what on your first day. Most of all he doesn't want you to hear about Hatcher. He was the one who informed on Hatcher and started the whole thing. He was the one who ruined Hatcher. That old woman I told you about who lives on the edge of town: she works for the company's chemical division, and Pilsen keeps an eye on her too. I heard from someone who works at one of the regional centers that the old woman was assigned to one of the company's biggest projects – a line of drugs that would treat very specific disorders, such as Hatcher's arachnophobia. It would have made Q. Org twice the company it is today, and on both sides of the border. But there was a problem.'

'I don't think I want to hear any more.'

'You should hear this. The old woman was almost taken off the company payroll because she was using more than just her esoteric knowledge of herbs and plants. The chemical engineers at company headquarters gave her detailed instructions to come up with variations on their basic formula. But she was moving in another direction entirely and following completely unsanctioned practices, primarily those of an occult nature.'

'You said she was *almost* taken off the company payroll.'

'That's right. They blamed her for Hatcher's disappearance. Hatcher was very important to them as an experimental subject. Everything was set up to make him a guinea pig – denying him his usual brand of cigarettes, taking him off his special diet and his medications. They went to a great deal of trouble. Hatcher was being cleansed for what the old woman, along with the company's chemical engineers, intended to put into him. The spider venom made some kind of sense. But, as I said, the old woman was also following practices that weren't sanctioned by the company. And they needed someone to blame for Hatcher's disappearance. That's why she was almost taken off the payroll.'

'So Hatcher was an experiment,' I said.

'That's what happens when you explode the way he did, ranting about the unending workload we were expected to handle and how the company always left us short-handed. The question remains, however. Was the Hatcher experiment a success or a failure?'

Ribello then looked at his wristwatch and said that we would talk further about Hatcher, the Quine Organization, and a host of other matters he wanted to share with me. 'I was so glad to see you walk into the office this morning. We have so many forms to process. So I'll be seeing you in, what, a few hours or so?' Without waiting for my response, Ribello rushed down the sidewalk toward the storefront office.

When I reached the door to my one-room apartment, everything within me was screaming out for sleep and medication. But I paused when I heard footsteps moving toward me from the end of the dim hallway. It was the woman who operated the apartment house, and she was carrying in her arms what looked like a bundle of dirty linen.

'Cobwebs,' she said without my asking her. She turned and pointed her head back toward a set of stairs down the hallway, the kind of pull-down steps that lead up to an attic. 'We do keep our houses clean here, no matter what some people from across the border may think. It's quite a job but at least I've made a start.'

I couldn't help but stare in silence at the incredible wadding of cobwebs the woman bore in her arms as she began to make her way downstairs. Some vague thoughts occurred to me, and I called to the woman. 'If you're finished for the time being I can put up those stairs to the attic.'

'That's good of you, thanks,' she shouted up the stairwell. 'I'll bring in the exterminator soon, just as you asked. I don't know exactly what's up there but I'm sure it's more than I can deal with myself.'

I understood what she meant only after I ascended into the attic and saw for myself what she had seen. At the top of the stairs there was only a single lightbulb which didn't begin to illuminate those vast and shadowed spaces. What I did see were the dead bodies, or parts of bodies, of more than a few rats. Some of these creatures looked as if they had escaped from just the sort of thick, heaping cobwebs which I had seen the woman who ran the apartment house carrying in her arms. They clung to the bodies of the rodents just as the dense, gray fog clung to everything in this town. Furthermore, all of these bodies seemed to be in a state of deformity ... or perhaps transition. When I looked closely at them I could see that, in addition to the four legs normally allowed them by nature, there were also four other legs that had begun sprouting from their undersides. Whatever had killed these vermin had also begun to change them.

But not all of the affected rodents had died or been partially eaten. Later investigations I made into the attic, once I had persuaded the woman who ran the apartment house to defer calling in the exterminator, revealed rats and other vermin with physical changes even more advanced. These changes explained the indefinable noises I had heard since moving into my one-room apartment just beneath the roof of the building, with the attic between.

Some of the things I saw had eight legs of equal length and were able to negotiate the walls of the attic and even crawl across the slanted ceiling just under the roof. Others had even begun making webs of their own. I think you would have recognized much of this, my friend, as something out of your own gruesome obsessions. Fortunately my own fears did not include arachnophobia, as was the case with Hatcher. (Nonetheless, I did ingest heavy doses of my medication before proceeding into the attic.) When I finally located him in the most remote corner of the attic I saw the knob-like head of a human being protruding from the pale, puffy body of a giant spider, or spider-thing. He was in the act of injecting his own venom into another verminous citizen of the attic. As soon as his pin-point eyes noticed mine he released the creature, which squeaked away to begin its own transformation.

I couldn't imagine that Hatcher desired to continue his existence in that state. As I approached him he made no move of either aggression or flight. And when I took out the carving knife I had brought with me it seemed that he lifted his head and showed me his tiny throat. He had made his decision, just as I had made mine: I never returned to the storefront office to process forms for the Quine Organization, in whose employ are all the doctors on this side of the border ... and perhaps also on your side. It is now my conviction that our own doctor has long been working for this company. At the very least I blame him for my exile to this remote, two-street town of fog and nightmares. At worst, I think it was his intention to deliver me across the border to become another slave or experimental subject for the company he serves.

I prepared two vials of the venom I extracted from Hatcher's body. The first I've already used on the doctor who has been treating me on this side of the border, even if the culmination of that treatment was to be imprisoned in a storefront office processing folders for an indefinite number of hours lasting the remainder of my indefinite existence. I'm still watching him suffer his painful mutations while I help myself to all the medications I please from the cabinets in his office. Before morning comes I'll put him out of his misery, and his medications will put me out of mine.

The second vial I offer to you, my friend. For so long you have suffered from such gruesome obsessions which our doctor did not, or would not, alleviate. Do with this medicine what you must. Do with it what your obsessions dictate. You might even consider, at just the right moment, giving the doctor my greetings ... and reminding him that nothing in this world is unendurable – nothing.

OUR TEMPORARY SUPERVISOR

I have sent this manuscript to your publication across the border, assuming that it ever arrives there, because I believe that the matters described in this personal anecdote have implications that should concern even those outside my homeland and beyond the influence, as far as I know, of the Quine Organization. These two entities, one of which may be designated a political entity and the other being a purely commercial entity, are very likely known to someone in your position of journalistic inquiry as all but synonymous. Therefore, on this side of the border one might as well call himself a *citizen* of the Quine Organization, or a Q. Org national, although I think that even someone like yourself cannot appreciate the full extent of this identity, which in my own lifetime has passed the point of identification between two separate entities and approached total assimilation of one by the other. Such a claim may seem alarmist or whimsical to those on your side of the border, where your closest neighbors – I know this – are often considered as a somewhat backward folk who inhabit small, decaying towns spread out across a low-lying land-scape blanketed almost year round by dense grayish fogs. This is how the Quine Organization, which is to say in the same breath my homeland, would deceptively present itself to the world, and this is precisely why I am anxious (for reasons that are not always explicit or punctiliously de-tailed) to relate my personal anecdote.

To begin with, I work in a factory situated just outside one of those small, decaying towns layered over with fogs for most of the year. The building is a nondescript, one-story structure made entirely of cinder blocks and cement. Inside is a working area that consists of a single room of floor space and a small corner office with windows of heavily frosted glass. Within the confines of this office are a few filing cabinets and a desk where the factory supervisor sits while the workers outside stand at one of several square 'assembly blocks.' Four workers are posi-tioned, one on each side of the square blocks, their only task being the assembly, by hand, of pieces of metal which are delivered to us from another factory. No one whom I have ever asked has the least notion of the larger machin-ery, if in fact it is some type of machinery, for which these pieces are destined.

When I first took this job at the factory it was not my intention to work there very long, for I once possessed higher hopes for my life, although the exact nature of these hopes remained rather vague in my youthful mind. While the work was not arduous, and my fellow workers congen-ial enough, I did not imagine myself standing forever at my designated assembly block, fitting together pieces of metal into other pieces of metal, with a few interruptions through-out the day for breaks that were supposed to refresh our minds from the tedium of our work or for meal breaks to allow us to nourish our bodies. Somehow it never occurred to me that the nearby town where I and the others at the factory lived, traveling to and from our jobs along the same fog-strewn road, held no higher opportunities for me or anyone else, which no doubt accounts for the vagueness, the wispy insubstantiality, of my youthful hopes.

As it happened, I had been employed at the factory only a few months when there occurred the only change that had ever disturbed its daily routine of piece-assembly, the only deviation from a ritual which had been going on for nobody knew how many years. The meaning of this digression in our working lives did not at first present any great cause for apprehension or anxiety, nothing that would require any of the factory's employees to reconsider the type or dosage of the medication which they were prescribed, since almost everyone on this side of the border, including myself, takes some kind of medication, a fact that is perhaps due in some part to an arrangement in my country whereby all doctors and pharmacists are on the payroll of the Quine Organization, a company which maintains a large chemical division.

In any case, the change of routine to which I have alluded was announced to us one day when the factory supervisor stepped out of his office and made one of his rare appearances on the floor where the rest of us stood positioned, in rather close quarters, around our designated assembly blocks. For the first time since I had taken this job, our work was called to a halt *between* those moments of pause when we took breaks for either mental refreshment or to nourish our bodies. Our supervisor, a Mr Frowley, was a massive individual, though not menacingly so, who moved and spoke with a lethargy that perhaps was merely a consequence of his bodily bulk, although his sluggishness might also have been caused by his medication, either as a side effect or possibly as the primary effect. Mr Frowley laboriously made his way to the central area of the factory floor and addressed us in his slow-mannered way.

'I'm being called away on company business,' he informed us. 'In my absence a new supervisor will be sent to take over my duties on a temporary basis. This situation will be in place tomorrow when you come to work. I can't say how long it will last.'

He then asked if any of us had questions for him regarding what was quite a momentous occasion, even though at the time I hadn't been working at the factory long enough to comprehend its truly anomalous nature. No one had any questions for Mr Frowley, or none that they voiced, and the factory supervisor then proceeded back to his small corner office with its windows of heavily frosted glass.

Immediately following Mr Frowley's announcement that he was being called away on company business and that in the interim the factory would be managed by a temporary supervisor, there were of course a few murmurings among my fellow workers about what all of this might mean. Nothing of this sort had ever happened at the factory, according to the employees who had worked there for any substantial length of time, including a few who were approaching an age when, I presumed, they would be able to leave their jobs behind them and enter a period of well-earned retirement after spending their entire adult lives standing at the same assembly blocks and fitting together pieces of metal. By the end of the day, however, these murmurings had long died out as we filed out of the factory and began making our way along the foggy road back to our homes in town.

That night, for no reason I could name, I was unable to fall asleep, something which previously I had had no trouble doing after being on my feet all day assembling pieces of metal in the same configuration one after the other. This activity of assemblage now burdened my mind, as I tossed about in my bed, with the full weight of its repetitiousness, its endlessness, and its disconnection from any purpose I could imagine. For the first time I wondered how those metal pieces that we assembled had come to be created, my thoughts futilely attempting to pursue them to their origins in the crudest form of substance which, I assumed, had been removed from the earth and undergone some process of refinement, then taken shape in some factory, or series of factories, before they arrived at the one where I was presently employed. With an even greater sense of futility I tried to imagine where these metal pieces were delivered once we had fitted them together as we had been trained to do, my mind racing in the darkness of my room to conceive of their ultimate destination and purpose. Until that night I had never been disturbed by questions of this kind. There was no point in occupying myself with such things, since I had always possessed higher hopes for my life beyond the time I needed to serve at the factory in order to support myself. Finally I got out of bed and took an extra dose of medication. This allowed me at least a few hours of sleep before I was required to be at my job.

When we entered the factory each morning, it was normal procedure for the first man who passed through the door to switch on the cone-shaped lamps which hung down on long rods from the ceiling. Another set of lights was located inside the supervisor's office, and Mr Frowley would switch those on himself when he came into work around the same time as the rest of us. That morning, however, no lights were on within the supervisor's office. Since this was the first day that a new supervisor was scheduled to assume Mr Frowley's duties, if only on a temporary basis, we naturally assumed that, for some reason, this person was not yet present in the factory. But when daylight shone through the fog beyond the narrow rectangular windows of the factory, which included the windows of the supervisor's office, we now began to suspect that the new supervisor – that is, our temporary supervisor – had been inside his office all along. I use the word 'suspect' because it simply was not possible to tell – in the absence of the office lights being switched on, with only natural daylight shining into the windows through the fog – whether or not there was someone on the other side of the heavily frosted glass that enclosed the supervisor's office. If the new supervisor that the Quine Organization had sent to fill in temporarily for Mr Frowley had in fact taken up residence in the office situated in a corner of the factory, he was not moving about in any way that would allow us to distinguish his form among the blur of shapes which could be detected through the heavily frosted glass of that room.

Even if no one said anything that specifically referred either to the new supervisor's presence or absence within the factory, I saw that nearly everyone standing around their assembly blocks had cast a glance at some point during the early hours of the day in the direction of Mr Frowley's office. The assembly block that served as my station was located closer than most to the supervisor's office, and we who were positioned there would seem to have been able to discern if someone was in fact inside. But those of us standing around the assembly block to which I was assigned, as well as others at blocks even closer to the supervisor's office, only exchanged furtive looks among ourselves, as if we were asking one another, 'What do you think?' But no one could say anything with certainty, or nothing that we could express in sensible terms.

Nevertheless, all of us behaved as if that corner office were indeed occupied and conducted ourselves in the manner of employees whose actions were subject to profound scrutiny and the closest supervision. As the hours passed it became more and more apparent that the supervisor's office was being inhabited, although the nature of its new resident had become a matter for question. During the first break of the day there were words spoken among some of us to the effect that the figure behind the heavily frosted glass could not be seen to have a definite shape or to possess any kind of stable or solid form. Several of my fellow workers mentioned a dark ripple they had spied several times moving behind or within the uneven surface of the glass which enclosed the supervisor's office. But whenever their eyes came to focus on this rippling movement, they said, it would suddenly come to a stop or simply disperse like a patch of fog. By the time we took our meal break there were more observations shared, many of them in agreement about sighting a slowly shifting outline, some darkish and globulant form like a thunderhead churning in a darkened sky. To some it appeared to have no more substance than a shadow, and perhaps that's all it was, they argued, although they had to concede that this shadow was unlike any other they had seen, for at times it moved in a seemingly purposeful way, tracing the same path over and over behind the frosted glass, as if it were a type of creature pacing about in a cage. Others swore they could discern a bodily configuration, however elusive and aberrant. They spoke only in terms of its 'head part' or 'arm-protrusions,' although even these more conventional descriptions were qualified by admissions that such quasi-anatomical components did not manifest themselves in any normal aspect inside the office. 'It doesn't seem to be sitting behind the desk,' one man asserted, 'but looks more like it's sticking up from the top, sort of sideways too.' This was something that I too had noted as I stood at my assembly block, as had the men who worked to the left and right of me. But the employee who stood directly across the block from where I was positioned, whose name was Blecher and who was younger than most of the others at the factory and perhaps no more than a few years older than I was, never spoke a single word about anything he might have seen in the supervisor's office. Moreover, he worked throughout that day with his eyes fixed upon his task of fitting together pieces of metal, his gaze locked at a downward angle, even when he moved away from the assembly block for breaks or to use the lavatory. Not once did I catch him glancing in the direction of that corner of the factory which the rest of us, as the hours dragged by, could barely keep our eyes from. Then, toward the end of the work day, when the atmosphere around the factory had been made weighty by our spoken words and unspoken thoughts, when the sense of an unknown mode of supervision hung ominously about us, as well as within us (such that I felt some inner shackles had been applied that kept both my body and my mind from straying far from the position I occupied at that assembly block), Blecher finally broke down.

'No more,' he said as if speaking only to himself. Then he repeated these words in a louder voice and with a vehemence that suggested something of what he had been holding within himself throughout the day. 'No more!' he shouted as he moved away from the assembly block and turned to look straight at the door of the supervisor's office, which, like the office windows, was a frame of heavily frosted glass.

Blecher moved swiftly to the door of the office. Without pausing for a moment, not even to knock or in any way announce his entrance, he stormed inside the cube-shaped room and slammed the door behind him. All eyes in the factory were now fixed on the office in the corner. While we had suffered so many confusions and conflicts over the physical definition of the temporary supervisor, we had no trouble at all seeing the dark outline of Blecher behind the heavily frosted glass and could easily follow his movements. Afterward, everything happened very rapidly, and the rest of us stood as if stricken with the kind of paralysis one sometimes experiences in a dream.

At first Blecher stood rigid before the desk inside the office, but this posture lasted only for a moment. Soon he was rushing about the room as if in flight from some pursuing agency, crashing into the filing cabinets and finally falling to the floor. When he stood up again he appeared to be fending off a swarm of insects, waving his arms wildly to forestall the onslaught of a cloudy and shifting mass that hovered about him like a trembling aura. Then his body slammed hard against the frosted glass of the door, and I thought he was going to break through. But he scrambled full about and came stumbling out of the office, pausing a second to stare at the rest of us, who were staring back at him. There was a look of derangement and incomprehension in his eyes, while his hands were shaking.

The door behind Blecher was left half open after his furious exit, but no one attempted to look inside the office. He seemed unable to move away from the place where he stood with the half-open office door only a few feet behind him. Then the door finally began to close slowly behind him, although no visible force appeared to be causing it to do so, however deliberately it moved on its hinges. A little click sounded when the door pushed back into its frame. But it was the sound of the lock being turned on the other side of the door that stirred Blecher from his frozen stance, and he went running out of the factory. Only seconds later the bell signaling the close of the work day rang with all the shrillness of an alarm, even though it was not quite time for us to leave our assembly blocks behind us.

Startled back into a fully wakened state, we exited the factory as a consolidated group, proceeding with a measured pace, unspeaking, until we had all filed out of the building. Outside there was no sign of Blecher, although I don't think that anyone expected to see him. In any case, the grayish fog was especially dense along the road leading back to town, and we could hardly see one another as we made our way home, none of us saying a word about what had happened, as if we were bound by a pact of silence. Any mention of the Blecher incident would have made it impossible, at least to my mind, to go back to the factory. And there was no other place we could turn to for our living.

That evening I went to bed early, taking a substantial dose of medication to insure that I would drop right off to sleep and not spend hour upon hour with my mind racing, as it had been the previous night, with thoughts about the origins (somewhere in the earth) and subsequent destination (at some other factory or series of factories) of the metal pieces I spent my days assembling. I awoke earlier than usual, but rather than lingering about my room, where I was likely to start thinking about the events of the day before, I went to a small diner in town which I knew would be open for breakfast at that time of the morning.

When I stepped inside the diner I saw that it was unusually crowded, the tables and booths and stools at the counter occupied for the most part by my fellow workers from the factory. For once I was glad to see these men whom I had previously considered 'lifers' in a job which I never intended to work at for very long, considering that I still possessed higher hopes of a vague sort for my future. I greeted a number of the others as I walked toward an unoccupied stool at the counter, but no one returned more than a nod to me, nor were they much engaged in talking with one another.

After taking a seat at the counter and ordering breakfast, I recognized the man on my right as someone who worked at the assembly block beside the one where I was positioned day after day. I was fairly sure that his name was Nohls, although I didn't use his name and simply said 'Good morning' to him in the quietest voice I could manage. For a moment Nohls didn't reply but simply continued to stare into the plate in front of him from which he was slowly and mechanically picking up small pieces of food with his fork and placing them into his mouth. Without turning to face me, Nohls said, in a voice even quieter than my own had been, 'Did you hear about Blecher?'

'No,' I whispered. 'What about him?'

'Dead,' said Nohls.

'Dead?' I responded in voice that was loud enough to cause everyone else in the diner to turn and look my way. Resuming our converation in extremely quiet tones, I asked Nohls what had happened to Blecher.

'That rooming house where he lives. The woman who runs the place said that he was acting strange after – after he came back from work yesterday.'

Later on, Nohls informed me, Blecher didn't show up for dinner. The woman who operated the boarding house took it upon herself to check up on Blecher, who didn't answer when she knocked on his door. Concerned, she asked one of her other male residents to look in on Mr Blecher. He was found lying face down on his bed, and on the nightstand were several open containers of the various medications which he was prescribed. He hadn't consumed the entire contents of these containers but had nevertheless died of an overdose of medication. Perhaps he simply wanted to put the events of the day out of his mind and get a decent night's sleep. I had done this myself, I told Nohls.

'Could be that's what happened,' Nohls replied. 'I don't suppose that anyone will ever know for sure.'

After finishing my breakfast, I kept drinking refill after refill of coffee, as I noticed others in the diner, including Nohls, were doing. We still had time before we needed to be at our jobs. Eventually, however, other patrons began to arrive and, as a group, we left for work.

When we arrived at the factory in the darkness and fog some hours before dawn, there were several other employees standing outside the door. None of them, it seemed, wanted to be the first to enter the building and switch on the lights. Only after the rest of us approached the factory did anyone go inside. It was then we found that someone had preceded us into work that morning, and had switched on the lights. His was a new face to us. He was standing in Blecher's old position, directly opposite mine at the same assembly block, and he had already done a considerable amount of work, his hands moving furiously as he fitted those small metal pieces together.

As the rest of us walked onto the floor of the factory to take position at our respective assembly blocks, almost everyone cast a suspicious eye upon the new man who was standing where Blecher used to stand and who, as I remarked, was working at a furious pace. But in fact it was only his hands that were working in a furious manner, manipulating those small pieces of metal like two large spiders spinning the same web. Otherwise he stood quite calmly and was very much a stock figure of the type of person that worked at the factory. He was attired in regulation gray work clothes that were well worn and was neither conspicuously older nor conspicuously younger than the other employees. The only quality that singled him out was the furiousness he displayed in his work, to which he gave his full attention. Even when the factory began to fill with other men in gray work clothes, almost all of whom cast a suspicious eye on the new man, he never looked up from the assembly block where he was manipulating those pieces of metal with such intentness, such complete absorption, that he gave no notice to anyone else around him.

If the new man seemed an unsettling presence, appearing as he did the morning after Blecher had taken an overdose of medication and standing in Blecher's position directly across from me at the same assembly block, at least he served to distract us from the darkened office which was inhabited by our temporary supervisor. Whereas the day before we were wholly preoccupied with this supervisory figure, our attention was now primarily drawn to the new employee among us. And even though he filled our minds with various speculations and suspicions, the new man did not contribute to the atmosphere of nightmarish thoughts and perceptions that had caused Blecher to become entirely deranged and led him to take action in the way he did.

Of course we could forbear for just so long before someone addressed the new man about his appearance at the factory that day. Since my fellow workers who stood to the right and left of me at the assembly block were doing their best to ignore the situation, the task of probing for some answers, I felt, had fallen upon me.

'Where are you from?' I asked the man who stood directly across from me where Blecher once stood on his side of the assembly block.

'The company sent me,' the man responded in a surprisingly forthcoming and casual tone, although he didn't for a second look up from his work.

I then introduced myself and the other two men at the assembly block, who nodded and mumbled their greetings to the stranger. That was when I discovered the limitations of the new man's willingness to reveal himself.

'No offense,' he said. 'But there's a lot of work that needs to be done around here.'

During our brief exchange the new man had continued to manipulate those pieces of metal before him without interruption. However, even though he kept his head angled downward, as Blecher had done for most of the previous day, I saw that he did allow his eyes to flash very quickly in the direction of the supervisor's office. Seeing that, I did not bother him any further, thinking that perhaps he would be more talkative during the upcoming break. In the meantime I let him continue his furious pace of work, which was far beyond the measure of productivity anyone else at the factory had ever attained.

Soon I observed that the men standing to the left and right of me at the assembly block were attempting to emulate the new man's style of so deftly fitting together those small metal pieces and even to compete with the incredibly productive pace at which he worked. I myself followed suit. At first our efforts were an embarrassment, our own hands fumbling to imitate the movements of his, which were so swift that our eyes could not follow them, nor our minds puzzle out a technique of working quite different from the one we had always practiced. Nevertheless, in some way unknown to us, we began to approach, if somewhat remotely, the speed and style of the new man's method of fitting together his pieces of metal. Our efforts and altered manner of working did not go unnoticed by the employees at the assembly blocks nearby. The new technique was gradually taken up and passed on to others around the factory. By the time we stopped for our first break of the day, everyone was employing the new man's methodology.

But we didn't stop working for very long. After it became obvious that the new man was not pausing for a second to join us in our scheduled break period, we all returned to our assembly blocks and continued working as furiously as we could. We surprised ourselves in the performance of what once seemed a dull and simple task, eventually rising to the level of virtuosity displayed by a man whose name we did not even know. I now looked forward to speaking to him about the change he had brought about in the factory, expecting to do so when the time came for our meal break. Yet the rest of us at the factory never anticipated the spectacle that awaited us when that time finally arrived.

For, rather than leaving his position at the assembly block during the meal break that the company had always sanctioned, the new man continued to work, consuming his meal with one hand while still assembling those metal pieces, although at a somewhat slower pace, with the other. This performance introduced the rest of us at the factory to a hitherto unknown level of virtuosity in the service of productivity. At first there was some resistance to this heightened level of dedication to our work to which the new man, without any ostentation, was leading us. But his purpose soon enough became evident. And it was simple enough: those employees who ceased working entirely during the meal break found themselves once again preoccupied, even tormented, by the troubling atmosphere that pervaded the factory, the source of which was attributed to the temporary supervisor who inhabited the office with heavily frosted windows. On the other hand, those employees who continued working at their assembly blocks seemed relatively unbothered by the images and influences which, although there was no consensus as to their exact nature, had plagued everyone the day before. Thus, it wasn't long before all of us learned to consume our meals with one hand while continuing to work with the other. It goes without saying that when the time came for our last break of the day, no one budged an inch from his assembly block.

It was only when the bell rang to signal the end of the work day, sounding several hours later than we were accustomed to hearing it, that I had a chance to speak with the new employee. Once we were outside the factory, and everyone was proceeding in a state of silent exhaustion back to town, I made a point of catching up to him as he strode at a quick pace through the dense, grayish fog. I didn't mince words. 'What's going on?' I demanded to know.

Unexpectedly he stopped dead in his tracks and faced me, although we could barely see each other through the fog. Then I saw his head turn slightly in the direction of the factory we had left some distance behind us. 'Listen, my friend,' he said, his voice filled with a grave sincerity. 'I'm not looking for trouble. I hope you're not either.'

'Wasn't I working right along with you?' I said. 'Wasn't everyone?'

'Yes. You all made a good start.'

'So I take it you're working with the new supervisor.'

'No,' he said emphatically. 'I don't know anything about that. I couldn't tell you anything about that.'

'But you've worked under similar conditions before, isn't that true?'

'I work for the company, just like you. The company sent me here.'

'But something must have changed at the company,' I said. 'Something new is happening.'

'Not really,' he replied. 'The Quine Organization is always making adjustments and refinements in the way it does business. It just took some time for it to reach you out here. You're a long way from company headquarters, or even the closest regional center.'

'There's more of this coming, isn't there?'

'Possibly. But there really isn't any point in discussing such things. Not if you want to continue working for the company. Not if you want to stay out of trouble.'

'What trouble?'

'I have to go. Please don't try to discuss this matter with me again.'

'Are you saying that you're going to report me?'

'No,' he said, his eyes looking back at the factory. 'That's not necessary these days.'

Then he turned and walked off at a quick pace into the fog.

The next morning I returned to the factory along with everyone else. We worked at an even faster rate and were even more productive. Part of this was due to the fact that the bell that signaled the end of the work day rang later than it had the day before. This lengthening of the time we spent at the factory, along with the increasingly fast rate at which we worked, became an established pattern. It wasn't long before we were allowed only a few hours away from the factory, only a few hours that belonged to us, although the only possible way we could use this time was to gain the rest we needed in order to return to the exhausting labors which the company now demanded of us.

But I had always possessed higher hopes for my life, hopes that were becoming more and more vague with each passing day. *I have to resign my position at the factory.* These were the words that raced through my mind as I tried to gain a few hours of rest before returning to my job. I had no idea what such a step might mean, since I had no other prospects for earning a living, and I had no money saved that would enable me to keep my room in the apartment building where I lived. In addition, the medications I required, that almost everyone on this side of the border requires to make their existence at all tolerable, were prescribed by doctors who were all employed by the Quine Organization and filled by pharmacists who also operated only at the sufferance of this company. All of that notwithstanding, I still felt that I had no choice but to resign my position at the factory.

At the end of the hallway outside my apartment there was a tiny niche in which was located a telephone for public use by the building's tenants. I would have to make my resignation using this telephone, since I couldn't imagine doing so in person. I couldn't possibly enter the office of the temporary supervisor, as Blecher had done. I couldn't go into that room enclosed by heavily frosted glass behind which I and my fellow workers had observed something that appeared in various forms and manifestations, from an indistinct shape that seemed to shift and churn like a dark cloud to something more defined that appeared to have a 'head part' and 'arm-protrusions.' Given this situation, I would use the telephone to call the closest regional center and make my resignation to the appropriate person in charge of such matters.

The telephone niche at the end of the hallway outside my apartment was so narrow that I had to enter it sideways. In the confines of that space there was barely enough room to make the necessary movements of placing coins in the telephone that hung on the wall and barely enough light to see what number one was dialing. I remember how concerned I was not to dial a wrong number and thereby lose a portion of what little money I had. After taking every possible precaution to insure that I would successfully complete my phone call, a process that seemed to take hours, I reached someone at the closest regional center operated by the company.

The phone rang so many times that I feared no one would ever answer. Finally the ringing stopped and, after a pause, I heard a barely audible voice. It sounded thin and distant.

'Quine Organization, Northwest Regional Center.'

'Yes,' I began. 'I would like to resign my position at the company,' I said.

'I'm sorry, did you say that you wanted to resign from the company? You sound so far away,' said the voice.

'Yes, I want to resign,' I shouted into the mouthpiece of the telephone. 'I want to resign. Can you hear me?'

'Yes, I can hear you. But the company is not accepting resignations at this time. I'm going to transfer you to our temporary supervisor.'

'Wait,' I said, but the transfer had been made and once again the phone began ringing so many times that I feared no one would answer.

Then the ringing stopped, although no voice came on the line. 'Hello,' I said. But all I could hear was an indistinct, though highly reverberant, noise – a low roaring sound that alternately faded and swelled as if it were echoing through vast spaces deep within the caverns of the earth or across a clouded sky. This noise, this low and bestial roaring, affected me with a dread I could not name. I held the telephone receiver away from my ear, but the roaring noise continued to sound within my head. Then I felt the telephone quivering in my hand, pulsing like something that was alive. And when I slammed the telephone receiver back into its cradle, this quivering and pulsing sensation continued to move up my arm, passing through my body and finally reaching my brain where it became synchronized with the low roaring noise which was now growing louder and louder, confusing my thoughts into an echoing insanity and paralyzing my movements so that I could not even scream for help.

I was never sure that I had actually made that telephone call to resign my position at the company. And if in fact I did make such a call, I could never be certain that what I experienced – what I heard and felt in that telephone niche at the end of the hallway outside my apartment – in any way resembled the dreams which recurred every night after I stopped showing up for work at the factory. No amount of medication I took could prevent the nightly onset of these dreams, and no amount of medication could efface their memory from my mind. Soon enough I had taken so much medication that I didn't have a sufficient amount left to overdose my system, as Blecher had done. And since I was no longer employed, I could not afford to get my prescription refilled and thereby acquire the medication I needed to tolerate my existence. Of course I might have done away with myself in some other manner, should I have been so inclined. But somehow I still retained higher hopes for my life. Accordingly, I returned to see if I could get my job back at the factory. After all, hadn't the person I spoke with at the regional center told me that the Quine Organization was not accepting resignations at this time?

Of course I couldn't be sure what I had been told over the telephone, or even if I had made such a call to resign my position with the company. It wasn't until I actually walked onto the floor of the factory that I realized I still had a job there if I wanted one, for the place where I had stood for such long hours at my assembly block was unoccupied. Already attired in my gray work clothes, I walked over to the assembly block and began fitting together, at a furious pace, those small metal pieces. Without pausing in my task I looked across the assembly block at the person I had once thought of as the 'new man.'

'Welcome back,' he said in a casual voice.

'Thank you,' I replied.

'I told Mr Frowley that you would return any day now.'

For a moment I was overjoyed at the implicit news that the temporary supervisor was gone and Mr Frowley was back managing the factory. But when I looked over at his office in the corner I noticed that behind the heavily frosted glass there were no lights on, although the large-bodied outline of Mr Frowley could be distinguished sitting behind his desk. Nevertheless, he was a changed man, as I discovered soon after returning to work. No one and nothing at the factory would ever again be as it once was. We were working practically around the clock now. Some of us began to stay the night at the factory, sleeping for an hour or so in a corner before going back to work at our assembly blocks.

After returning to work I no longer suffered from the nightmares that had caused me to go running back to the factory in the first place. And yet I continued to feel, if somewhat faintly, the atmosphere of those nightmares, which was so like the atmosphere our temporary supervisor had brought to the factory. I believe that this feeling of the overseeing presence of the temporary supervisor was a calculated measure on the part of the Quine Organization, which is always making adjustments and refinements in the way it does business.

The company retained its policy of not accepting resignations. It even extended this policy at some point and would not allow retirements. We were all prescribed new medications, although I can't say exactly how many years ago that happened. No one at the factory can remember how long we've worked here, or how old we are, yet our pace and productivity continues to increase. It seems as if neither the company nor our temporary supervisor will ever be done with us. Yet we are only human beings, or at least physical beings, and one day we must die. This is the only retirement we can expect, even though none of us is looking forward to that time. For we can't keep from wondering what might come afterward – what the company could have planned for us, and the part our temporary supervisor might play in that plan. Working at a furious pace, fitting together those small pieces of metal, helps keep our minds off such things.

IN A FOREIGN TOWN, IN A FOREIGN LAND

HIS SHADOW SHALL RISE TO A HIGHER HOUSE

In the middle of the night I lay wide awake in bed, listening to the dull black drone of the wind outside my window and the sound of bare branches scraping against the shingles of the roof just above me. Soon my thoughts became fixed upon a town, picturing its various angles and aspects, a remote town near the northern border. Then I remembered that there was a hilltop graveyard that hovered not far beyond the edge of town. I have never told a soul about this graveyard, which for a time was a source of great anguish for those who had retreated to the barren landscape of the northern border.

It was within the hilltop graveyard, a place that was far more populated than the town over which it hovered, that the body of Ascrobius had been buried. Known throughout the town as a recluse who possessed an intensely contemplative nature, Ascrobius had suffered from a disease that left much of his body in a grossly deformed condition.

Nevertheless, despite the distinguishing qualities of his severe deformity and his intensely contemplative nature, the death of Ascrobius was an event that passed almost entirely unnoticed. All of the notoriety gained by the recluse, all of the comment I attached to his name, occurred sometime after his disease-mangled body had been housed among the others in the hilltop graveyard.

At first there was no specific mention of Ascrobius, but only a kind of twilight talk – dim and pervasive murmurs that persistently revolved around the graveyard outside of town, often touching upon more general topics of a morbid character, including some abstract discourse, as I interpreted it, on the phenomenon of the grave. More and more, whether one moved about the town or remained in some secluded quarter of it, this twilight talk became familiar and even invasive. It emerged from shadowed doorways along narrow streets, from half-opened windows of the highest rooms of the town's old houses, and from the distant corners of labyrinthine and resonant hallways. Everywhere, it seemed, there were voices that had become obsessed to the point of hysteria with a single subject: the 'missing grave.' No one mistook these words to mean a grave that somehow had been violated, its ground dug up and its contents removed, or even a grave whose headstone had absconded, leaving the resident of some particular plot in a state of anonymity. Even I, who was less intimate than many others with the peculiar nuances of the northern border town, understood what was meant by the words 'a missing grave' or 'an absent grave.' The hilltop graveyard was so dense with headstones and its ground so riddled with interments that such a thing would be astonishingly apparent: where there once had been a grave like any other, there was now, in the same precious space, only a patch of virgin earth.

For a certain period of time, speculation arose concerning the identity of the occupant of the missing grave. Because there existed no systematic record-keeping for any particular instance of burial in the hilltop graveyard – when or where or for whom an interment took place – the dis-cussions over the occupant of the missing grave, or the *former* occupant, always degenerated into outbursts of the wildest nonsense or simply faded into a vaporous and sullen confusion. Such a scene was running its course in the cellar of an abandoned building where several of us had gathered one evening. It was on this occasion that a gentleman calling himself Dr Klatt first suggested 'Ascrobius' as the name upon the headstone of the missing grave. He was almost offensively positive in this assertion, as if there were not an abundance of headstones on the hilltop graveyard with erroneous or unreadable names, or none at all.

For some time Klatt had been advertising himself around town as an individual who possessed a distinguished background in some discipline of a vaguely scientific nature. This persona or imposture, if it was one, would not have been unique in the history of the northern border town. However, when Klatt began to speak of the recent anomaly not as a *missing* grave, even an absent grave, but as an *uncreated* grave, the others began to listen. Soon enough it was the name of Ascrobius that was mentioned most frequently as the occupant of the missing – now *uncreated* – grave. At the same time the reputation of Dr Klatt became closely linked to that of the deceased individual who was well known for both his grossly deformed body and his intensely contemplative nature.

During this period it seemed that anywhere in town one happened to find oneself, Klatt was there holding forth on the subject of his relationship to Ascrobius, whom he now called his 'patient.' In the cramped back rooms of shops long gone out of business or some other similarly out-of-the-way locale – a remote street corner, for instance – Klatt spoke of the visits he had made to the high backstreet house of Ascrobius and of the attempts he had made to treat the disease from which the recluse had long suffered. In addition, Klatt boasted of insights he had gained into the deeply contemplative personality whom most of us had never met, let alone conversed with at any great length. While Klatt appeared to enjoy the attention he received from those who had previously dismissed him as just another impostor in the northern border town, and perhaps still considered him as such, I believe he was unaware of the profound suspicion, and even dread, that he inspired due to what certain persons called his 'meddling' in the affairs of Ascrobius. 'Thou shalt not meddle' was an unspoken, though seldom observed, commandment of the town, or so it seemed to me. And Klatt's exposure of the formerly obscure existence of Ascrobius, even if the doctor's anecdotes were misleading or totally fabricated, would be regarded as a highly perilous form of meddling by many longtime residents of the town.

Nonetheless, nobody turned away whenever Klatt began talking about the diseased, contemplative recluse: nobody tried to silence or even question whatever claims he made concerning Ascrobius. 'He was a monster,' said the doctor to some of us who were gathered one night in a ruined factory on the outskirts of the town. Klatt frequently stigmatized Ascrobius as either a 'monster' or a 'freak,' though these epithets were not intended simply as a reaction to the grotesque physical appearance of the notorious recluse. It was in a strictly metaphysical sense, according to Klatt, that Ascrobius should be viewed as most monstrous and freakish, qualities that emerged as a consequence of his intensely contemplative nature. 'He had incredible powers available to him,' said the doctor. 'He might even have cured himself of his diseased physical condition; who can say? But all of his powers of contemplation, all of those incessant *meditations* that took place in his high backstreet house, were directed toward another purpose altogether.' Saying this much, Dr Klatt fell silent in the flickering, makeshift illumination of the ruined factory. It was almost as if he were waiting for one of us to prompt his next words, so that we might serve as accomplices in this extraordinary gossip over his deceased patient, Ascrobius.

Eventually someone did inquire about the contemplative powers and meditations of the recluse, and toward what end they might have been directed. 'What Ascrobius sought,' the doctor explained, 'was not a remedy for his physical disease, not a cure in any usual sense of the word. What he sought was an absolute *annulment*, not only of his disease but of his entire existence. On rare occasions he even spoke to me,' the doctor said, 'about the *uncreation* of his whole life.' After Dr Klatt had spoken these words there seemed to occur a moment of the most profound stillness in the ruined factory where we were gathered. No doubt everyone had suddenly become possessed, as was I, by a single object of contemplation – the absent grave, which Dr Klatt described as an uncreated grave, within the hilltop graveyard outside of town. 'You see what has happened,' Dr Klatt said to us. 'He has annulled his diseased and nightmarish existence, leaving us with an uncreated grave on our hands.' Nobody who was at the ruined factory that night, nor anyone else in the northern border town, believed there would not be a price to pay for what had been revealed to us by Dr Klatt. Now all of us had become meddling accomplices in those events which came to be euphemistically described as the 'Ascrobius escapade.'

Admittedly the town had always been populated by hysterics of one sort or another. Following the Ascrobius escapade, however, there was a remarkable plague of twilight talk about 'unnatural repercussions' that were either in the making or were already taking place throughout the town. *Someone would have to atone for that uncreated existence*, or such was the general feeling as it was expressed in various obscure settings and situations. In the dead of night one could hear the most reverberant screams arising at frequent intervals from every section of town, particularly the backstreet areas, far more than the usual nocturnal outbursts. And upon subsequent overcast days the streets were all but deserted. Any talk confronting the specifics of the town's night terrors was either precious or entirely absent: perhaps, I might even say, it was as uncreated as Ascrobius himself, at least for a time.

It was inevitably the figure of Dr Klatt who, late one afternoon, stepped forward from the shadows of an old warehouse to address a small group of persons assembled there. His shape barely visible in the gauzy light that pushed its way through dusty windowpanes, Klatt announced that he might possess the formula for solving the new-found troubles of the northern border town. While the warehouse gathering was as wary as the rest of us of any further meddling in the matter of Ascrobius, they gave Klatt a hearing in spite of their reservations. Included among this group was a woman known as Mrs Glimm, who operated a lodging house – actually a kind of brothel – that was patronized for the most part by out-of-towners, especially business travelers stopping on their way to some destination across the border. Even though Klatt did not directly address Mrs Glimm, he made it quite clear that he would require an assistant of a very particular type in order to carry out the measures he had in mind for delivering us all from those intangible traumas that had lately afflicted everyone in some manner. 'Such an assistant,' the doctor emphasized, 'should not be anyone who is exceptionally sensitive or intelligent.

'At the same time,' he continued, 'this person must have a definite handsomeness of appearance, even a fragile beauty.' Further instructions from Dr Klatt indicated that the requisite assistant should be sent up to the hilltop graveyard that same night, for the doctor fully expected that the clouds which had choked the sky throughout the day would linger long into the evening, thus cutting off the moonlight that often shone so harshly on the closely huddled graves. This desire for optimum darkness seemed to be a conspicuous giveaway on the doctor's part. Everyone present at the old warehouse was of course aware that such 'measures' as Klatt proposed were only another instance of meddling by someone who was almost certainly an impostor of the worst sort. But we were already so deeply implicated in the Ascrobius escapade, and so lacking in any solutions of our own, that no one attempted to discourage Mrs Glimm from doing what she could to assist the doctor with his proposed scheme.

So the moonless night came and went, and the assistant sent by Mrs Glimm never returned from the hilltop graveyard. Yet nothing in the northern border town seemed to have changed. The chorus of midnight outcries continued and the twilight talk now began to focus on both the 'terrors of Ascrobius' and the 'charlatan Dr Klatt,' who was nowhere to be found when a search was conducted throughout every street and structure of the town, excepting of course the high backstreet house of the dreadful recluse. Finally a small party of the town's least hysterical persons made its way up the hill which led to the graveyard. When they approached the area of the absent grave, it was immediately apparent what 'measures' Klatt had employed and the fashion in which the assistant sent by Mrs Glimm had been used in order to bring an end to the Ascrobius escapade.

The message which those who had gone up to the graveyard carried back to town was that Klatt was nothing but a common butcher. 'Well, perhaps not a *common* butcher,' said Mrs Glimm, who was among the small graveyard party. Then she explained in detail how the body of the doctor's assistant, its skin finely shredded by countless incisions and its parts numerously dismembered, had been arranged with some calculation on the spot of the absent grave: the raw head and torso were propped up in the ground as if to serve as the headstone for a grave, while the arms and legs were disposed in a way that might be seen to demarcate the rectangular space of a graveyard plot. Someone suggested giving the violated body a proper burial in its own gravesite, but Mrs Glimm, for some reason unknown even to herself, or so she said, persuaded the others that things should be left as they were. And perhaps her intuition in this matter was felicitous, for not many days later there was a complete cessation of all terrors associated with the Ascrobius escapade, however indefinite or possibly nonexistent such occurrences might have been from the start. Only later, by means of the endless murmurs of twilight talk, did it become apparent why Dr Klatt might have abandoned the town, even though his severe measures seemed to have worked the exact cure which he had promised.

Although I cannot say that I witnessed anything myself, others reported signs of a 'new occupation,' not at the site of the grave of Ascrobius, but at the high backstreet house where the recluse once spent his intensely contemplative days and nights. There were sometimes lights behind the curtained windows, these observers said, and the passing figure outlined upon those curtains was more outlandishly grotesque than anything they had ever seen while the resident of that house had lived. But no one ever approached the house. Afterward all speculation about what had come to be known as the 'resurrection of the uncreated' remained in the realm of twilight talk. Yet as I now lie in my bed, listening to the wind and the scraping of bare branches on the roof just above me, I cannot help remaining wide awake with visions of that deformed specter of Ascrobius and pondering upon what unimaginable planes of contemplation it dreams of another act of uncreation, a new and far-reaching effort of great power and more certain permanence. Nor do I welcome the thought that one day someone may notice that a particular house appears to be missing, or absent, from the place it once occupied along the backstreet of a town near the northern border.

THE BELLS WILL SOUND FOREVER

I was sitting in a small park on a drab morning in early spring when a gentleman who looked as if he should be in a hospital sat down on the bench beside me. For a time we both silently stared out at the colorless and soggy grounds of the park, where things were still thawing out and signs of a revived natural life remained only tentative, the bare branches of trees finely outlined against a gray sky. I had seen the other man on previous visits to the park and, when he introduced himself to me by name, I seemed to remember him as a businessman of some sort. The words 'commercial agent' came to my mind as I sat gazing up at the thin dark branches and, beyond them, the gray sky. Somehow our quiet and somewhat halting conversation touched upon the subject of a particular town near the northern border, a place where I once lived. 'It's been many years,' the other man said, 'since I was last in that town.' Then he proceeded to tell me about an experience he had had there in the days when he often traveled to remote locales for the business firm he represented and which, until that time, he had served as a longterm and highly dedicated employee.

It was late at night, he told me, and he needed a place to stay before moving on to his ultimate destination across the northern border. I knew, as a one-time resident of the town, that there were two principal venues where he might have spent the night. One of them was a lodging house on the west side of town that, in actuality, functioned primarily as a brothel patronized by travelling commercial agents. The other was located somewhere on the east side of town in a district of once-opulent, but now for the most part unoccupied houses, one of which, according to rumor, had been converted into a hostel of some kind by an old woman named Mrs Pyk, who was reputed to have worked in various carnival sideshows – first as an exotic dancer, and then later as a fortune-teller – before settling in the northern border town. The commercial agent told me that he could not be sure if it was misdirection or deliberate mischief that sent him to the east side of town, where there were only a few lighted windows here and there. Thus he easily spotted the VACANCY sign that stood beside the steps leading up to an enormous house which had a number of small turrets that seemed to sprout like so many warts across its façade and even emerged from the high peaked roof that crowned the structure. Despite the grim appearance of the house (a 'miniature ruined castle,' as my companion in the park expressed it), not to mention the generally desolate character of the surrounding neighborhood, the commercial agent said that he was not for a moment deterred from ascending the porch steps. He pressed the doorbell, which he said was a 'buzzer-type bell,' as opposed to the type that chimed or tolled its signal. However, in addition to the buzzing noise that was made when he pressed the button for the doorbell, he claimed that there was also a 'jingle-jangle sound' similar to that of sleigh bells. When the door finally opened, and the commercial agent confronted the heavily made-up face of Mrs Pyk, he simply asked, 'Do you have a room?'

Upon entering the vestibule to the house, he was made to pause by Mrs Pyk, who gestured with a thin and palsied hand toward a registration ledger which was spread open on a lectern in the corner. There were no other visitors listed on the pages before him, yet the commercial agent unhesitatingly picked up the fountain pen that lay in the crux of the ledger book and signed his name: Q. H. Crumm. Having done this, he turned back toward Mrs Pyk and stooped down to retrieve the small suitcase he had brought in with him. At that moment he first saw Mrs Pyk's left hand, the non-palsied hand, which was just as thin as the other but which appeared to be a prosthetic device resembling the pale hand of an old mannikin, its enameled epidermis having flaked away in several places. It was then that Mr Crumm fully realized, in his own words, the 'deliriously preposterous' position in which he had placed himself. Yet he said that he also felt a great sense of excitation relating to things which he could not precisely name, things which he had never imagined before and which it seemed were not even possible for him to imagine with any clarity at the time.

The old woman was aware that Crumm had taken note of her artificial hand. 'As you can see,' she said in a slow and raspy voice, 'I'm perfectly capable of taking care of myself, no matter what some fool tries to pull on me. But I don't receive as many gentleman travelers as I once did. I'm sure I wouldn't have any at all, if it were up to certain people,' she finished. *Deliriously preposterous*, Mr Crumm thought to himself. Nevertheless, he followed Mrs Pyk like a little dog when she guided him into her house, which was so poorly lighted that one was at a loss to distinguish any features of the décor, leaving Crumm with the heady sensation of being enveloped by the most sumptuous surroundings of shadows. This feeling was only intensified when the old woman reached out for a small lamp that was barely glowing in the darkness and, with a finger of her real hand, turned up its wick, the light pushing back some of the shadows while grotesquely enlarging many others. She then began escorting Crumm up the stairs to his room, holding the lamp in her real hand while simply allowing her artificial hand to hang at her side. And with each step that Mrs Pyk ascended, the commercial agent seemed to detect the same jingle-jangle of bells that he had first heard when he was standing outside the house, waiting for someone to answer his ring. But the sound was so faint, as if heavily muffled, that Mr Crumm willingly believed it to be only the echo of a memory or his wandering imagination.

The room in which Mrs Pyk finally deposited her guest was on the highest floor of the house, just down a short, narrow hallway from the door leading to the attic. 'By that time there seemed nothing at all preposterous in this arrangement,' Mr Crumm told me as we sat together on the park bench looking out at that drab morning in early spring. I replied that such lapses in judgment were not uncommon where Mrs Pyk's lodging house was concerned; at least such were the rumors I had heard during the period when I was living in the town near the northern border.

When they had reached the hallway of the highest floor of the house, Crumm informed me, Mrs Pyk set aside the lamp she was carrying on a table positioned near the top of the last flight of stairs. She then extended her hand and pushed a small button that protruded from one of the walls, thereby activating some lighting fixtures along either wall. The illumination remained dismal – actively dismal, as Crumm described it – but served to reveal the densely patterned wallpaper and the even more densely patterned carpeting of the hallway which led, in one direction, to the opening onto the attic and, in the other direction, to the room in which the commercial agent was supposed to sleep that night. After Mrs Pyk unlocked the door to this room and pushed another small button upon the wall inside, Crumm observed how cramped and austere was the chamber in which he was being placed, unnecessarily so, he thought, considering the apparent spaciousness, or 'dark sumptuousness,' as he called it, of the rest of the house. Yet Crumm made no objection (nor felt any, he insisted), and with mute obedience set down his suitcase beside a tiny bed which was not even equipped with a headboard. 'There's a bathroom just a little way down the hall,' Mrs Pyk said before she left the room, closing the door behind her. And in the silence of that little room, Crumm thought that once again he could hear the jingle-jangle sound of bells fading into the distance and the darkness of that great house.

Although he had put in quite a long day, the commercial agent did not feel in the least bit tired, or possibly he had entered into a mental state beyond the boundaries of absolute fatigue, as he himself speculated when we were sitting on that bench in the park. For some time he lay on the undersized bed, still fully clothed, and stared at a ceiling that had several large stains spread across it. After all, he thought, he had been placed in a room that was directly below the roof of the house, and apparently this roof was damaged in some way which allowed the rain to enter freely through the attic on stormy days and nights. Suddenly his mind became fixed in the strangest way upon the attic, the door to which was just down the hall from his own room. *The mystery of an old attic*, Crumm whispered to himself as he lay on that miniature bed in a room at the top of an enormous house of enveloping shadows. Feelings and impulses that he had never experienced before arose in him as he became more and more excited about the attic and its mysteries. He was a traveling commercial agent who needed his rest to prepare himself for the next day, and yet all he could think about was getting up from his bed and walking down the dimly lighted hallway toward the door leading to the attic of Mrs Pyk's shadowy house. He could tell anyone who cared to know that he was only going down the hall to use the bathroom, he told himself. But Crumm proceeded past the door to the bathroom and soon found himself helplessly creeping into the attic, the door to which had been left unlocked.

The air inside smelled sweet and stale. Moonlight entered by way of a small octagonal window and guided the commercial agent among the black clutter toward a light-bulb that hung down from a thick black cord. He reached up and turned a little dial that protruded from the side of the lightbulb fixture. Now he could see the treasures surrounding him, and he was shaking with the excitation of his discovery. Crumm told me that Mrs Pyk's old attic was like a costume shop or the dressing room of a theater. All around him was a world of strange outfits spilling forth from the depths of large open trunks or dangling in the shadows of tall open wardrobes. Later he became aware that these curious clothes were, for the most part, remnants from Mrs Pyk's days as an exotic dancer, and subsequently a fortune-teller, for various carnival sideshows. Crumm himself remembered observing that mounted along the walls of the attic were several faded posters advertising the two distinct phases of the old woman's former life. One of these posters portrayed a dancing girl posed in mid-turn amidst a whirl of silks, her face averted from the silhouetted heads representing the audience at the bottom of the picture, a mob of bald pates and bowler hats huddled together. Another poster displayed a pair of dark staring eyes with long spidery lashes. Above the eyes, printed in a serpentine style of lettering, were the words: Mistress of Fortune. Below the eyes, spelled in the same type of letters, was a simple question: WHAT IS YOUR WILL?

Aside from the leftover garments of an exotic dancer or a mysterious fortune teller, there were also other clothes, other costumes. They were scattered all over the attic – that 'paradise of the past,' as Crumm began to refer to it. His hands trembled as he found all sorts of odd disguises lying about the floor or draped across a wardrobe mirror, elaborate and clownish outfits in rich velvets and shiny, colorful satins. Rummaging among this delirious attic-world, Crumm finally found what he barely knew he was seeking. There it was, buried at the bottom of one of the largest trunks – a fool's motley complete with soft slippers turned up at the toes and a two-pronged cap that jangled its bells as he pulled it over his head. The entire suit was a mad patchwork of colored fabrics and fitted him perfectly, once he had removed all of the clothing he wore as a commercial agent. The double peaks of the fool's cap resembled the twin horns of a snail, Crumm noticed when he looked at his image in the mirror, except that they drooped this way and that whenever he shook his head to make the bells jangle. There were also bells sewn into the turned-up tips of the slippers and hanging here and there upon the body of the jester's suit. Crumm made them all go jingle-jangle, he explained to me, as he pranced before the wardrobe mirror gazing upon the figure that he could not recognize as himself, so lost was he in a world of feelings and impulses he had never before imagined. He no longer retained the slightest sense, he said, of his existence as a travelling commercial agent. For him, there was now only the jester's suit hugging his body, the jingle-jangle of the bells, and the slack face of a fool in the mirror.

After a time he sank face-down upon the cold wooden floor of the attic, Crumm informed me, and lay absolutely still, exhausted by the contentment he had found in that musty paradise. Then the sound of the bells started up again, although Crumm could not tell from where it was coming. His body remained unmoving upon the floor in a state of sleepy paralysis, and yet he heard the sound of the jangling bells. Crumm thought that if he could just open his eyes and roll over on the floor he could see what was making the sound of the bells. But soon he lost all confidence in this plan of action, because he could no longer feel his own body. The sound of the bells became even louder, jangling about his ears, even though he was incapable of making his head move in any way and thus shaking the bells on his two-pronged fool's cap. Then he heard a voice say to him, 'Open your eyes . . . and see your surprise.' And when he opened his eyes he finally saw his face in the wardrobe mirror: it was a tiny face on a tiny fool's head . . . and the head was at the end of a stick, a kind of baton with stripes on it like a candy cane, held in the wooden hand of Mrs Pyk. She was shaking the striped stick like a baby's rattle, making the bells on Crumm's tiny head go jingle-jangle so wildly. There in the mirror he could also see his body still lying helpless and immobile upon the attic floor. And in his mind was a single consuming thought: *to be a head on a stick held in the wooden hand of Mrs Pyk. Forever . . . forever.*

When Crumm awoke the next morning, he heard the sound of raindrops on the roof just above the room in which he lay fully clothed on the bed. Mrs Pyk was shaking him gently with her real hand, saying, 'Wake up, Mr Crumm. It's late and you have to be on your way. You have business across the border.' Crumm wanted to say something to the old woman then and there, confront her with what he described to me as his 'adventure in the attic.' But Mrs Pyk's brusque, businesslike manner and her entirely ordinary tone of voice told him that any inquiries would be useless. In any case, he was afraid that openly bringing up this peculiar matter with Mrs Pyk was not something he should do if he wished to remain on good terms with her. Soon thereafter he was standing with his suitcase in his hand at the door of the enormous house, lingering for a moment to gaze upon the heavily made-up face of Mrs Pyk and secure another glimpse of the artificial hand which hung down at her side.

'May I come to stay again?' Crumm asked.

'If you wish,' answered Mrs Pyk, as she held open the door for her departing guest.

Once he was outside on the porch Crumm quickly turned about-face and called out, 'May I have the same room?'

But Mrs Pyk had already closed the door behind him, and her answer to his question, if it actually was one, was a faint jingle-jangle sound of tiny bells.

After consummating his commercial dealings on the other side of the northern border, Mr Crumm returned to the location of Mrs Pyk's house, only to find that the place had burned to the ground during the brief interval he had been away. I told him, as we sat on that park bench looking out upon a drab morning in early spring, that there had always been rumors, a sort of irresponsible twilight talk, about Mrs Pyk and her old house. Some persons, hysterics of one sort or another, suggested that Mrs Glimm, who operated the lodging house on the west side of town, was the one behind the fire which brought to an end Mrs Pyk's business activities on the east side. The two of them had apparently been associates at one time, in a sense partners, whose respective houses on the west and east sides of the northern border town were operated for the mutual benefit of both women. But a rift of some kind appeared to turn them into bitter enemies. Mrs Glimm, who was sometimes character-ized as a 'person of uncanny greed,' became intolerant of the competition posed by her former ally in business. It came to be understood throughout the town near the northern border that Mrs Glimm had arranged for someone to assault Mrs Pyk in her own house, an attack which culminated in the severing of Mrs Pyk's left hand. However, Mrs Glimm's plan to discourage the ambitions of her competitor ultimately backfired, it seemed, for after this attack on her person Mrs Pyk appeared to undergo a dramatic change, as did her method of running things at her east side house. She had always been known as a woman of exceptional will and extraordinary gifts, this one-time exotic dancer and later Mistress of Fortune, but following the dismemberment of her left hand, and its replacement by an artificial wooden hand, she seemed to have attained unheard-of powers, all of which she directed toward one aim – that of putting her ex-partner, Mrs Glimm, out of business. It was then that she began to operate her lodging house in an entirely new manner and in accordance with unique methods, so that whenever traveling commercial agents who patronized Mrs Glimm's west side lodging house came to stay at Mrs Pyk's, they always returned to Mrs Pyk's house on the east side and never again to Mrs Glimm's west-side place.

I mentioned to Mr Crumm that I had lived in that northern border town long enough to have been told on various occasions that a guest could visit Mrs Pyk just so many times before he discovered one day that he could never leave her again. Such talk, I continued, was to some extent substantiated by what was found in the ruins of Mrs Pyk's house after the fire. It seemed there were rooms all over the house, and even in the farthest corners of its vast cellar regions, where the charred remains of human bodies were found. To all appearances, given the intensely destructive nature of that conflagration, each of the incinerated corpses was dressed in some outlandish clothing, as if the whole structure of the house were inhabited by a nest of masqueraders. In light of all the stories we had heard in the town, no one bothered to remark on how unlikely it was, how preposterous even, that none of the lodgers at Mrs Pyk's house had managed to escape. Nevertheless, as I disclosed to Crumm, the body of Mrs Pyk herself was never found, despite a most diligent search that was conducted by Mrs Glimm.

Yet even as I brought all of these facts to his attention as we sat on that park bench, Crumm's mind seemed to have drifted off to other realms and more than ever he looked as if he belonged in a hospital. Finally he spoke, asking me to confirm what I had said about the absence of Mrs Pyk's body among those found in the ashes left by the fire. I confirmed the statement I had made, begging him to consider the place and the circumstances which were the source of this and all my other remarks, as well as his own, that were made that morning in early spring. 'Remember your own words,' I said to Crumm.

'Which words were those?' he asked.

'Deliriously preposterous,' I replied, trying to draw out the sound of each syllable, as if to imbue them with some actual sense or at least a dramatic force of some kind. 'You were only a pawn,' I said. 'You and all those others were nothing but pawns in a struggle between forces you could not conceive. Your impulses were not your own. They were as artificial as Mrs Pyk's wooden hand.'

For a moment Crumm seemed to become roused to his senses. Then he said, as if to himself, 'They never found her body.'

'No, they did not,' I answered.

'Not even her hand,' he said in a strictly rhetorical tone of voice. Again I affirmed his statement.

Crumm fell silent after that juncture in our conversation, and when I left him that morning he was staring out at the drab and soggy grounds of that park with the look of someone in a hysterical trance, remaining quietly attentive for some sound or sign to reach his awareness. That was the last time I saw him.

Occasionally, on nights when I find it difficult to sleep, I think about Mr Crumm the commercial agent and the conversation we had that day in the park. I also think about Mrs Pyk and her house on the east side of a northern border town where I once lived. In these moments it is almost as if I myself can hear the faint jingle-jangle of bells in the blackness, and my mind begins to wander in pursuit of a desperate dream that is not my own. Perhaps this dream ultimately belongs to no one, however many persons, including commercial agents, may have belonged to it.

A SOFT VOICE WHISPERS NOTHING

Long before I suspected the existence of the town near the northern border, I believe that I was in some way already an inhabitant of that remote and desolate place. Any number of signs might be offered to support this claim, although some of them may seem somewhat removed from the issue. Not the least of them appeared during my childhood, those soft gray years when I was stricken with one sort or another of life-draining infirmity. It was at this early stage of development that I sealed my deep affinity with the winter season in all its phases and manifestations. Nothing seemed more natural to me than my impulse to follow the path of the snow-topped roof and the ice-crowned fence-post, considering that I, too, in my illness, exhibited the marks of an essentially hibernal state of being. Under the plump blankets of my bed I lay freezing and pale, my temples sweating with shiny sickles of fever. Through the frosted panes of my bedroom window I watched in awful devotion as dull winter days were succeeded by blinding winter nights. I remained ever awake to the possibility, as my young mind conceived it, of an 'icy transcendence.' I was therefore cautious, even in my frequent states of delirium, never to indulge in a vulgar sleep, except perhaps to dream my way deeper into that landscape where vanishing winds snatched me up into the void of an ultimate hibernation.

No one expected I would live very long, not even my attending physician, Dr Zirk. A widower far along into middle age, the doctor seemed intensely dedicated to the well-being of the living anatomies under his care. Yet from my earliest acquaintance with him I sensed that he too had a secret affinity with the most remote and desolate locus of the winter spirit, and therefore was also allied with the town near the northern border. Every time he examined me at my bedside he betrayed himself as a fellow fanatic of a disconsolate creed, embodying so many of its stigmata and gestures. His wiry, white-streaked hair and beard were thinning, patchy remnants of a former luxuriance, much like the bare, frost-covered branches of the trees outside my window. His face was of a coarse complexion, rugged as frozen earth, while his eyes were overcast with the cloudy ether of a December afternoon. And his fingers felt so frigid as they palpated my neck or gently pulled at the underlids of my eyes.

One day, when I believe that he thought I was asleep, Dr Zirk revealed the extent of his initiation into the barren mysteries of the winter world, even if he spoke only in the cryptic fragments of an overworked soul in extremis. In a voice as pure and cold as an arctic wind the doctor made reference to 'undergoing certain ordeals,' as well as speaking of what he called 'grotesque discontinuities in the order of things.' His trembling words also invoked an epistemology of 'hope and horror,' of exposing once and for all the true nature of this 'great gray ritual of existence' and plunging headlong into an 'enlightenment of inanity.' It seemed that he was addressing me directly when in a soft gasp of desperation he said, 'To make an end of it, little puppet, in your own way. To close the door in one swift motion and not by slow, fretful degrees. If only this doctor could show you the way of such cold deliverance.' I felt my eyelashes flutter at the tone and import of these words, and Dr Zirk immediately became silent. Just then my mother entered the room, allowing me a pretext to display an aroused consciousness. But I never betrayed the confidence or indiscretion the doctor had entrusted to me that day.

In any case, it was many years later that I first discovered the town near the northern border, and there I came to understand the source and significance of Dr Zirk's mumblings on that nearly silent winter day. I noticed, as I arrived in the town, how close a resemblance it bore to the winterland of my childhood, even if the precise time of year was still slightly out of season. On that day, everything – the streets of the town and the few people traveling upon them, the store windows and the meager merchandise they displayed, the weightless pieces of debris barely animated by a half-dead wind – everything looked as if it had been drained entirely of all color, as if an enormous photographic flash had just gone off in the startled face of the town. And somehow beneath this pallid façade I intuited what I described to myself as the 'all-pervasive aura of a place that has offered itself as a haven for an interminable series of delirious events.'

It was definitely a mood of delirium that appeared to rule the scene, causing all that I saw to shimmer vaguely in my sight, as if viewed through the gauzy glow of a sickroom: a haziness that had no precise substance, distorting without in any way obscuring the objects behind or within it. There was an atmosphere of disorder and commotion that I sensed in the streets of the town, as if its delirious mood were only a soft prelude to great pandemonium. I heard the sound of something that I could not identify, an approaching racket that caused me to take refuge in a narrow passageway between a pair of high buildings. Nestled in this dark hiding place I watched the street and listened as that nameless clattering grew louder. It was a medley of clanging and creaking, of groaning and croaking, a dull jangle of something unknown as it groped its way through the town, a chaotic parade in honor of some special occasion of delirium.

The street that I saw beyond the narrow opening between the two buildings was now entirely empty. The only thing I could glimpse was a blur of high and low structures which appeared to quiver slightly as the noise became louder and louder, the parade closing in, though from which direction I did not know. The formless clamor seemed to envelop everything around me, and then suddenly I could see a passing figure in the street. Dressed in loose white garments, it had an egg-shaped head that was completely hairless and as white as paste, a clown of some kind who moved in a way that was both casual and laborious, as if it were strolling underwater or against a strong wind, tracing strange patterns in the air with billowed arms and pale hands. It seemed to take forever for this apparition to pass from view, but just before doing so it turned to peer into the narrow passage where I had secreted myself, and its greasy white face was wearing an expression of bland malevolence.

Others followed the lead figure, including a team of ragged men who were harnessed like beasts and pulled long bristling ropes. They also moved out of sight, leaving the ropes to waver slackly behind them. The vehicle to which these ropes were attached – by means of enormous hooks – rolled into the scene, its great wooden wheels audibly grinding the pavement of the street beneath them. It was a sort of platform with huge wooden stakes rising from its perimeter to form the bars of a cage. There was nothing to secure the wooden bars at the top, and so they wobbled with the movement of the parade.

Hanging from the bars, and rattling against them, was an array of objects haphazardly tethered by cords and wires and straps of various kinds. I saw masks and shoes, household utensils and naked dolls, large bleached bones and the skeletons of small animals, bottles of colored glass, the head of a dog with a rusty chain wrapped several times around its neck, and sundry scraps of debris and other things I could not name, all knocking together in a wild percussion. I watched and listened as that ludicrous vehicle passed by in the street. Nothing else followed it, and the enigmatic parade seemed to be at an end, now only a delirious noise fading into the distance. Then a voice called out behind me.

'What are you doing back here?'

I turned around and saw a fat old woman moving toward me from the shadows of that narrow passageway between the two high buildings. She was wearing a highly decorated hat that was almost as wide as she was, and her already ample form was augmented by numerous layers of colorful scarves and shawls. Her body was further weighted down by several necklaces which hung like a noose around her neck and many bracelets about both of her chubby wrists. On the thick fingers of either hand were a variety of large gaudy rings.

'I was watching the parade,' I said to her. 'But I couldn't see what was inside the cage, or whatever it was. It seemed to be empty.'

The woman simply stared at me for some time, as if contemplating my face and perhaps surmising that I had only recently arrived in the northern border town. Then she introduced herself as Mrs Glimm and said that she ran a lodging house. 'Do you have a place to stay?' she asked in an aggressively demanding tone. 'It should be dark soon,' she said, glancing slightly upward. 'The days are getting shorter and shorter.'

I agreed to follow her back to the lodging house. On the way I asked her about the parade. 'It's all just some nonsense,' she said as we walked through the darkening streets of the town. 'Have you seen one of these?' she asked, handing me a crumpled piece of paper that she had stuffed among her scarves and shawls.

Smoothing out the page Mrs Glimm had placed in my hands, I tried to read in the dimming twilight what was printed upon it.

At the top of the page, in capital letters, was a title: METAPHYSICAL LECTURE I. Below these words was a brief text which I read to myself as I walked with Mrs Glimm. 'It has been said,' the text began, 'that after undergoing certain ordeals – whether ecstatic or abysmal – we should be obliged to change our names, as we are no longer who we once were. Instead the opposite rule is applied: our names linger long after anything resembling what we were, or thought we were, has disappeared entirely. Not that there was ever much to begin with – only a few questionable memories and impulses drifting about like snowflakes in a gray and endless winter. But each soon floats down and settles into a cold and nameless void.'

After reading this brief 'metaphysical lecture,' I asked Mrs Glimm where it came from. 'They were all over town,' she replied. 'Just some nonsense, like the rest of it. Personally I think this sort of thing is bad for business. Why should I have to go around picking up customers in the street? But as long as someone's paying my price I will accommodate them in whatever style they wish. In addition to operating a lodging house or two, I am also licensed to act as an undertaker's assistant and a cabaret stage manager. Well, here we are. You can go inside – someone will be there to take care of you. At the moment I have an appointment elsewhere.' With these concluding words, Mrs Glimm walked off, her jewelry rattling with every step she took.

Mrs Glimm's lodging house was one of several great structures along the street, each of them sharing similar features and all of them, I later discovered, in some way under the proprietorship or authority of the same person – that is, Mrs Glimm. Nearly flush with the street stood a series of high and almost styleless houses with institutional façades of pale gray mortar and enormous dark roofs. Although the street was rather wide, the sidewalks in front of the houses were so narrow that the roofs of these edifices slightly overhung the pavement below, creating a sense of tunnel-like enclosure. All of the houses might have been siblings of my childhood residence, which I once heard someone describe as an 'architectural moan.' I thought of this phrase as I went through the process of renting a room in Mrs Glimm's lodging house, insisting that I be placed in one that faced the street. Once I was settled into my apartment, which was actually a single, quite expansive bedroom, I stood at the window gazing up and down the street of gray houses, which together seemed to form a procession of some kind, a frozen funeral parade. I repeated the words 'architectural moan' over and over to myself until exhaustion forced me away from the window and under the musty blankets of the bed. Before I fell asleep I remembered that it was Dr Zirk who had used this phrase to describe my childhood home, a place that he had visited so often.

So it was of Dr Zirk that I was thinking as I fell asleep in that expansive bedroom in Mrs Glimm's lodging house. And I was thinking of him not only because he had used the phrase 'architectural moan' to describe the appearance of my childhood home, which so closely resembled those high-roofed structures along that street of gray houses in the northern border town, but also, and even primarily, because the words of the brief metaphysical lecture I had read some hours earlier reminded me so much of the words, those fragments and mutterings, that the doctor had spoken as he sat upon my bed and attended to the life-draining infirmities from which everyone expected I would die at a very young age. Lying under the musty blankets of my bed in that strange lodging house, with a little moonlight shining through the window to illuminate the dreamlike vastness of the room around me, I once again felt the weight of someone sitting upon my bed and bending over my apparently sleeping body, ministering to it with unseen gestures and a soft voice. It was then, while pretending to be asleep as I used to do in my childhood, that I heard the words of a second 'metaphysical lecture.' They were whispered in a slow and resonant monotone.

'We should give thanks,' the voice said to me, 'that a poverty of knowledge has so narrowed our vision of things as to allow the possibility of feeling something about them. How could we find a pretext to react to anything if we understood . . . everything? None but an absent mind was ever victimized by the adventure of intense emotional feeling. And without the suspense that is generated by our benighted state – our status as beings possessed by our own bodies and the madness that goes along with them – who could take enough interest in the universal spectacle to bring forth even the feeblest yawn, let alone exhibit the more dramatic manifestations which lend such unwonted color to a world that is essentially composed of shades of gray upon a background of blackness? Hope and horror, to repeat merely two of the innumerable conditions dependent on a faulty insight, would be much the worse for an ultimate revelation that would expose their lack of necessity. At the other extreme, both our most dire and most exalted emotions are well served every time we take some ray of knowledge, isolate it from the spectrum of illumination, and then forget it completely. All our ecstasies, whether sacred or from the slime, depend on our refusal to be schooled in even the most superficial truths and our maddening will to follow the path of forgetfulness. Amnesia may well be the highest sacrament in the great gray ritual of existence. To know, to understand in the fullest sense, is to plunge into an enlightenment of inanity, a wintry landscape of memory whose substance is all shadows and a profound awareness of the infinite spaces surrounding us on all sides. Within this space we remain suspended only with the aid of strings that quiver with our hopes and our horrors, and which keep us dangling over the gray void. How is it that we can defend such puppetry, condemning any efforts to strip us of these strings? The reason, one must suppose, is that nothing is more enticing, nothing more vitally idiotic, than our desire to have a name – even if it is the name of a stupid little puppet – and to hold on to this name throughout the long ordeal of our lives as if we could hold on to it forever. If only we could keep those precious strings from growing frayed and tangled, if only we could keep from falling into an empty sky, we might continue to pass ourselves off under our assumed names and perpetuate our puppet's dance throughout all eternity . . .'

The voice whispered more words than this, more than I can recall, as if it would deliver its lecture without end. But at some point I drifted off to sleep as I had never slept before, calm and gray and dreamless.

The next morning I was awakened by some noise down in the street outside my window. It was the same delirious cacophony I had heard the day before when I first arrived in the northern border town and witnessed the passing of that unique parade. But when I got up from my bed and went to the window, I saw no sign of the uproarious procession. Then I noticed the house directly opposite the one in which I had spent the night. One of the highest windows of that house across the street was fully open, and slightly below the ledge of the window, lying against the gray façade of the house, was the body of a man hanging by his neck from a thick white rope. The cord was stretched taut and led back through the window and into the house. For some reason this sight did not seem in any way unexpected or out of place, even as the noisy thrumming of the unseen parade grew increasingly loud and even when I recognized the figure of the hanged man, who was extreme-ly slight of build, almost like a child in physical stature. Although many years older than when I had last seen him, his hair and beard now radiantly white, clearly the body was that of my old physician, Dr Zirk.

Now I could see the parade approaching. From the far end of the gray, tunnel-like street, the clown creature strolled in its loose white garments, his egg-shaped head scanning the high houses on either side. As the creature passed beneath my window it looked up at me for a moment with that same expression of bland malevolence, and then passed on. Following this figure was the formation of ragged men harnessed by ropes to a cage-like vehicle that rolled along on wooden wheels. Countless objects, many more than I saw the previous day, clattered against the bars of the cage. The grotesque inventory now included bottles of pills that rattled with the contents inside them, shining scalpels and instruments for cutting through bones, needles and syringes strung together and hung like ornaments on a Christmas tree, and a stethoscope that had been looped about the decapitated dog's head. The wooden stakes of the caged platform wobbled to the point of breaking with the additional weight of this cast-off clutter. Because there was no roof covering this cage, I could see down into it from my window. But there was nothing inside, at least for the moment. As the vehicle passed directly below, I looked across the street at the hanged man and the thick rope from which he dangled like a puppet. From the shadows inside the open window of the house, a hand appeared that was holding a polished steel straight razor. The fingers of that hand were thick and wore many gaudy rings. After the razor had worked at the cord for a few moments, the body of Dr Zirk fell from the heights of the gray house and landed in the open vehicle just as it passed by. The procession which was so lethargic in its every aspect now seemed to disappear quickly from view, its muffled riot of sounds fading into the distance.

To make an end of it, I thought to myself – *to make an end of it in whatever style you wish*.

I looked at the house across the street. The window that was once open was now closed, and the curtains behind it were drawn. The tunnel-like street of gray houses was absolutely quiet and absolutely still. Then, as if in answer to my own deepest wish, a sparse showering of snowflakes began to descend from the gray morning sky, each one of them a soft whispering voice. For the longest time I continued to stare out from my window, gazing upon the street and the town that I knew was my home.

WHEN YOU HEAR THE SINGING, YOU WILL KNOW IT IS TIME

I had lived in the town near the northern border long enough so that, with the occult passing of time, I had begun to assume that I would never leave there, at least not while I was alive.

I would die by my own hand, I might have believed, or possibly by the more usual means of some violent misadventure or some wasting disease. But certainly I had begun to assume that my life's end, as if by right, would take place either within the town itself or in close proximity to its outskirts, where the dense streets and structures of the town started to thin out and eventually dissolved into a desolate and seemingly endless countryside. Following my death, I thought, or had begun unwittingly to assume, I would be buried in the hilltop graveyard outside the town. I had no idea that there were others who might have told me that it was just as likely I would not die in the town and therefore would not be buried, or interred in any way whatsoever, within the hilltop graveyard. Such persons might have been regarded as hysterics of some kind, or possibly some type of impostor, since everyone who was a permanent resident of the northern border town seemed to be either one or the other and often both of them at once. These individuals might have suggested to me that it was also entirely possible neither to die in the town nor ever to leave it. I began to learn how such a thing might happen during the time I was living in a small backstairs apartment on the ground floor of a large rooming house located in one of the oldest parts of town.

It was the middle of the night, and I had just awakened in my bed. More precisely, I had *started into wakefulness*, much as I had done throughout my life. This habit of starting into wakefulness in the middle of the night enabled me to become aware, on that particular night, of a soft droning sound which filled my small, one-room apartment and which I might not have heard had I been the sort of person who remains asleep all night long. The sound was emanating from under the floorboards and rose up to reverberate in the moonlit darkness of the entire room. After a few moments sitting up in my bed, and then getting out of bed to step quietly around my small apartment, it seemed to me that the soft droning sound I heard was made by a voice, a very deep voice, which spoke as if it were delivering a lecture of some kind or addressing an audience with the self-assured inflections of authority. Yet I could not discern a single word of what the voice was saying, only its droning intonations and its deeply reverberant quality as it rose up from beneath the floorboards of my small backstairs apartment.

Until that night I had not suspected that there was a cellar below the rooming house where I lived on the ground floor. I was even less prepared to discover, as I eventually did, that hidden under a small, worn-down carpet, which was the only floor covering in my room, was a trap door – an access, it seemed, to whatever basement or cellar might have existed (beyond all my suspicions) below the large rooming house. But there was something else unusual about this trap door, aside from its very presence in my small apartment room and the fact that it implied the existence of some type of rooming-house cellar. Although the trap door was somehow set into the floorboards of my room, it did not in any way appear to be *of a piece* with them. The trap door, as I thought of it, did not at all seem to be constructed of wood but of something that was more of a leathery consistency, all withered and warped and cracked in places as though it did not fit in with the roughly parallel lines of the floorboards in my room but clearly opposed them both in its shape and its angles, which were highly irregular by any standards that might conceivably apply to a rooming-house trap door. I could not even say if this leathery trap door had four sides to it or possibly five sides or more, so elusive and misshapen was its crude and shriveled construction, at least as I saw it in the moonlight after starting into wakefulness in my small backstairs apartment. Yet I was absolutely certain that the deeply reverberant voice which continued to drone on and on as I inspected the trap door was in fact emanating from a place, a cellar or basement of some kind, directly below my room. I knew this to be true because I placed my hand, very briefly, on the trap door's leathery and irregular surface, and in that moment I could feel that it was *pulsing* in a way that corresponded to the force and rhythms of the voice which echoed its indecipherable words throughout the rest of that night, fading only moments before daylight.

Having remained awake for most of the night, I left my backstairs apartment and began to wander the streets of the northern border town on a cold and overcast morning in late autumn. Throughout the whole of that day I saw the town, where I had already lived for some time, under an aspect I had not known before. I have stated that this town near the northern border was a place where I had assumed I would one day die, and I may even say it was a place where I actually desired to make an end of it, or such was the intention or wish that I *entertained* at certain times and in certain places, including my residence in one of the oldest sections of the town. But as I wandered the streets on that overcast morning in late autumn, and throughout the day, my entire sense of my surroundings, as well as my intuition that my existence would be terminated within those surroundings, had become altered in a completely unexpected manner. The town had, of course, always displayed certain peculiar and often profoundly surprising qualities and features. Sooner or later everyone who was a permanent resident there was confronted with something of a nearly insupportable oddity or corruption.

As I wandered along one byway or another throughout that morning and into late afternoon, I recalled a specific street near the edge of town, a dead-end street where all the houses and other buildings seemed to have grown into one another, melding their diverse materials into a bizarre and jagged conglomerate of massive architectural proportions, with peaked roofs and soaring chimneys or towers visibly swaying and audibly moaning even in the calm of an early summer twilight. I had thought that this was the absolute limit, only to find out at exactly the moment of having this thought that there was something further involved with this street, something that caused persons living in the area to repeat a special slogan or incantation to whomever would listen. *When you hear the singing*, they said, *you will know it is time*. These words were spoken, and I heard them myself, as if the persons uttering them were attempting to absolve or protect themselves in some way that was beyond any further explication. And whether or not one heard the singing or had ever heard what was called the *singing*, and whether or not that obscure and unspeakable *time* ever came, or would ever come to those who arrived in that street with its houses and other buildings all mingled together and tumbling into the sky, there nevertheless remained within you the feeling that this was still the place – the town near the northern border – where you came to live and where you might believe you would be a permanent resident until either you chose to leave it or until you died, possibly by violent misadventure or some wasting disease, if not by your own hand. Yet on that overcast morning in late autumn I could no longer maintain this feeling, not after having started into wakefulness the night before, not after having heard that droning voice which delivered some incomprehensible sermon for hours on end, and not after having seen that leathery trap door which I placed my hand upon for only a brief moment and thereafter retreated to the furthest corner of my small apartment until daylight.

And I was not the only one to notice a change within the town, as I discovered when twilight drew on and more of us began to collect on street corners or in back alleys, as well as in abandoned storefront rooms or old office buildings where most of the furniture was badly broken and out-of-date calendars hung crooked on the walls. It was difficult for some persons to refrain from observing that there seemed to be fewer of us as the shadows of twilight gathered that day. Even Mrs Glimm, whose lodging house-plus-brothel was as populous as ever with its out-of-town clientele, said that among the permanent residents of the northern border town there was a 'noticeably diminished' number of persons.

A man named Mr Pell (sometimes *Doctor* Pell) was to my knowledge the first to use the word 'disappearances' in order to illuminate, during the course of one of our twilight gatherings, the cause of the town's slightly reduced population. He was sitting in the shadows on the other side of an overturned desk or bookcase, so his words were not entirely audible as he whispered them in the direction of a darkened doorway, perhaps speaking to someone who was standing, or possibly lying down, in the darkness beyond the aperture. But once this concept – of 'disappearances,' that is – had been introduced, it seemed that quite a few persons had something to say on the subject, especially those who had lived in the town longer than most of us or who had lived in the oldest parts of the town for more years than I had. It was from one of the latter, a veteran of all kinds of hysteria, that I learned about the demonic preacher Reverend Cork, whose sermonizing I had apparently heard during the previous night as it reverberated through the leathery trap door in my apartment room. 'You didn't happen to open that trap door, did you?' the old hysteric asked in a somewhat coy tone of voice. We were sitting, just the two of us, on some wooden crates we had found in the opening to a narrow alley. 'Tell me,' he urged as the light from a streetlamp shone upon his thin face in the darkening twilight. 'Tell me that you didn't just take a little peek inside that trap door.' I then told him I had done nothing of the sort. Suddenly he began to laugh hysterically in a voice that was both high-pitched and extremely coarse. 'Of course you didn't take a little peek inside the trap door,' he said when he finally settled down. 'If you had, then you wouldn't be *here* with *me*, you would be *there* with *him*.'

The antics and coy tone of the old hysteric notwithstanding, there was a meaning in his words that resonated with my experience in my apartment room and also with my perception that day of a profound change in the town near the northern border. At first I tended to conceive of the figure of Reverend Cork as a spirit of the dead, someone who had 'disappeared' by wholly natural means. In these terms I was able to think of myself as having been the victim of a haunting at the large rooming house where, no doubt, many persons had ended their lives in one way or another. This metaphysical framework seemed to apply nicely to my recent experiences and did not conflict with what I had been told in that narrow alley as twilight turned into evening. I was indeed *here*, in the northern border town with the old hysteric, and not *there*, in the land of the dead with Reverend Cork the demonic preacher.

But as the night wore on, and I moved among other residents of the town who had lived there far longer than I, it became evident that Reverend Cork, whose voice I had heard 'preaching' the night before, was neither dead, in the usual sense of the word, nor among those who had only recently 'disappeared,' many of whom, I learned, had not disappeared in any mysterious way at all but had simply abandoned the northern border town without notifying anyone. They had made this hasty exodus, according to several hysterics or impostors I spoke with that night, because they had 'seen the signs,' even as I had seen that leathery trap door whose existence in my apartment room was previously and entirely unsuspected.

Although I had not recognized it as such, this trap door, which appeared to lead to a cellar beneath the rooming house where I lived, was among the most typical of the so-called 'signs.' All of them, as numerous persons hysterically avowed, were indications of some type of *threshold* – doorways or passages that one should be cautious not to enter, or even to approach. Most of these signs, in fact, took the form of doors of various types, particularly those which might be found in odd, out-of-the-way places, such as a miniature door at the back of a broom closet or a door appearing on the inner wall of a fireplace, and even doors that might not seem to lead to any sensible space, as would be the case with a trap door in an apartment on the ground floor of a rooming house that did not have a cellar, nor had ever had one that could be accessed in such a way. I did hear about other such 'threshold-signs,' including window frames in the most queer locations, stairways that spiraled downward into depths beneath a common basement or led below ground level along lonely sidewalks, and even entrances to streets that were not formerly known to exist, with perhaps a narrow gate swinging open in temptation.

Yet all of these signs or thresholds gave themselves away by their distinctive appearance, which, according to many of those knowledgeable of such things, was very much like that withered and leathery appearance of the trap door in my apartment room, not to mention displaying the same kind of shapes and angles that were strikingly at odds with their surroundings.

Nevertheless, there were still those who, for one reason or another, chose to ignore the signs or were unable to resist the enticements of thresholds that simply cropped up overnight in the most unforeseen places around the northern border town. To all appearances, at that point, the demonic preacher Reverend Cork had been one of the persons who had 'disappeared' in this way. I now became aware, as the evening progressed into a brilliantly star-filled night, that I had not been the victim of a *haunting*, as I had earlier supposed, but had actually witnessed a phenomenon of quite a different sort.

'The reverend has been gone since the last disappearances,' said an old woman whose face I could barely see in the candlelight that illuminated the enormous, echoing lobby of a defunct hotel where some of us had gathered after midnight. But someone took issue with the old woman, or 'idiot-hag,' as this person called her. The preacher, this other person contended in exactly the following words, was *old town*. This was my first exposure to the phrase 'old town,' but before I could take in its full meaning or implications it began to undergo a metamorphosis among those gathered after midnight in the lobby of that defunct hotel. While the person who called the old woman an idiot-hag continued to speak of the 'old town,' where he said Reverend Cork resided or was originally *from*, the old woman and a few of those who sided with her spoke only about the *other* town. 'No one is *from* the other town,' the woman said to the person who was calling her an idiot-hag. 'There are only those who disappear *into* the other town, among them the demonic preacher Reverend Cork, who may have been a ludicrous impostor but was never what anyone would call *demonic* until he disappeared into that trap door in the room where this gentleman,' she said, referring to me, 'heard him preaching only last night.'

'You idiot-hag,' said the other person, 'the old town existed on the very spot where this northern border town now exists . . . until the day when it disappeared, along with everyone who lived in it, including the demonic preacher Reverend Cork.'

Then someone else, who was lying deep in the cushions of an old divan in the lobby, added the following words: 'It was a *demon town* and was inhabited by demonic entities of all sorts who made the whole thing invisible. Now they throw out these *thresholds* as a way to lure another group of us who only want to live in this town near the northern border and not in some intolerable demon town.'

Nonetheless, the old woman and the few others who sided with her persisted in speaking not about an *old town* or an invisible *demon town*, but about the *other* town, which, they all agreed, never had any concrete existence to speak of, but was simply a metaphysical backdrop to the northern border town that we all knew and that was a place where many of us fervently desired to make an end of our lives. Whatever the facts in this matter, one point was hammered into my brain over and over again: there was simply no peace to be had no matter where you hid yourself away. Even in a northern border town of such intensely chaotic oddity and corruption there was still some greater chaos, some deeper insanity, than one had counted on, or could ever be taken into account – wherever there was anything, there would be chaos and insanity to such a degree that one could never come to terms with it, and it was only a matter of time before your world, whatever you thought it to be, was undermined, if not completely overrun, by another world.

Throughout the late hours of that night the debates and theories and fine qualifications continued regarding the spectral towns and the tangible thresholds that served to reduce the number of permanent residents of the northern border town, either by causing them to disappear through some out-of-the-way door or window or down a spiraling stairway or phantom street, or by forcing them to abandon the town because, for whatever reason, it had become, or seemed to become, something quite different from the place they had known it to be, or believed it to be, for so long. Whether or not they arrived at a resolution of their conflicting views I will never know, since I left the defunct hotel while the discussion was still going strong. But I did not go back to my small apartment in one of the oldest parts of town. Instead I wandered out to the hilltop graveyard outside of town and stood among the graves until the following morning, which was as cold and overcast as the one before it. I knew then that I would not die in the northern border town, either by means of a violent misadventure or a wasting disease, or even by my own hand, and therefore I would not be buried in the hilltop graveyard where I stood that morning looking down on the place where I had lived for so long. I had already wandered the streets of the northern border town for the last time and found, for whatever reason, that they had become something different from what they had been, or had once seemed to be. This was the only thing that was now certain in my mind. For a moment I considered returning to the town and seeking out one of the newly appeared thresholds in order to enter it before all of them mysteriously disappeared again, so that I might disappear along with them into the other town, or the old town, where perhaps I might find once more what I seemed to have lost in the northern border town. Possibly there might have been something there – on the other side of the town – that was like the dead-end street where, it was said, 'When you hear the singing, you will know it is time.' And while I might never be able to die in the town near the northern border, neither would I ever have to leave it. To have such thoughts was, of course, only more chaos and insanity. But I had not slept for two nights. I was tired and felt the ache of every broken dream I had ever carried within me. Perhaps I would one day seek out another town in another land where I could make an end of it, or at least where I could wait in a fatalistic delirium for the end to come. Now it was time to just walk away in silence.

Years later I learned there was a movement to 'clean up' the northern border town of what was elsewhere perceived to be its 'contaminated' elements. On arriving in the town, however, the investigators assigned to this task discovered a place that was all but deserted, the only remaining residents being a few hysterics or impostors who muttered endlessly about 'other towns' or 'demon towns,' and even of an 'old town.' Among these individuals was a large and gaudily attired old woman who styled herself as the owner of a lodging house and several other properties. These venues, she said, along with many others throughout the town, had been rendered uninhabitable and useless for any practical purpose. This statement seemed to capsulize the findings of the investigators, who ultimately composed a report that was dismissive of any threat that might be posed by the town near the northern border, which, whatever else it may have been, or seemed to be, was always a genius of the most insidious illusions.

THE DAMAGED AND THE DISEASED

TEATRO GROTTESCO

T he first thing I learned was that no one *anticipates* the arrival of the Teatro. One would not say, or even think, 'The Teatro has never come to this city – it seems we're due for a visit,' or perhaps, 'Don't be surprised when you-know-what turns up. It's been years since the last time.' Even if the city in which one lives is exactly the kind of place favored by the Teatro, there can be no basis for predicting its appearance. No warnings are given, no fanfare to announce that a Teatro season is about to begin, or that *another* season of that sort will soon be upon us. But if a particular city possesses what is sometimes called an 'artistic underworld,' and if one is in close touch with this society of artists, the chances are optimal for being among those who discover that things have already started. This is the most one can expect.

For a time it was all rumors and lore, hearsay and dreams. Anyone who failed to show up for a few days at the usual club or bookstore or special artistic event was the subject of speculation. But most of the crowd I am referring to led highly unstable, even precarious lives. Any of them might have packed up and disappeared without notifying a single soul. And almost all of the supposedly 'missing ones' were, at some point, seen again. One such person was a filmmaker whose short movie *Private Hell* served as the featured subject of a local one-night festival. But he was nowhere to be seen either during the exhibition or at the party afterward. 'Gone with the Teatro,' someone said with a blasé knowingness, while others smiled and clinked glasses in a sardonic farewell toast.

Yet only a week later the filmmaker was spotted in one of the back rows of a pornographic theater. He later explained his absence by insisting he had been in the hospital following a thorough beating at the hands of some people he had been filming who did not consent or desire to be filmed. This sounded plausible, given the subject matter of the man's work. But for some reason no one believed his hospital story, despite the evidence of bandages he was still required to wear. 'It has to be the Teatro,' argued a woman who always dressed in shades of purple and who was a good friend of the filmmaker. '*His* stuff and *Teatro* stuff,' she said, holding up two crossed fingers for everyone to see.

But what was meant by 'Teatro stuff'? This was a phrase I heard spoken by a number of persons, not all of them artists of a pretentious or self-dramatizing type. Certainly there is no shortage of anecdotes that have been passed around which purport to illuminate the nature and workings of this 'cruel troupe,' an epithet used by those who are too superstitious to invoke the Teatro Grottesco by name. But sorting out these accounts into a coherent *profile*, never mind their truth value, is another thing altogether.

For instance, the purple woman I mentioned earlier held us all spellbound one evening with a story about her cousin's roommate, a self-styled 'visceral artist' who worked the night shift as a stock clerk for a supermarket chain in the suburbs. On a December morning, about an hour before sun-up, the artist was released from work and began his walk home through a narrow alley that ran behind several blocks of various stores and businesses along the suburb's main avenue. A light snow had fallen during the night, settling evenly upon the pavement of the alley and glowing in the light of a full moon which seemed to hover just at the alley's end. The artist saw a figure in the distance, and something about this figure, this winter-morning vision, made him pause for a moment and stare. Although he had a trained eye for sizing and perspective, the artist found this silhouette of a person in the distance of the alley intensely problematic. He could not tell if it was short or tall, or even if it was moving – either toward him or away from him – or was standing still. Then, in a moment of hallucinated wonder, the figure stood before him in the middle of the alley.

The moonlight illuminated a little man who was entirely unclothed and who held out both of his hands as if he were grasping at a desired object just out of his reach. But the artist saw that something was wrong with these hands. While the little man's body was pale, his hands were dark and were too large for the tiny arms on which they hung. At first the artist believed the little man to be wearing oversized mittens. His hands seemed to be covered by some kind of fuzz, just as the alley in which he stood was layered with the fuzziness of the snow that had fallen during the night. His hands looked soft and fuzzy like the snow, except that the snow was white and his hands were black.

In the moonlight the artist came to see that the mittens worn by this little man were more like the paws of an animal. It almost made sense to the artist to have thought that the little man's hands were actually paws which had only appeared to be two black mittens. Then each of the paws separated into long thin fingers that wriggled wildly in the moonlight. But they could not have been the fingers of a hand, because there were too many of them. So what appeared to be fingers could not have been fingers, just as the hands were not in fact hands nor the paws really paws

– no more than they were mittens. And all of this time the little man was becoming smaller and smaller in the moonlight of that alley, as if he were moving into the distance far away from the artist who was hypnotized by this vision. Finally a little voice spoke which the artist could barely hear, and it said to him: 'I cannot keep them away from me anymore, I am becoming so small and weak.' These words suddenly made this whole winter-morning scenario into something that was too much even for the self-styled 'visceral artist.'

In the pocket of his coat the artist had a tool which he used for cutting open boxes at the supermarket. He had cut into flesh in the past, and, with the moonlight glaring upon the snow of that alley, the artist made a few strokes which turned that white world red. Under the circumstances what he had done seemed perfectly justified to the artist, even an act of mercy. The man was becoming so small.

Afterward the artist ran through the alley without stopping until he reached the rented house where he lived with his roommate. It was she who telephoned the police, saying there was a body lying in the snow at such and such a place and then hanging up without giving her name. For days, weeks, the artist and his roommate searched the local newspapers for some word of the extraordinary thing the police must have found in that alley. But nothing ever appeared.

'You see how these incidents are hushed up,' the purple woman whispered to us. 'The police know what is going on. There are even *special police* for dealing with such matters. But nothing is made public, no one is questioned. And yet, after that morning in the alley, my cousin and her roommate came under surveillance and were followed everywhere by unmarked cars. Because these special policemen know that it is artists, or highly artistic persons, who are *approached* by the Teatro. And they know whom to watch after something has happened. It is said that these police may be party to the deeds of that "company of nightmares."'

But none of us believed a word of this Teatro anecdote told by the purple woman, just as none of us believed the purple woman's friend, the filmmaker, when he denied all innuendos that connected him to the Teatro. On the one hand, our imaginations had sided with this woman when she asserted that her friend, the creator of the short movie *Private Hell*, was somehow in league with the Teatro; on the other hand, we were mockingly dubious of the story about her cousin's roommate, the self-styled visceral artist, and his encounter in the snow-covered alley.

This divided reaction was not as natural as it seemed. Never mind that the case of the filmmaker was more credible than that of the visceral artist, if only because the first story was lacking the extravagant details which burdened the second. Until then we had uncritically relished all we had heard about the Teatro, no matter how bizarre these accounts may have been and no matter how much they opposed a verifiable truth or even a coherent portrayal of this phenomenon. As artists we suspected that it was in our interest to have our heads filled with all kinds of Teatro craziness. Even I, a writer of nihilistic prose works, savored the inconsistency and the flamboyant absurdity of what was told to me across a table in a quiet library or a noisy club. In a word, I delighted in the *unreality* of the Teatro stories. The truth they carried, if any, was immaterial. And we never questioned any of them until the purple woman related the episode of the visceral artist and the small man in the alley.

However, this new disbelief was not in the least inspired by our sense of reason or reality. It was in fact based solely on fear; it was driven by the will to negate what one fears. No one gives up on something until it turns on them, whether or not that thing is real or unreal. In some way all of this Teatro business had finally worn upon our nerves; the balance had been tipped between a madness that intoxicated us and one that began to menace our minds. As for the woman who always dressed herself in shades of purple . . . we avoided her. It would have been typical of the Teatro, someone said, to use a person like that for their purposes.

Perhaps our judgment of the purple woman was unfair. No doubt her theories concerning the 'approach of the Teatro' made us all uneasy. But was this reason enough to cast her out from that artistic underworld which was the only society available to her? Like many societies, of course, ours was founded on fearful superstition, and this is always reason enough for any kind of behavior. She had been permanently stigmatized by too closely associating herself with something unclean in its essence. Because even after her theories were discredited by a newly circulated Teatro tale, her status did not improve.

I am now referring to a story that was going around in which an artist was not *approached* by the Teatro but rather took the first step *toward* the Teatro, as if acting under the impulse of a sovereign will.

The artist in this case was a photographer of the I-am-a-camera type. He was a studiedly bloodless specimen who quite often, and for no apparent reason, would begin to stare at someone and to continue staring until that person reacted in some manner, usually by fleeing the scene but on occasion by assaulting the photographer, who invariably pressed charges. It was therefore not entirely surprising to learn that he tried to engage the services of the Teatro in the way he did, for it was his belief that this cruel troupe could be hired to, in the photographer's words, 'utterly destroy someone.' And the person he wished to destroy was his landlord, a small balding man with a mustache who, after the photographer had moved out of his apartment, refused to remit his security deposit, perhaps with good reason but perhaps not.

In any case, the photographer, whose name incidentally was Spence, made inquiries about the Teatro over a period of some months. Following up every scrap of information, no matter how obscure or suspect, the tenacious Spence ultimately arrived in the shopping district of an old suburb where there was a two-story building that rented space to various persons and businesses, including a small video store, a dentist, and, as it was spelled out on the building's directory, the Theatre Grottesco. At the back of the first floor, directly below a studio for dancing instruction, was a small suite of offices whose glass door displayed some stencilled lettering that read: TG VENTURES. Seated at a desk in the reception area behind the glass door was a young woman with long black hair and black-rimmed eyeglasses. She was thoroughly engrossed in writing something on a small blank card, several more of which were spread across her desk. The way Spence told it, he was undeterred by all appearances that seemed to suggest the Teatro, or Theatre, was not what he assumed it was. He entered the reception area of the office, stood before the desk of the young woman, and introduced himself by name and occupation, believing it important to communicate as soon as possible his identity as an artist, or at least imply as best he could that he was a highly artistic photographer, which undoubtedly he was. When the young woman adjusted her eyeglasses and asked, 'How can I help you?' the photographer Spence leaned toward her and whispered, 'I would like to enlist the services of the Teatro, or Theatre if you like.' When the receptionist asked what he was planning, the photographer answered, 'To utterly destroy someone.' The young woman was absolutely unflustered, according to Spence, by this declaration. She began calmly gathering the small blank cards that were spread across her desk and, while doing this, explained that TG Ventures was, in her words, an 'entertainment service.' After placing the small blank cards to one side, she removed from her desk a folded brochure outlining the nature of the business, which provided clowns, magicians, and novelty performances for a variety of occasions, their specialty being children's parties.

As Spence studied the brochure, the receptionist placidly sat with her hands folded and gazed at him from within the black frames of her eyeglasses. The light in that suburban office suite was bright but not harsh; the pale walls were incredibly clean and the carpeting, in Spence's description, was conspicuously new and displayed the exact shade of purple found in turnips. The photographer said that he felt as if he were standing in a mirage. 'This is all a front,' Spence finally said, throwing the brochure on the receptionist's desk. But the young woman only picked up the brochure and placed it back in the same drawer from which it had come. 'What's behind that door?' Spence demanded, pointing across the room. And just as he pointed at that door there was a sound on the other side of it, a brief rumbling as if something heavy had just fallen to the floor. 'The dancing classes,' said the receptionist, her right index finger pointing up at the floor above. 'Perhaps,' Spence allowed, but he claimed that this sound that he heard, which he described as having an 'abysmal resonance,' caused a sudden rise of panic within him. He tried not to move from where he was standing, but his body was overwhelmed by the impulse to leave that suite of offices. The photographer turned away from the receptionist and saw his reflection in the glass door. She was watching him from behind the lenses of black-framed eyeglasses, and the stencilled lettering on the glass door read backward, as if in a mirror. A few seconds later Spence was outside the building in the old suburb. All the way home, he asserted, his heart was pounding.

The following day Spence paid a visit to his landlord's place of business, which was a tiny office in a seedy downtown building. Having given up on the Teatro, he would have to deal in his own way with this man who would not return his security deposit. Spence's strategy was to plant himself in his landlord's office and stare him into submission with a photographer's unnerving gaze. After he arrived at his landlord's rented office on the sixth floor of what was a thoroughly depressing downtown building, Spence seated himself in a chair looking across a filthy desk at a small balding man with a mustache. But the man merely looked back at the photographer. To make things worse, the landlord (whose name was Herman Zick) would lean toward Spence every so often and in a quiet voice say, 'It's all perfectly legal, you know.' Then Spence would continue his staring, which he was frustrated to find ineffective against this man Zick, who of course was not an artist, nor even a highly artistic person, as were the usual victims of the photographer. Thus the battle kept up for almost an hour, the landlord saying, 'It's all perfectly legal,' and Spence trying to hold a fixed gaze upon the man he wished to utterly destroy.

Ultimately Spence was the first to lose control. He jumped out of the chair in which he was sitting and began to shout incoherently at the landlord. Once Spence was on his feet, Zick swiftly maneuvered around the desk and physically evicted the photographer from the tiny office, locking him out in the hallway. Spence said that he was in the hallway for only a second or two when the doors opened to the elevator that was directly across from Zick's sixth-floor office. Out of the elevator compartment stepped a middle-aged man in a dark suit and black-framed eyeglasses. He wore a full, well-groomed beard which, Spence observed, was slightly streaked with gray. In his left hand the gentleman was clutching a crumpled brown bag, holding it a few inches in front of him. He walked up to the door of the landlord's office and with his right hand grasped the round black doorknob, jiggling it back and forth several times. There was a loud click that echoed down the hallway of that old downtown building. The gentleman turned his head and looked at Spence for the first time, smiling briefly before admitting himself to the office of Herman Zick.

Again the photographer experienced that surge of panic he had felt the day before when he visited the suburban offices of TG Ventures. He pushed the down button for the elevator, and while waiting he listened at the door of the landlord's office. What he heard, Spence claimed, was that terrible sound that had sent him running out into the street from TG Ventures, that 'abysmal resonance,' as he defined it. Suddenly the gentleman with the well-groomed beard and black-rimmed glasses emerged from the tiny office. The door to the elevator had just opened, and the man walked straight past Spence to board the empty compartment. Spence himself did not get in the elevator but stood outside, helplessly staring at the bearded gentleman, who was still holding that small crumpled bag. A split second before the elevator doors slid closed, the gentleman looked directly at Spence and winked at him. It was the assertion of the photographer that this wink, executed from behind a pair of black-framed eyeglasses, made a mechanical clicking sound which echoed down the dim hallway. Prior to his exit from the old downtown building, leaving by way of the stairs rather than the elevator, Spence tried the door to his landlord's office. He found it unlocked and cautiously stepped inside. But there was no one on the other side of the door.

The conclusion to the photographer's adventure took place a full week later. Delivered by regular post to his mail box was a small square envelope with no return address. Inside was a photograph. He brought this item to Des Esseintes' Library, a bookstore where several of us were giving a late-night reading of our latest literary efforts. A number of persons belonging to the local artistic under-world, including myself, saw the photograph and heard Spence's rather frantic account of the events surrounding it. The photo was of Spence himself staring stark-eyed into the camera, which apparently had taken the shot from inside an elevator, a panel of numbered buttons being partially visible along the right-hand border of the picture. 'I could see no camera,' Spence kept repeating. 'But that wink he gave me . . . and what's written on the reverse side of this thing.' Turning over the photo Spence read aloud the following handwritten inscription: 'The little man is so much littler these days. Soon he will know about the soft black stars.

And your payment is past due.' Someone then asked Spence what they had to say about all this at the offices of TG Ventures. The photographer's head swivelled slowly in exasperated negation. 'Not there anymore,' he said over and over. With the single exception of myself, that night at Des Esseintes' Library was the last time anyone would see Spence.

After the photographer ceased to show up at the usual meeting places and special artistic events, there were no cute remarks about his having 'gone with the Teatro.' We were all of us beyond that stage. I was perversely proud to note that a degree of philosophical maturity had now developed among those in the artistic underworld of which I was a part. There is nothing like fear to complicate one's consciousness, inducing previously unknown levels of reflection. Under such mental stress I began to organize my own thoughts and observations about the Teatro, specifically as this phenomenon related to the artists who seemed to be its sole objects of attention.

Whether or not an artist was approached by the Teatro or took the initiative to approach the Teatro himself, it seemed the effect was the same: the end of an artist's work. I myself verified this fact as thoroughly as I could. The filmmaker whose short movie *Private Hell* so many of us admired had, by all accounts, become a full-time dealer in pornographic videos, none of them his own productions. The self-named visceral artist had publicly called an end to those stunts of his which had gained him a modest underground reputation. According to his roommate, the purple woman's cousin, he was now managing the supermarket where he had formerly labored as a stock clerk. As for the purple woman herself, who was never much praised as an artist and whose renown effectively began and ended with the 'cigar box assemblage' phase of her career, she had gone into selling real estate, an occupation in which she became quite a success. This roster of ex-artists could be extended considerably, I am sure of that. But for the purposes of this report or confession (or whatever else you would like to call it) I must end my list of no-longer-artistic persons with myself, while attempting to offer some insights into the manner in which the Teatro Grottesco could transform a writer of nihilistic prose works into a non-artistic, more specifically a *post-artistic* being.

It was after the disappearance of the photographer Spence that my intuitions concerning the Teatro began to crystallize and become explicit thoughts, a dubious process but one to which I am inescapably subject as a prose writer. Until that point in time, everyone tacitly assumed that there was an intimacy of *kind* between the Teatro and the artists who were either approached by the Teatro or themselves approached this cruel troupe by means of some overture, as in the case of Spence, or perhaps by gestures more subtle, even purely noetic (I retreat from writing *unconscious*, although others might argue with my intellectual reserve). Many of us even spoke of the Teatro as a manifestation of super-art, a term which we always left conveniently nebulous. However, following the disappearance of the photographer, all knowledge I had acquired about the Teatro, fragmentary as it was, became configured in a completely new pattern. I mean to say that I no longer considered it possible that the Teatro was in any way related to a super-art, or to an art of any kind – quite the opposite in fact. To my mind the Teatro was, and is, a phenomenon intensely destructive of everything that I conceived of as art. Therefore, the Teatro was, and is, intensely destructive of all artists and even of highly artistic persons. Whether this destructive force is a matter of intention or is an epiphenomenon of some unrelated, perhaps greater design, or even if there exists anything like an intention or design on the part of the Teatro, I have no idea (at least none I can elaborate in comprehensible terms). Nonetheless, I feel certain that for an artist to encounter the Teatro there can be only one consequence: the end of that artist's work. Strange, then, that knowing this fact I still acted as I did.

I cannot say if it was I who approached the Teatro or vice versa, as if any of that stupidness made a difference. The important thing is that from the moment I perceived the Teatro to be a profoundly anti-artistic phenomenon I conceived the ambition to make my form of art, by which I mean my nihilistic prose writings, into an *anti-Teatro* phenomenon. In order to do this, of course, I required a penetrating knowledge of the Teatro Grottesco, or of some significant aspect of that cruel troupe, an insight of a deeply subtle, even dreamlike variety into its nature and workings.

The photographer Spence had made a great visionary advance when he intuited that it was in the nature of the Teatro to act on his request to utterly destroy someone (although the exact meaning of the statement 'he will know about the soft black stars,' in reference to Spence's landlord, became known to both of us only sometime later). I realized that I would need to make a similar leap of insight in my own mind. While I had already perceived the Teatro to be a profoundly anti-artistic phenomenon, I was not yet sure what in the world would constitute an anti-Teatro phenomenon, nor how in the world I could turn my own prose writings to such a purpose.

Thus, for several days I meditated on these questions. As usual, the psychic demands of this meditation severely taxed my bodily processes, and in my weakened state I contracted a virus, specifically an *intestinal virus*, which confined me to my small apartment for a period of one week. Nonetheless, it was during this time that things fell into place regarding the Teatro and the insights I required to oppose this company of nightmares in a more or less efficacious manner.

Suffering through the days and nights of an illness, especially an intestinal virus, one becomes highly conscious of certain realities, as well as highly sensitive to the *functions* of these realities, which otherwise are not generally subject to prolonged attention or meditation. Upon recovery from such a virus, the consciousness of these realities and their functions necessarily fades, so that the once-stricken person may resume his life's activities and not be driven to insanity or suicide by the acute awareness of these most unpleasant facts of existence. Through the illumination of analogy, I came to understand that the Teatro operated in much the same manner as the illness from which I had recently suffered, with the consequence that the person exposed to the Teatro-disease becomes highly conscious of certain realities and their functions, ones quite different of course from the realities and functions of an intestinal virus. However, an intestinal virus ultimately succumbs, in a reasonably healthy individual, to the formation of antibodies (or something of that sort). But the disease of the Teatro, I now understood, was a disease for which no counteracting agents, or antibodies, had ever been created by the systems of the individuals – that is, the *artists* – it attacked. An encounter with any disease, including an intestinal virus, serves to alter a person's mind, making it intensely aware of certain realities, but this mind cannot remain altered once this encounter has ended or else that person will never be able to go on living in the same way as before. In contrast, an encounter with the Teatro appears to remain within one's system and to alter a person's mind permanently. For the artist the result is not to be driven into insanity or suicide (as might be the case if one assumed a permanent mindfulness of an intestinal virus) but the absolute termination of that artist's work. The simple reason for this effect is that there are no antibodies for the disease of the Teatro, and therefore no relief from the consciousness of the realities which an encounter with the Teatro has forced upon an artist.

Having progressed this far in my contemplation of the Teatro – so that I might discover its nature or essence and thereby make my prose writings into an anti-Teatro phenomenon – I found that I could go no further. No matter how much thought and meditation I devoted to the subject I did not gain a definite sense of having revealed to myself the true realities and functions that the Teatro communicated to an artist and how this communication put an end to that artist's work. Of course I could vaguely imagine the species of awareness that might render an artist thenceforth incapable of producing any type of artistic efforts. I actually arrived at a fairly detailed and disturbing idea of such an awareness – a *world-awareness*, as I conceived it. Yet I did not feel I had penetrated the mystery of 'Teatrostuff.' And the only way to know about the Teatro, it seemed, was to have an encounter with it. Such an encounter between myself and the Teatro would have occurred in any event as a result of the discovery that my prose writings had been turned into an anti-Teatro phenomenon: this would constitute an *approach* of the most outrageous sort to that company of nightmares, forcing an encounter with all its realities and functions. Thus it was not necessary, at this point in my plan, to have actually succeeded in making my prose writings into an anti-Teatro phenomenon. I simply had to make it known, falsely, that I had done so.

As soon as I had sufficiently recovered from my intestinal virus I began to spread the word. Every time I found myself among others who belonged to the so-called artistic underworld of this city I bragged that I had gained the most intense awareness of the Teatro's realities and functions, and that, far from finishing me off as an artist, I had actually used this awareness as inspiration for a series of short prose works. I explained to my colleagues that merely to exist – let alone create artistic works – we had to keep certain things from overwhelming our minds. However, I continued, in order to keep these things, such as the realities of an intestinal virus, from overwhelming our minds we attempted to deny them any voice whatsoever, neither a voice in our minds nor, certainly, a precise and clear voice in works of art. The voice of madness, for instance, is barely a whisper in the babbling history of art because its realities are themselves too maddening to speak of for very long –

and those of the Teatro have no voice at all, given their imponderably grotesque nature. Furthermore, I said, the Teatro not only propagated an intense awareness of these things, these realities and functionings of realities – it was *identical* with them. And I, I boasted, had allowed my mind to be overwhelmed by all manner of Teatro stuff, while also managing to use this experience as material for my prose writings. 'This,' I practically shouted one day at Des Esseintes' Library, 'is the super-art.' Then I promised that in two days' time I would give a reading of my series of short prose pieces.

Nevertheless, as we sat around on some old furniture in a corner of Des Esseintes' Library, several of the others challenged my statements and assertions regarding the Teatro. One fellow writer, a poet, spoke hoarsely through a cloud of cigarette smoke, saying to me: 'No one knows what this Teatro stuff is all about. I'm not sure I believe it myself.' But I answered that Spence knew what it was all about, thinking that very soon I too would know what he knew. '*Spence!*' said a woman in a tone of exaggerated disgust (she once lived with the photographer and was a photographer herself). 'He's not telling us about anything these days, never mind the Teatro.' But I answered that, like the purple woman and the others, Spence had been overwhelmed by his encounter with the Teatro, and his artistic impulse had been thereby utterly destroyed. 'And *your* artistic impulse is still intact,' she said snidely. I answered that, yes, it was, and in two days I would prove it by reading a series of prose works that exhibited an intimacy with the most overwhelmingly grotesque experiences and gave voice to them. 'That's because you have no idea what you're talking about,' said someone else, and almost everyone supported this remark. I told them to be patient, wait and see what my prose writings revealed to them. 'Reveal?' asked the poet. 'Hell, no one even knows why it's called the Teatro Grottesco.' I did not have an answer for that, but I repeated that they would understand much more about the

Teatro in a few days, thinking to myself that within this period of time I would have either succeeded or failed in my attempt to provoke an encounter with the Teatro and the matter of my nonexistent anti-Teatro prose writing would be immaterial.

On the very next day, however, I collapsed in Des Esseintes' Library during a conversation with a different congregation of artists and highly artistic persons. Although the symptoms of my intestinal virus had never entirely disappeared, I had not expected to collapse the way I did and ultimately to discover that what I thought was an intestinal virus was in fact something far more serious. As a consequence of my collapse, my unconscious body ended up in the emergency room of a nearby hospital, the kind of place where borderline indigents like myself always end up – a backstreet hospital with dated fixtures and a staff of sleepwalkers.

When I next opened my eyes it was night. The bed in which they had put my body was beside a tall paned window that reflected the dim fluorescent light fixed to the wall behind me, creating a black glare in the windowpanes that allowed no view of anything beyond them, only a broken image of myself and the room where I had been assigned for treatment. There was a long row of these tall paned windows and several other beds in the ward, each of them supporting a sleeping body that, like mine, was damaged in some way and therefore had been committed to that backstreet hospital.

I felt none of the extraordinary pain that had caused me to collapse in Des Esseintes' Library. At that moment, in fact, I could feel nothing of the experiences of my past life: it seemed I had always been an occupant of that dark hospital wards and always would be. This sense of estrangement from both myself and everything else made it terribly difficult to remain in the hospital bed where I had been placed. At the same time I felt uneasy about any movement *away* from that bed, especially any movement that would cause me to approach the open doorway which led into a half-lighted backstreet hospital corridor. Compromising between my impulse to get out of my bed and my fear of moving away from the bed and approaching that corridor, I positioned myself so that I was sitting on the edge of the mattress with my bare feet grazing the cold linoleum floor. I had been sitting on the edge of that mattress for quite a while before I heard the voice out in the corridor.

The voice came over the public address system, but it was not a particularly loud voice. In fact I had to strain my attention for several minutes simply to discern the peculiar qualities of the voice and to decipher what it said. It sounded like a child's voice, a sing-song voice full of taunts and mischief. Over and over it repeated the same phrase – *paging Dr Groddeck, paging Dr Groddeck*. The voice sounded incredibly hollow and distant, garbled by all kinds of interference. *Paging Dr Groddeck*, it giggled from the other side of the world.

I stood up and slowly approached the doorway leading out into the corridor. But even after I had crossed the room in my bare feet and was standing in the open doorway, that child's voice did not become any louder or any clearer. Even when I actually moved out into that long dim corridor with its dated lighting fixtures, the voice that was calling Dr Groddeck sounded just as hollow and distant. And now it was as if I were in a dream in which I was walking in my bare feet down a backstreet hospital corridor, hearing a crazy voice that seemed to be eluding me as I moved past the open doorways of innumerable ward full of damaged bodies. But then the voice died away, calling to Dr Groddeck one last time before fading like the final echo in a deep well. At the same moment that the voice ended its hollow outcrying, I paused somewhere toward the end of that shadowy corridor. In the absence of the mischievous voice I was able to hear something else, a sound like quiet, wheezing laughter. It was coming from the room just ahead of me along the right-hand side of the corridor. As I approached this room I saw a metal plaque mounted at eye level on the wall, and the words displayed on this plaque were these: Dr T. Groddeck.

A strangely glowing light emanated from the room where I heard that quiet and continuous wheezing laughter. I peered around the edge of the doorway and saw that the source of the laughter was an old gentleman seated behind a desk, while the strangely glowing light was coming from a large globular object positioned on top of the desk directly in front of him. The light from this object – a globe of solid glass, it seemed – shone on the old gentleman's face, which was a crazy-looking face with a neatly clipped beard that was pure white and a pair of spectacles with slim rectangular lenses resting on a slender nose. When I moved to stand in the doorway of that office, the eyes of Dr Groddeck did not gaze up at me but continued to stare into the strange, shining globe and at the things that were inside it.

What were these things inside the globe that Dr Groddeck was looking at? To me they appeared to be tiny star-shaped flowers evenly scattered throughout the glass, just the thing to lend a mock-artistic appearance to a common paperweight. Except that these flowers, these spidery chrysanthemums, were pure black. And they did not seem to be firmly fixed within the shining sphere, as one would expect, but looked as if they were floating in position, their starburst of petals wavering slightly like tentacles. Dr Groddeck appeared to delight in the subtle movements of those black appendages. Behind rectangular spectacles his eyes rolled about as they tried to take in each of the hovering shapes inside the radiant globe on the desk before him.

Then the doctor slowly reached down into one of the deep pockets of the lab coat he was wearing, and his wheezing laughter grew more intense. From the open doorway I watched as he carefully removed a small paper bag from his pocket, but he never even glanced at me. With one hand he was now holding the crumpled bag directly over the globe. When he gave the bag a little shake, the things inside the globe responded with an increased agitation of their thin black arms. He used both hands to open the top of the bag and quickly turned it upside down.

From out of the bag something tumbled onto the globe, where it seemed to stick to the surface. It was not actually adhering to the surface of the globe, however, but sinking into the interior of the glass. It squirmed as those soft black stars inside the globe gathered to pull it down to themselves. Before I could see what it was that they had captured, the show was over. Afterward they returned to their places, floating slightly once again within the glowing sphere.

I looked at Dr Groddeck and saw that he was finally looking back at me. He had stopped his asthmatic laughter, and his eyes were staring frigidly into mine, completely devoid of any readable meaning. Yet somehow these eyes provoked me. Even as I stood in the open doorway of that hideous office in a backstreet hospital, Dr Groddeck's eyes provoked in me an intense outrage, an astronomical resentment of the position I had been placed in. Even as I had consummated my plan to encounter the Teatro and experience its most devastating realities and functions (in order to turn my prose works into an anti-Teatro phenomenon) I was outraged to be standing where I was standing and resentful of the staring eyes of Dr Groddeck. It no longer mattered whether I had approached the Teatro, the Teatro had approached me, or we had both approached each other. I realized that there is such a thing as being approached in order to force one's hand into making what only appears to be an approach, which is actually a non-approach that negates the whole concept of approaching. It was all a fix from the start because I belonged to an artistic underworld, because I was an artist whose work would be brought to an end by an encounter with the Teatro Grottesco. And so I was outraged by the eyes of Dr Groddeck, which were the eyes of the Teatro, and I was resentful of all the insane realities and the excruciating functions of the Teatro. Although I knew that the persecutions of the Teatro were not exclusively focused on the artists and highly artistic persons of the world, I was nevertheless outraged and resentful to be singled out for *special treatment*. I wanted to punish those persons in this world who are not the object of such special treatment. Thus, at the top of my voice, I called out in the dim corridor – I cried out the summons for others to join me before the stage of the Teatro. Strange that I should think it necessary to compound the nightmare of all those damaged bodies in that backstreet hospital, as well as its staff of sleepwalkers who moved within a world of outdated fixtures. But by the time anyone arrived Dr Groddeck was gone, and his office became nothing more than a room full of dirty laundry.

My escapade that night notwithstanding, I was soon released from the hospital, even though the results of several tests I had been administered were still pending. I was feeling as well as ever, and the hospital, like any hospital, always needed bed space for more damaged bodies. They said I would be contacted in the next few days.

It was in fact on the following day that I was informed of the outcome of my stay in the hospital. 'Hello again,' began the letter, which was typed on a plain, though waterstained sheet of paper. 'I was so pleased to finally meet you in person. I thought your performance during our interview at the hospital was really first rate, and I am authorized to offer you a position with us. There is an opening in our organization for someone with your resourcefulness and imagination. I'm afraid things didn't work out with Mr Spence. But he certainly did have a camera's eye, and we have gotten some wonderful pictures from him. I would especially like to share with you his last shots of the soft black stars, or S.B.S., as we sometimes refer to them. Veritable super-art, if there ever was such a thing!

'By the way, the results of your tests – some of which you have yet to be subjected to – are going to come back positive. If you think an intestinal virus is misery, just wait a few more months. So think fast, sir. We will arrange another meeting with you in any case. And remember – *you* approached *us*. Or was it the other way around?

'As you might have noticed by now, all this artistic business can only keep you going so long before you're left speechlessly gaping at the realities and functions of . . . well, I think you know what I'm trying to say. I was forced into this realization myself, and I'm quite mindful of what a blow this can be. Indeed, it was I who invented the appellative for our organization as it is currently known. Not that I put any stock in names, nor should you. Our company is so much older than its own name, or any other name for that matter. (And how many it's had over the years – The Ten Thousand Things, Anima Mundi, Nethescurial.) You should be proud that we have a special part for you to play, such a talented artist. In time you will forget yourself entirely in your work, as we all do eventually. Myself, I go around with a trunkful of aliases, but do you think I can say who I once was *really*? A man of the theater, that seems plausible. Possibly I was the father of Faust or Hamlet – or merely Peter Pan.

'In closing, I do hope you will seriously consider our offer to join us. We can do something about your medical predicament. We can do just about anything. Otherwise, I'm afraid that all I can do is welcome you to your own private hell, which will be as unspeakable as any on earth.'

The letter was signed Dr Theodore Groddeck, and its prognostication of my physical health was accurate: I have taken more tests at the backstreet hospital and the results are somewhat grim. For several days and sleepless nights I have considered the alternatives the doctor proposed to me, as well as others of my own devising, and have yet to reach a decision on what course to follow. The one conclusion that keeps forcing itself upon me is that it makes no difference what choice I make or do not make. You can never anticipate the Teatro – or anything else. You can never know what you are approaching or what is approaching you. Soon enough my thoughts will lose all clarity, and

I will no longer be aware that there was ever a decision to be made. The soft black stars have already begun to fill the sky.

GAS STATION CARNIVALS

Outside the walls of the Crimson Cabaret was a world of rain and darkness. At intervals, whenever someone entered or exited through the front door of the club, one could actually see the steady rain and was allowed a brief glimpse of the darkness. Inside it was all amber light, tobacco smoke, and the sound of the raindrops hitting the windows, which were all painted black. On such nights, as I sat at one of the tables in that drab little place, I was always filled with an infernal merriment, as if I were waiting out the apocalypse and could not care less about it. I also liked to imagine that I was in the cabin of an old ship during a really vicious storm at sea or in the club car of a luxury passenger train that was being rocked on its rails by ferocious winds and hammered by a demonic rain. Sometimes, when I was sitting in the Crimson Cabaret on a rainy night, I thought of myself as occupying a waiting room for the abyss (which of course was exactly what I was doing) and between sips from my glass of wine or cup of coffee I smiled sadly and touched the front pocket of my coat where I kept my imaginary ticket to oblivion.

However, on that particular rainy November night I was not feeling very well. My stomach was slightly queasy, as if signalling the onset of a virus or even food poisoning. Another source for my malaise, I thought to myself, might well have been my longstanding nervous condition, which fluctuated from day to day but was always with me in some form and manifested itself in a variety of symptoms both physical and psychic. I was in fact experiencing a faint sensation of panic, although this in no way ruled out the possibility that the queasiness of my stomach was due to a strictly physical cause, either viral or toxic. Neither did it rule out a third possibility which I was trying to ignore at that point in the evening. Whatever the etiology of my stomach disorder, I felt the need to be in a public place that night, so that if I should collapse – an eventuality I often feared – there would be people around who might attend to me, or at least shuttle my body off to the hospital. At the same time I was not seeking close contact with any of these people, and I would have been bad company in any case, sitting there in the corner of the club drinking mint tea and smoking mild cigarettes out of respect for my ailing stomach. For all these reasons I had brought my notebook with me that night and had it lying open on the table before me, as if to say that I wanted to be left alone to mull over some literary matters. But when Stuart Quisser entered the club at approximately ten o'clock, the sight of me sitting at a corner table with my open notebook, drinking mint tea and smoking mild cigarettes so that I might stay on top of the situation with my queasy stomach, did not in the least discourage him from walking directly to my table and taking the seat across from me. A waitress came over to us. Quisser ordered some kind of white wine, while I asked for another cup of mint tea.

'So now it's mint tea,' Quisser said as the girl left us.

'I'm surprised you're showing your face around here,' I said by way of reply.

'I thought I might try to make up with the old crimson woman.'

'Make up? That doesn't sound like you.'

'Nevertheless, have you seen her tonight?'

'No, I haven't. You humiliated her at that party. I haven't seen her since, not even in her own club. I don't know if you're aware of this, but she's not someone you want to have as an enemy.'

'Meaning what?' he asked.

'Meaning that she has connections you know absolutely nothing about.'

'And of course *you* know all about it. I've read your stories. You're a confessed paranoid, so what's your point?'

'My point,' I said, 'is that there's hell in every handshake, never mind an outright and humiliating insult.'

'I had too much to drink, that's all.'

'You called her a *deluded no-talent*.'

Quisser looked up at the waitress as she approached with our drinks, and he made a hasty hand-signal to me for silence. When she was gone he said, 'I happen to know that our waitress is very loyal to the crimson woman. She will very probably inform her about my visiting the club tonight. I wonder if she would be willing to act as a go-between with her boss and deliver a second-hand apology from me.'

'Look around at the walls,' I said.

Quisser set down his glass of wine and scanned the room.

'Hmm,' he said when he had finished looking. 'This is more serious than I thought. She's taken down all her old paintings. And the new ones don't look like her work at all.'

'They're not. You *humiliated* her.'

'And yet she seems to have done up the stage since I last saw it. New paint job or something.'

The so-called stage to which Quisser referred was a small platform in the opposite corner of the club. This area was entirely framed by four long panels, each of them painted with black and gold sigils against a glossy red background. Various events occurred on this stage: poetry readings, *tableaux vivants*, playlets of sundry types, puppet shows, artistic slideshows, musical performances, and so on. That night, which was a Tuesday, the stage was dark. I observed nothing different about it and asked Quisser what he imagined he thought was new.

'I can't say exactly, but something seems to have been done. Maybe it's those black and gold ideographs or whatever they're supposed to be. The whole thing looks like the cover of a menu in a Chinese restaurant.'

'You're quoting yourself,' I said.

'What do you mean?'

'The Chinese menu remark. You used that in your review of the Marsha Corker exhibit last month.'

'Did I? I don't remember.'

'Are you just saying you don't remember, or do you really not remember?' I asked this question in the spirit of trivial curiosity, my queasy stomach discouraging the strain of any real antagonism on my part.

'I *remember*, all right? Which reminds me, there's something I wanted to talk to you about. It came to me the other day, and I immediately thought of you and your . . . stuff,' he said, gesturing toward my notebook of writings open on the table between us. 'I can't believe it's never come up before. You of all people should know about them. No one else seems to. It was years ago, but you're old enough to remember them. You've got to remember them.'

'Remember what?' I asked, and after the briefest pause he replied:

'The gas station carnivals.'

And he said these words as if he were someone delivering a punchline to a joke, the proud bringer of a surprising and profound hilarity. I was supposed to express an astonished recognition, that much I knew. It was not a phenomenon of which I was *entirely ignorant*, and memory is such a tricky thing. This, at least, is what I told Quisser. But as Quisser told me *his* memories, trying to arouse mine, I gradually realized the true nature and purpose of the so-called gas station carnivals. During this time it was all I could do to conceal how badly my stomach was acting up on me, queasy and burning. I kept telling myself, as Quisser was talking about his memories of the gas station carnivals, that I was certainly experiencing the onset of a virus, if in fact I had not been the victim of food poisoning. Quisser, nevertheless, was so caught up in his story that he seemed not to notice my agony.

Quisser said that his recollections of the gas station carnivals derived from his early childhood. His family, meaning his parents and himself, would go on long vacations by car, often driving great distances, to a variety of destinations. Along the way, naturally, they would need to stop at any number of gas stations that were located in towns and cities, as well as those that they came upon in more isolated, rural locales. These were the places, Quisser said, where one was most likely to discover those hybrid enterprises which he called gas station carnivals.

Quisser did not claim to know when or how these specialized *carnivals*, or perhaps specialized *gas stations*, came into existence, nor how widespread they might have been. His father, whom Quisser believed would be able to answer such questions, had died some years ago, while his mother was no longer mentally competent, having suffered a series of psychic catastrophes not long after the death of Quisser's father. Thus, all that remained to Quisser was the memory of these childhood excursions with his parents, during which they would find themselves in some rural area, perhaps at the crossroads of two highways (and often, he seemed to recall, around sunset), and discover in this isolated location one of those curiosities which he described to me as gas station carnivals.

They were invariably *filling stations*, Quisser emphasized, and not *service stations*, which might have facilities for doing extensive repairs on cars and other vehicles. There would be, in those days, four gas pumps at most, often only two, and some kind of modest building which usually had so many signs and advertisements applied to its exterior that no one could say if anything actually stood beneath them.

Quisser said that as a child he always took special notice of the signs that advertised chewing tobacco, and that as an adult, in his capacity as an art critic, he still found the sight of chewing-tobacco packages very appealing, and he could not understand why some artist had not successfully exploited their visual and imaginative qualities. It seemed to me, as we sat that night in the Crimson Cabaret, that this chewing-tobacco material was intended to lend greater credence to Quisser's story. This detail was so vivid to him. But when I asked Quisser if he recalled any particular brands of chewing tobacco being advertised at these filling stations which had carnivals attached to them, he became slightly defensive, as if my question were intended to challenge the accuracy of his childhood recollection. He then shifted the focus of the issue I had raised by asserting that the carnival aspect of these places was not exactly *attached* to the gas station aspect, but that they were never very far away from each other and there was definitely a commercial liaison between them. His impression, which had been instilled in him like some founding principle of a dream, was that a substantial purchase of gasoline allowed the driver and passengers of a given vehicle free access to the nearby carnival.

At this point in his story Quisser became anxious to explain that these gas station carnivals were by no means elaborate – quite the opposite, in fact. Situated on some empty stretch of land that stood alongside, or sometimes behind, a rural filling station, they consisted of only the remnants of fully fledged carnivals, the *bare bones* of much larger and grander entertainments. There was usually a tall, arched entranceway with colored lightbulbs that provided an eerie contrast to the vast and barren landscape surrounding it. Especially around sunset, which was usually, or possibly always, when Quisser and his parents found themselves in one of these remote locales, the colorful illumination of a carnival entranceway created an effect that was both festive and sinister. But once a visitor had gained admittance to the actual grounds of the carnival, there came a moment of letdown at the thing itself – that spare assemblage of equipment that appeared to have been left behind by a travelling amusement park in the distant past.

There were always only a few carnival rides, Quisser said, and these were very seldom in actual operation. He supposed that at some time they had been in functioning order, probably when they were first installed as an annex to the gas stations. But this period, he speculated, could not have lasted long. And no doubt at the earliest sign of malfunction each of the rides had been shut down. Quisser said that he himself had never been on a single ride at a gas station carnival, though he insisted that his father once allowed him to sit atop one of the wooden horses on a defunct merry-go-round. 'It was a miniature merry-go-round,' Quisser told me, as if that gave his recollected experience an aura of meaning or substance. All the rides, it seemed, were miniature, he asserted – small-scale versions of carnival rides he had elsewhere known and had actually ridden upon. Beside the miniature merry-go-round, which never moved an inch and always stood dark and silent in a remote rural landscape, there would be a miniature ferris wheel (no taller than a bungalow-style house, Quisser said), and sometimes a miniature tilt-a-whirl or a miniature roller coaster. And they were always closed down because once they had malfunctioned, if in fact any of them were ever in operation, they were never subsequently repaired. Possibly they never could be repaired, Quisser thought, given the antiquated parts and mechanisms of these miniature carnival rides.

Yet there was a single, quite crucial amusement that one could almost always expect to see open to the public, or at least to those whose car had been filled with the requisite amount of gasoline and who were therefore free to pass through the brightly lit entranceway upon which the word CARNIVAL was emblazoned in colored lights against a vast and haunting sky at sundown somewhere out in a rural wasteland. Quisser posed to me a question: how could a place advertise itself as a carnival, even a gas station carnival, if it did not include that most vital carnivalesque feature – a sideshow? Perhaps there was some special law or ordinance regulating such matters, Quisser imagined out loud, an old statute of some kind that would have particular force in remote areas where certain traditions have an endurance unknown to urban centers. This would account for the fact that, except under extraordinary circumstances (such as dangerously bad weather), there was always some type of sideshow performance at these gas station carnivals, even though everything else on the grounds stood dark and damaged.

Of course these sideshows, as Quisser described them, were not terribly sophisticated, even by the standards of the average carnival, let alone those that served as commercial enticements for some out-of-the-way gas station. There would be only a single sideshow attraction at a given site, and outwardly they each presented the same image to the carnival's patrons: a small tent of torn and filthy canvas. At some point along the perimeter of the tent would be a loose flap of material through which Quisser and his parents, though sometimes only Quisser himself, would gain entrance to the sideshow. Inside the tent were a few wooden benches that had sunk a little bit into the hard dirt beneath them and, some distance away, a small stage area that was raised perhaps just a foot or so above ground level. Illumination was provided by two ordinary floor lamps – one on either side of the stage – that were without lampshades or any other kind of covering, so that their bare lightbulbs burned harshly and cast dramatic shadows throughout the interior of the tent. Quisser said that he always noticed the frayed electrical cords that trailed off from the base of each lamp and, by means of several extension cords, ultimately found a source of power at the gas station – that is, from within the small brick building which was obscured by so many signs advertising chewing tobacco and other products.

When visitors to a gas station carnival entered the sideshow tent and took their places on one of the benches in front of the stage, they were not usually alerted to the particular nature of the performance or spectacle that they would witness. Quisser remarked that there was no marquee or billboard of any type that might offer such a notice to the carnival-goers either before they entered the sideshow tent or after they were inside and seated on one of the old wooden benches. However, with one important exception, each of the performances, or spectacles, was much the same rigmarole. The audience would settle itself on the wooden benches, most of which were about to collapse or (as Quisser observed) were so unevenly sunk into the ground that it was impossible to sit on them, and the show would begin.

The attractions varied from sideshow to sideshow, and Quisser said he was unable to remember all of the ones he had seen. He did recall what he described as the Human Spider. This was a very brief spectacle during which someone in a clumsy costume scuttled from one side of the stage to the other and back again, exiting through a slit at the back of the tent. The person wearing the costume, Quisser added, was presumably the attendant who pumped gas, washed windows, and performed various services around the filling station. In many sideshow performances, such as that of the Hypnotist, Quisser remembered that a gas station attendant's uniform (greasy gray or blue coveralls) was quite visible beneath the performer's stage clothes. Quisser did admit that he was unsure why he designated this particular sideshow act the 'Hypnotist,' since there was no hypnotism involved in the performance, and of course no marquee or billboard existed either outside the tent or within it that might lead the public to expect any kind of mesmeric routines. The performer was simply clothed in a long, loose overcoat and wore a plastic mask, which was a plain, very pale replica of a human face, with the exception that instead of eyes (or eyeholes) there were two large discs with spiral designs painted upon them. The Hypnotist would gesticulate chaotically in front of the audience for some moments, no doubt because his vision was obscured by the spiral-patterned discs over the eyes of his mask, and then stumble offstage.

There were numerous other sideshow acts that Quisser claimed to have seen, including the Dancing Puppet, the Worm, the Hunchback, and Dr Fingers. With one important exception, the routine was always the same: Quisser and his parents would enter the sideshow tent and sit upon one of the rotted benches, soon after which some performer would appear briefly on the small stage that was lit up by two ordinary floor lamps. The single deviation from this routine was an attraction that Quisser called the Showman.

Whereas every other sideshow act began and ended *after* Quisser and his parents had entered the special tent and seated themselves, the one called the Showman always seemed to be *in progress*. As soon as Quisser stepped inside the tent – invariably preceding his parents, he claimed – he saw the figure standing perfectly still upon the small stage *with his back to the audience*. For whatever reason, there were never any other patrons when Quisser and his parents stopped at twilight and visited one of these gas station carnivals – with their second-hand, defective amusements – eventually making their way into the sideshow tent. This situation did not seem strange or troubling to the young Quisser except on those occasions when he entered the sideshow tent and saw that it was the Showman onstage with his back to a few rows of empty benches that looked as if they might break up altogether if one attempted to sit on them. Whenever faced with this scene, Quisser immediately wanted to turn around and leave the place. But then his parents would come pushing into the tent behind him, he said, and before he knew it they would all be sitting on one of the benches in the very first row looking at the Showman. His parents never knew how terrified he was of this peculiar sideshow figure, Quisser repeated several times.

Furthermore, visiting these gas station carnivals, and especially taking in the sideshows, was all done for Quisser's benefit, since his father and mother would have preferred simply filling up the family car with gasoline and moving on toward whatever vacation spot was next on their itinerary.

Quisser contended that his parents actually enjoyed watching him sit in terror before the Showman, until he could not stand it any longer and asked to go back to the car. At the same time he was quite transfixed by the sight of this sideshow character, who was unlike any other he could remember. There he was, Quisser said, standing with his back to the audience and wearing an old top hat and a long cape that touched the dirty floor of the small stage on which he stood. Sticking out from beneath the top hat were the dense and lengthy shocks of the Showman's stiff red hair, Quisser said, which looked like some kind of sickening vermin's nest. When I asked Quisser if this hair might actually have been a wig, deliberately testing his memory and imagination, he gave me a contemptuous look, as if to stress that *I* was not the one who had seen the stiff red hair; *he* was the one who had seen it sticking out from beneath the Showman's old top hat. The only other features that were visible to the audience, Quisser continued, were the fingers of the Showman which grasped the edges of his long cape. These fingers appeared to Quisser to be somehow deformed, curling together into little claws, and were a pale greenish color. Apparently, as Quisser viewed it, the entire stance of the figure was calculated to suggest that at any moment he might twirl about and confront the audience full-face, his moldy fingers lifting up the edges of his cape, reaching to the height of his stiff red hair. Yet the figure never budged. Sometimes it did seem to Quisser that the Showman was moving his head a little to the left or a little to the right, threatening to reveal one side of his face or the other, playing a horrible game of peek-a-boo. But ultimately Quisser concluded that these perceived movements were illusory and that the Showman was always posed in perfect stillness, a nightmarish mannikin that invited all kinds of imaginings by its very forbearance of any gesture.

'It was all a nasty pretense,' Quisser said to me and then paused to finish off his glass of wine.

'But what if he had turned around to face the audience?' I asked. While awaiting his response, I sipped some of my mint tea, which did not seem to be doing much good for my queasy stomach, yet at the same time was causing no harm either. I lit one of the mild cigarettes that I was smoking on that occasion. 'Did you hear what I said?' I said to Quisser, who had been looking toward the stage located in the opposite corner of the Crimson Cabaret. 'The stage is the same,' I said to Quisser quite sternly, attracting some glances from persons sitting at the other tables in the club. 'The panels are the same and the designs on them are also the same.'

Quisser played nervously with his empty wine glass. 'When I was very young,' he said, 'there were certain occasions on which I would see the Showman, but he wasn't in his natural habitat, so to speak, of the sideshow tent.'

'I think I've heard enough tonight,' I interjected, my hand pressing against my queasy stomach.

'What are you saying?' asked Quisser. 'You remember them, don't you? The gas station carnivals. Maybe just a *faint* memory. I was sure you would be the one to know about them.'

'I think I can say,' I said to Quisser, 'I've heard enough of your gas station carnival story to know what it's all about.'

'What do you mean, "what it's all about"?' asked Quisser, who was still looking over at the small stage across the room.

'Well, for one thing, your later memories, your *purported* memories, of that Showman character. You were about to tell me that throughout your childhood you repeatedly saw this figure at various times and in various places. Perhaps you saw him in the distance of a schoolyard, standing with his back to you. Or you saw him on the other side of a busy street, but when you crossed the street he wasn't there any longer.'

'Something like that, yes.'

'And you were then going to tell me that lately you've been seeing this figure, or faint suggestions of this figure – sketchy reflections in store windows along the sidewalk, flashing glimpses in the rear-view mirror of your car.'

'It's very much like one of your stories.'

'In some ways it is,' I said, 'and in some ways it isn't. You feel that if you ever see the Showman figure turn his head around to look at you ... that something terrible will happen, most likely that you'll perish on the spot from some kind of monumental shock.'

'Yes,' agreed Quisser. 'An unsustainable horror. But I haven't told you the strangest part. You're right that lately I have had glimpses of ... that figure, and I did see him during my childhood, outside of the sideshow tent, I mean. But the strangest part is that I remember seeing him in other places even *before* I first saw him at the gas station carnivals.'

'This is just my point,' I said.

'What is?'

'That there *are no gas station carnivals*. There never were any gas station carnivals. Nobody remembers them because they never existed. The whole idea is preposterous.'

'But my parents were there with me.'

'Exactly – your dead father and your mentally incompetent mother. Do you remember ever discussing with them your vacation experiences at these special gas stations with the carnivals supposedly annexed to them?'

'No, I don't.'

'That's because you never went to any such places with them. Think about how ludicrous it all sounds. That there should be filling stations out in the sticks that entice customers with free admission to broken-down carnivals – it's all so ridiculous. Miniature carnival rides? Gas station attendants doubling as sideshow performers?'

'Not the Showman,' interrupted Quisser. 'He was never a gas station attendant.'

'No, of course he wasn't a gas station attendant, because he was a delusion. The whole thing is an outrageous delusion, but it's also a very particular type of delusion.'

'And what type would that be?' asked Quisser, who was still sneaking glances at the stage area across the room of the Crimson Cabaret.

'It's not some type of common psychological delusion, if that's what you were thinking I was about to say. I have no interest at all in such things. But I am very interested when someone is suffering from a *magical* delusion. Even more precisely, I am interested in delusions that are a result of *art-magic*. And do you know how long you've been under the influence of this art-magic delusion?'

'You've lost me,' said Quisser.

'It's simple,' I said. 'How long have you imagined all this nonsense about the gas station carnivals, and specifically about this character you describe as the Showman?'

'I guess it would be more or less absurd at this point to insist to you that I've seen this figure since childhood, even if that's exactly how it seems and that's exactly what I remember.'

'Of course it would be absurd, because you're definitely delusional.'

'So I'm delusional about the Showman, but you're not delusional about . . . what do you call it?'

'Art-magic. For as long as you've been a victim of this particular art-magic, this is how long you've been delusional about the gas station carnivals and all related phenomena.'

'And how long is that?' asked Quisser.

'Since you humiliated the crimson woman by calling her a *deluded no-talent*. I told you that she had connections you knew absolutely nothing about.'

'I'm talking about something from my childhood, something I've remembered my entire life. You're talking about a matter of days.'

'That's because a matter of days is exactly the term that you've been delusional. Don't you see that through her art-magic she has caused you to suffer from the worst kind of delusion, which might be called a *retroactive* delusion. And it's not only you who's been afflicted in the past days and weeks and even months. Everyone around here has sensed the threat of this art-magic for some time now. I'm beginning to think that I've found out about it too late myself, much too late. You know what it is to suffer from a delusion of the retroactive type, but do you know what it's like to be the victim of a severe stomach disorder? I've been sitting here in the crimson woman's club drinking mint tea served by a waitress who is the crimson woman's friend, thinking that mint tea is just the thing for my stomach when it very well may be aggravating my condition or even causing it to transform, in accordance with the principles of art-magic, into something more serious and more strange. But the crimson woman is not the only one practicing this art-magic. It's happening everywhere around here. It drifted in unexpectedly like a fog at sea, and so many of us are becoming lost in it. Look at the faces in this room and then tell me that you alone are the victim of a horrible art-magic. The crimson woman has quite a few adversaries, just as she is connected with powerful allies. How can I say exactly who they are – some group specializing in art-magic, no doubt, but I can't just say, with a fatuous certainty, "Yes, it must be some particular gang of illuminati," or *esoteric scientists*, as so many have begun styling themselves these days.'

'But it all sounds like one of your stories,' Quisser protested.

'Of course it does, don't you think *she* knows that? But I'm not the one with that grotesque yarn about the gas station carnivals and the sideshow tent with a small stage not unlike the stage on the opposite side of this room. You can't keep your eyes off it, I can see that and so can the other people around the room. And I know what you think you're seeing over there.'

'Assuming *you* know what you're talking about,' said Quisser, who was now forcing himself to look away from the stage area across the room, 'what am I supposed to do about it?'

'You can start by keeping your eyes off that stage across the room. There's nothing you can see over there except an art-magic delusion. There is nothing necessarily fatal or permanent about the affliction. But you must believe that you will recover, just as you would if you were suffering from some non-fatal physical disease. Otherwise these delusions may turn into something far more deadly, on either a physical level or a psychic level, or both. Take my advice, as someone who dabbles in tales of extraordinary doom, and walk away from all of this madness. There are enough fatalities of a mundane sort. Find a quiet place and wait for one of them to carry you off.'

I could now see that the intense conviction carried by my words had finally had its effect on Quisser. His gaze was no longer drawn toward the small stage on the opposite side of the room but was directed full upon me. He did remain somewhat distraught in the face of the truth about his delusion, yet he seemed to have settled down considerably.

I lit another of my mild cigarettes and glanced around the room, not looking for anything or anyone in particular but merely gauging the atmosphere. The tobacco smoke drifting through the club was so much thicker, the amber light several shades darker, and the sound of raindrops still played against the black painted windows of the Crimson Cabaret. I was now back in the cabin of that old ship as it was being cast about in a vicious storm at sea, utterly insecure in its bearings and profoundly threatened by uncontrollable forces. Quisser excused himself to go to the rest room, and his form passed across my field of vision like a shadow through dense fog.

I have no idea how long Quisser was gone from the table. My attention became fully absorbed by the other faces in the club and the deep anxiety they betrayed to me, an anxiety that was not of the natural, existential sort but one that was caused by peculiar concerns of an uncanny nature. *What a season is upon us*, these faces seemed to say. And no doubt their voices would have spoken directly of certain peculiar concerns had they not been intimidated into weird equivocations and double entendres by the fear of falling victim to the same kind of unnatural affliction that had made so much trouble in the mind of the art critic Stuart Quisser. Who would be next? What could a person say these days, or even think, without feeling the dread of repercussion from powerfully connected groups and individuals? I could almost hear their voices asking, 'Why here, why now?' But of course they could have just as easily been asking, 'Why not here, why not now?' It would not occur to this crowd that there were no special rules involved; it would not occur to them, even though they were a crowd of imaginative artists, that the whole thing was simply a matter of random, purposeless terror that converged upon a particular place at a particular time for no particular reason. On the other hand, it would also not have occurred to them that they might have wished it all upon themselves, that they might have had a hand in bringing certain powerful forces and connections into our district simply by wishing them to come. They might have wished and wished for an unnatural evil to fall upon them but, for a while at least, nothing happened. Then the wishing stopped, the old wishes were forgotten yet at the same time gathered in strength, distilling themselves into a potent formula (who can say!), until one day the terrible season began. Because had they really told the truth, this artistic crowd might also have expressed what a sense of meaning (although of a negative sort), not to mention the vigorous thrill (although of an excruciating type), this season of unnatural evil had brought to their lives. What does it mean to be alive except to court disaster and suffering at every moment? For every diversion, for every *thrill* our born nature requires in this carnival world, even to the point of apocalypse, there are risks to be

taken. No one is safe, not even art-magicians or esoteric
scientists, who are the most deluded among us because they
are the most tempted by amusements of an uncanny and
unnatural kind, fumbling as any artist or scientist does with
the *inherent chaos of things*. It was during the moments that
I was looking at all the faces in the Crimson Cabaret, and
thinking my own thoughts about those faces, that a shadow
again passed across my foggy field of vision. While I
expected to find that this shadow was Quisser, my table
companion for that evening, on the way back from his trip
to the rest room, I instead found myself confronted by the
waitress who Quisser had claimed was so loyal to the
crimson woman. She asked if I wanted to order yet another
cup of mint tea, saying it in exactly these words, *yet another
cup of mint tea*. Trying not to become irritated by her
queerly sarcastic tone of voice, which would only have
further aggravated my already queasy stomach, I answered
that I was just about to leave for the night. Then I added
that perhaps my friend wanted to drink *yet another* glass of
wine, pointing across the table to indicate the empty glass
Quisser had left behind when he excused himself to use the
rest room. But there was no empty wine glass across the
table; there was only my empty cup of mint tea. I
immediately accused the waitress of taking away the empty
wine glass while I was distracted by my reverie upon the
faces in the Crimson Cabaret. But she denied ever serving
any glass of wine to anyone at my table, insisting that I had
been alone from the moment I arrived at the club and sat
down at the table across the room from the small stage area.
After a thorough search of the rest room, I returned and
tried to find someone else in the club who had seen the art
critic Quisser talking to me at great length about his gas
station carnivals. But all of them said they had seen no one
of the kind.

Even Quisser himself, when I tracked him down the next
day to a hole-in-the-wall art gallery, maintained that he had
not seen me the night before. He said that he had spent the

entire evening at home by himself, claiming that he had suffered some indisposition – some *bug*, he said – from which he had since fully recovered. When I called him a liar, he stepped right up to me as we stood in the middle of that hole-in-the-wall art gallery, and in a tense whisper he said that I should 'Watch my words.' I was always shooting off my mouth, he said, and in the future I should use more discretion in what I said and to whom I said it. He then asked me if I really thought it was wise to open my mouth at a party and call someone a *deluded no-talent*. There were certain persons, he said, that had powerful connections, and I, of all people, he said, should know better, considering my awareness of such things and the way I displayed this awareness in the stories I wrote. 'Not that I disagreed with what you said about you-know-who,' he said. 'But I would not have made such an open declaration. You *humiliated* her. And these days such a thing can be very perilous, if you know what I mean.'

Of course I did know what he meant, though I did not yet understand why he was now saying these words to me, rather than I to him. Was it not enough, I later thought, that I was still suffering a terrible stomach disorder? Did I also have to bear the burden of another's delusion? But even this explanation eventually fell to pieces upon further inquiry. The stories multiplied about the night of that party, accounts proliferated among my acquaintances and peers concerning exactly *who* had committed the humiliating offence and even who had been the *offended party*. 'Why are you telling me these things?' the crimson woman said to me when I proffered my deepest apologies. 'I barely know who you are. And besides, I've got enough problems of my own. That bitch of a waitress here at the club has taken down all my paintings and replaced them with her own.'

All of us had problems, it seemed, whose sources were untraceable, crossing over one another like the trajectories of countless raindrops in a storm, blending to create a fog of delusion and counter-delusion. Powerful forces and connections were undoubtedly at play, yet they seemed to have no faces and no names, and it was anybody's guess what we – a crowd of deluded no-talents – could have possibly done to offend them. We had been caught up in a season of hideous magic from which nothing could offer us deliverance. More and more I found myself returning to those memories of gas station carnivals, seeking an answer in the twilight of remote rural areas where miniature merry-go-rounds and ferris wheels lay broken in a desolate landscape.

But there is no one here who will listen even to my most abject apologies, least of all the Showman, who may be waiting behind any door (even that leading to the rest room of the Crimson Cabaret). And any room that I enter may become a sideshow tent where I must take my place upon a rickety old bench on the verge of collapse. Even now the Showman stands before my eyes. His stiff red hair moves a little toward one shoulder, as if he is going to turn his gaze upon me, and moves back again; then his head moves a little toward the other shoulder in this never-ending game of horrible peek-a-boo. I can only sit and wait, knowing that one day he will turn full around, step down from his stage, and claim me for the abyss I have always feared. Perhaps then I will discover what it was I did – what any of us did – to deserve this fate.

THE BUNGALOW HOUSE

E arly last September I discovered among the exhibits in a
local art gallery a sort of performance piece in the form
of an audiotape. This, I later learned, was the first of a series
of tape-recorded dream monologues by an unknown artist.
The following is a brief and highly typical excerpt from the
opening section of this work. I recall that after a few
seconds of hissing tape noise, the voice began speaking:
'There was far more to deal with in the bungalow house
than simply an infestation of vermin,' it said, 'although that
too had its questionable aspects.' Then the voice went on: 'I
could see only a few of the bodies where the moonlight
shone through the open blinds of the living-room windows
and fell upon the carpet. Only one of the bodies seemed to
be moving, and that very slowly, but there may have been
more that were not yet dead. Aside from the chair in which
I sat in the darkness there was very little furniture in the
room, or elsewhere in the bungalow house for that matter.
But a number of lamps were positioned around me, floor
lamps and table lamps and even two tiny lamps on the
mantel above the fireplace.'

A brief pause occurred here in the opening section of the tape-recorded dream monologue, as I remember it, after which the voice continued: 'The bungalow house was built with a fireplace, I said to myself in the darkness, thinking how long it had been since anyone had made use of this fireplace, or anything else in the house. Then my attention returned to the lamps, and I began trying each of them one by one, twisting their little grooved switches in the darkness. The moonlight fell upon the lampshades without shining through them, so I could see that none of the lamps was equipped with a lightbulb, and each time I turned the switch of a floor lamp or a table lamp or one of the tiny lamps on the mantel, nothing changed in the dark living room of the bungalow house: the moonlight shone through the dusty blinds and revealed the bodies of insects and other vermin on the pale carpet.'

'The challenges and obstacles facing me in that bungalow house were becoming more and more oppressive,' whispered the voice on the tape. 'There was something so desolate about being in that place in the dead of night, even if I did not know precisely what time it was. And to see upon the pale, threadbare carpet those verminous bodies, some of which were still barely alive; then to try each of the lamps and find that none of them was in working order – everything, it seemed, was in opposition to my efforts, everything aligned against my taking care of the problems I faced in the bungalow house. For the first time I noticed that the bodies lying for the most part in total stillness on the moonlit carpet were not like any species of vermin I had ever seen,' the voice on the tape recording said. 'Some of them seemed to be deformed, their naturally revolting forms altered in ways I could not discern. I knew that I would require specialized implements for dealing with these creatures, an arsenal of advanced tools of extermination. It was the idea of poisons – the toxic solutions and vapors I would need to use in my assault upon the bungalow hordes – that caused me to become overwhelmed by the complexities of the task before me and the paucity of my resources for dealing with them.'

At this point, and many others on the tape (as I recall), the voice became nearly inaudible. 'The bungalow house,' it said, 'was such a bleak environment in which to make a stand: the moonlight through the dusty blinds, the bodies on the carpet, the lamps without any lightbulbs. And the incredible silence. It was not the absence of sounds that I sensed, but the stifling of innumerable sounds and even voices, the muffling of all the noises one might expect to hear in an old bungalow house in the dead of night, as well as countless other sounds and voices. The forces required to accomplish this silence filled me with awe. *The infinite terror and dreariness of an infested bungalow house*, I whispered to myself. *A bungalow universe*, I then thought without speaking aloud. Suddenly I was overcome by a feeling of euphoric hopelessness which passed through my body like a powerful drug and held all my thoughts and all my movements in a dreamy, floating suspension. In the moonlight that shone through the blinds of that bungalow house I was now as still and as silent as everything else.'

The title of the tape-recorded artwork from which I have just quoted was *The Bungalow House (Plus Silence)*. I discovered this and other dream monologues by the same artist at Dalha D. Fine Arts, which was located in the near vicinity of the public library (main branch) where I was employed in the Language and Literature department. Sometimes I spent my lunch breaks at the gallery, even consuming my brown-bag meals on the premises. There were a few chairs and benches on the floor of the gallery, and I knew that the woman who owned the place did not discourage any kind of traffic, however lingering. Her actual livelihood was in fact not derived from the gallery itself. How could it have been? Dalha D. Fine Arts was a hole in the wall. One would think it no trouble at all to keep up the premises where there was so little floor space, just a single room that was by no means overcrowded with artworks or art-related merchandise. But no attempt at such upkeeping seemed ever to have been made. The display window was so filmy that someone passing by could barely make out the paintings and sculptures behind it (the same ones year after year). From the street outside, this tiny front window presented the most desolate hallucination of bland colors and shapeless forms, especially on late November afternoons. Further inside the gallery, things were in a similar state – from the cruddy linoleum floor, where some cracked tiles revealed the concrete foundation, to the rather high ceiling, which occasionally sent down small chips of plaster. If every artwork and item of art-related merchandise had been cleared out of that building, no one would think that an art gallery had once occupied this space and not some enterprise of a lesser order. But as many persons were aware, if only through second-hand sources, the woman who operated Dalha D. Fine Arts did not make her living by dealing in those artworks and related items, which only the most desperate or scandalously naïve artist would allow to be put on display in that gallery. By all accounts, including my own brief lunchtime conversations with the woman, she had pursued a variety of careers in her time. She herself had worked as an artist at one point, and some of her works – messy assemblages inside old cigar boxes – were exhibited in a corner of her gallery. But evidently her art gallery business was not self-sustaining, despite minimal overhead, and she made no secret of her true means of income.

'Who wants to buy such junk?' she once explained to me, gesturing with long fingernails painted emerald green. This same color also seemed to dominate her wardrobe of long, loose garments, with many of her outfits featuring incredible scarves or shawls that dragged along the floor as she moved about the art gallery. She paused and with the pointed toe of one of her emerald-green shoes gave a little kick at a wire wastebasket that was filled with the miniature limbs of dolls, all of them individually painted in a variety of colors. 'What are people thinking when they make these things? What was I thinking with those stupid cigar boxes? But no more of that, definitely no more of that sort of thing.'

And she made no secret, beyond a certain reasonable caution, of what sort of thing now engaged her energies as a businesswoman. The telephone was always ringing at her art gallery, always upsetting the otherwise dead calm of the place with its cracked, warbling voice that called out from the back room. She would then quickly disappear behind a curtain that hung in the doorway separating the front and back sections of the art gallery. I might be eating a sandwich or a piece of fruit, and then suddenly, for the fourth or fifth time in a half-hour, the telephone would scream from the back room, eventually summoning this woman behind the curtain. But she never answered the telephone with the name of the art gallery or employed any of the stock phrases of business protocol. Not so much as a 'Good afternoon, may I help you?' did I ever hear from the back room as I sat eating my midday meal in the front section of the art gallery. She always answered the telephone in the same way with the same quietly expectant tone in her voice. *This is Dalha*, she always said.

Before I had known her very long even I found myself using her name in the most familiar way. The mere saying of this name instilled in me a sense of *access* to what she offered all those telephone-callers, not to mention those individuals who personally visited the art gallery to make or confirm an appointment. Whatever someone was eager to try, whatever step someone was willing to take – Dalha could arrange it. This was the true stock in trade of the art gallery, these *arrangements*. When I returned to the library after my lunch break, I continued to imagine Dalha back at the art gallery, racing between the front and back sections of the building, making all kinds of arrangements over the telephone, and sometimes in person.

On the day that I first noticed the new artwork entitled *The Bungalow House*, Dalha's telephone was extremely vocal. While she was talking to her clients in the back section of the art gallery, I was left alone in the front section. Just for a thrill I went over to the wire wastebasket full of dismembered doll parts and helped myself to one of the painted arms (emerald green!), hiding it in the inner pocket of my sportcoat. It was then that I spotted the old audiotape recorder on a small plastic table in the corner. Beside the machine was a business card on which the title of the artwork had been hand-printed, along with the following instructions: PRESS PLAY. PLEASE REWIND AFTER LISTENING. DO NO REMOVE TAPE. I placed the headphones over my ears and pressed the PLAY button. The voice that spoke through the headphones, which were enormous, sounded distant and was somewhat distorted by the hissing of the tape. Nevertheless, I was so intrigued by the opening passages of this dream monologue, which I have already transcribed, that I sat down on the floor next to the small plastic table on which the tape recorder was positioned and listened to the entire tape, exceeding my allotted lunchtime by over half an hour. By the time the tape had ended I was in another world – that is, the world of the infested bungalow house, with all its dreamlike crumminess and foul charms.

'Don't forget to rewind the tape,' said Dalha, who was now standing over me, her long gray hair, like steel wool, almost brushing against my face.

I pressed the REWIND button on the tape recorder and got up from the floor. 'Dalha, may I use your lavatory?' I asked. She pointed to the curtain leading to the back section of the art gallery. 'Thank you,' I said.

The effect of listening to the first dream monologue was very intense for reasons I will soon explain. I wanted to be alone for a few moments in order to preserve the state of mind which the voice on the tape had induced in me, much as one might attempt to hold on to the images of a dream just after waking. However, I felt that the lavatory at the library, despite its peculiar virtues which I have appreciated

over the years, would somehow undermine the sensations
and mental state created by the dream monologue, rather
than preserving this experience and even enhancing it, as I
hoped the lavatory in the back section of Dalha's art gallery
would do.

The very reason why I spent my lunchtimes in the
surroundings of Dalha's art gallery, which were so different
from those of the library, was exactly why I now wanted to
use the lavatory in the back section of that art gallery and
definitely not the lavatory at the library, even if I was
already overdue from my lunch break. And, indeed, this
lavatory had the same qualities as the rest of the art gallery,
as I hoped it would. The fact that it was located in the back
section of the art gallery, a region of mysteries to my mind,
was significant. Just outside the door of the lavatory stood
a small, cluttered desk upon which was positioned the
telephone that Dalha used in her true business of making
arrangements. The telephone was centered in the weak light
of a desk lamp, and I noticed, as I passed into the lavatory,
that it was an unwieldy object with a straight – that is,
uncoiled – cord connecting the receiver to the telephone
housing, with its enormous circular dial. But although
Dalha answered several calls during the time I was in the
lavatory, these seemed to be entirely legitimate conversations having to do either with her personal life or with
practical matters relating to the art gallery.

'How long are you going to be in there?' Dalha asked
through the door of the lavatory. 'I hope you're not sick,
because if you're sick you'll have to go somewhere else.'

I called out that there was nothing wrong (quite the
opposite) and a moment later emerged from the lavatory. I
was about to ask for details of the art performance tape I
had just heard, anxious to know about the artist and what
it would cost me to own the work entitled *The Bungalow
House*, as well as any similar works that might exist. But
the phone began ringing again. Dalha answered it with her
customary greeting as I stood by in the back section of the

art gallery, which was a dark, though relatively uncluttered space that now put me in mind of the living room of the bungalow house that I had heard described on the tape-recorded dream monologue. The conversation in which Dalha was engaged (another non-arrangement call) seemed interminable, and I was becoming nervously aware how long past my lunch break I had stayed at the storefront art gallery.

'I'll see you tomorrow,' I said to Dalha, who responded with a look from her emerald eyes while continuing to speak to the other party on the telephone. And she was smiling at me, *like muted laughter*, I remember thinking as I passed through the curtained doorway into the front section of the art gallery. I glanced at the tape recorder standing on the plastic table but decided against taking the audiocassette back to the library (and afterward home with me). It would be there when I visited on my lunch break the following day. Hardly anyone ever bought anything out of the front section of Dalha's art gallery.

For the rest of the day – both at the library and at my home – I thought about the bungalow house tape. Especially while riding the bus home from the library, I thought of the images and concepts described on the tape, as well as the voice that described them and the phrases it used throughout the dream monologue on the bungalow house. Much of my commute from my home to the library, and back home again, took me past numerous streets lined from end to end with desolate-looking houses, any of which might have been the inspiration for the bungalow house audiotape. I say that these streets were lined from 'end to end' with such houses, even though the bus never turned down any of them, and I therefore never actually viewed even a single street from 'end to end.' In fact, as I looked through the window next to my seat on the bus – on either side of the bus I always sat in the window seat, never in the aisle seat – the streets I saw appeared endless, vanishing from my sight toward an infinity of old houses, many of them derelict houses and a great many of them being dwarfish and desolate-looking houses of the bungalow type.

The tape-recorded dream monologue, as I recalled it that day while riding home on the bus and staring out the window, described several features of the infested bungalow house – the dusty window blinds through which the moonlight shone, the lamps with all their lightbulb sockets empty, the threadbare carpet, and the dead or barely living vermin that littered the carpet. Thus, I was afforded an interior view of the bungalow house by the voice on the tape, not a view from the exterior. Conversely, the houses I gazed upon with such intensity as I rode the bus to and from the library were seen by me only from an exterior perspective, their interiors being visible solely in my imagination. Of course my sense of these interiors, being entirely an imaginative projection, was highly vague, lacking the precise physical layout provided by the bungalow house audiotape. Similarly, the dreams I often had of these houses were highly vague. Yet the sensations and the mental state created by my imaginative projections *into* and my dreams *of* these houses perfectly corresponded to those I had experienced at Dalha's art gallery when I listened to the tape entitled *The Bungalow House*. That feeling of being in a trance while occupying, all alone, the most bleak and pathetic surroundings of an old bungalow house was communicated to me in the most powerful way by the voice on the tape, which described a silent and secluded world where one existed in a state of abject hypnosis. While sitting on the floor of the art gallery listening to the voice as it spoke through those enormous headphones, I had the sense that I was not simply *hearing* the words of that dream monologue but also *reading* them. What I mean is that whenever I have the occasion to read words on a page, any words on any page, the voice that I hear saying these words in my head is always recognizable in some way as my own, even though the words are those of another. Perhaps it is even more accurate to say that whenever I read words on a page, the voice in my head is my own voice *as it becomes merged* (or lost) within the words that I am reading. Conversely, when I have the occasion to write words on a page, even a simple note or memo at the library, the voice that I hear dictating these words does *not* sound like my own – until, of course, I read the words back to myself, at which time everything is all right again. The bungalow house tape was the most dramatic example of this phenomenon I had ever known. Despite the poor overall quality of the recording, the distorted voice reading this dream monologue became merged (or lost) within my own perfectly clear voice in my head, even though I was listening to its words over a pair of enormous headphones and not reading the words on a page. As I rode the bus home from the library, observing street after street of houses so reminiscent of the one described on the tape-recorded dream monologue, I regretted not having acquired this artwork on the spot or at least discovered more about it from Dalha, who had been occupied with what seemed an unusual number of telephone calls that afternoon.

The following day at the library I was anxious for lunchtime to arrive so that I could get over to the art gallery and find out everything I possibly could about the bungalow house tape, as well as discuss terms for its acquisition. Entering the art gallery, I immediately looked toward the corner where the tape recorder had been set on the small plastic table the day before. For some reason I was relieved to find the exhibit still in place, as if any artwork in that gallery could possibly have come and gone in a single day.

I walked over to the exhibit with the purpose of verifying that everything I had seen (and heard) the previous day was exactly as I remembered it. I checked that the audiocassette was still inside the recording machine and picked up the little business card on which the title of the exhibit was given, along with instructions for properly operating the tape-recorded artwork. It was then that I realized that this was a different card from the first one. Printed on this card was the title of a new artwork, which was called *The Derelict Factory with a Dirt Floor and Voices.*

While I was very excited to find a new work by this artist, I also felt intense apprehension at the absence of the bungalow house dream monologue, which I had planned to purchase with some extra money I brought with me to the art gallery that day. Just at that moment in which I experienced the dual sensations of excitement and apprehension, Dalha emerged from behind the curtain separating the back and front sections of the art gallery. I had intended to be thoroughly blasé in negotiating the purchase of the bungalow house artwork, but Dalha caught me off-guard in a state of disoriented conflict.

'What happened to the bungalow house tape that was here yesterday?' I asked, the tension in my voice betraying desires that were all to her advantage.

'That's gone now,' she replied in a frigid tone as she walked slowly and pointlessly about the gallery, her emerald skirt and scarves dragging along the floor.

'I don't understand. It was an artwork exhibited on that small plastic table.'

'Yes,' she agreed.

'Now, after only a single day on exhibit, it's gone?'

'Yes, it's gone.'

'Somebody bought it,' I said, assuming the worst.

'No,' she said, 'that one was not for sale. It was a performance piece. There was a charge, but *you* didn't pay.'

A sickly confusion now became added to the excitement and disappointment already mingling inside me. 'There was no notice of a charge for listening to the dream monologue,' I insisted. 'As far as I knew, as far as anyone could know, it was an item for sale like everything else in this place.'

'The dream monologue, as you call it, was an exclusive piece. The charge was on the back of the card on which the title was written, just as the charge is on the back of that card you are holding in your hand.'

I turned the card to the reverse side, where the words 'twenty-five dollars' were written in the same hand that appeared on all the price tags around the gallery. Speaking in the tones of an outraged customer, I said to Dalha, 'You wrote the price only on this card. There was nothing written on the bungalow house card.' But even as I said these words I lacked the conviction that they were true. In any case, I knew that if I wanted to hear the tape recording about the derelict factory I would have to pay what I owed, or what Dalha claimed I owed, for listening to the bungalow house tape.

'Here,' I said, removing my wallet from my back pocket, 'ten, twenty, twenty-five dollars for the bungalow house, and another twenty-five for listening to the tape now in the machine.'

Dalha stepped forward, took the fifty dollars I held out to her, and in her coldest voice said, 'This only covers yesterday's tape about the bungalow house, which was clearly priced at fifty dollars. You must still pay twenty-five dollars if you wish to listen to the tape today.'

'But why should the bungalow house tape cost twenty-five dollars more than the tape about the derelict factory?'

'That is simply because this is a less ambitious work than the one dealing with the bungalow house.'

In fact the tape recording entitled *The Derelict Factory with a Dirt Floor and Voices* was of shorter duration than *The Bungalow House (Plus Silence)*, but I found it no less wonderful in picturing the same 'infinite terror and dreariness.' For approximately fifteen minutes (on my lunch break) I embraced the degraded beauty of the derelict factory – a narrow ruin that stood isolated upon a vast plain, its broken windows allowing only the most meager haze of moonlight to shine across its floor of hard-packed dirt where dead machinery lay buried in a grave of shadows and languished in the echoes of hollow, senseless voices. How utterly desolate, yet all the same wonderfully comforting, was the voice that communicated its message to me through the medium of a tape recording. To think that another person shared my love for the *icy bleakness of things*. The satisfaction I felt at hearing that monotonal and somewhat distorted voice speaking so intimately of scenes and sensations that perfectly echoed certain aspects of my own deepest nature – this was an experience that even then, as I sat on the floor of Dalha's art gallery listening to the tape through enormous headphones, might have been heartbreaking. But I wanted to believe that the artist who created these dream monologues about the bungalow house and the derelict factory had not set out to break my heart or anyone's heart. I wanted to believe that this artist had escaped the dreams and demons of all *sentiment* in order to explore the foul and crummy delights of a universe where everything had been reduced to three stark principles: first, that there was nowhere for you to go; second, that there was nothing for you to do; and third, that there was no one for you to know. Of course I knew that this view was an illusion like any other, but it was also one that had sustained me so long and so well – as long and as well as any other illusion and perhaps longer, perhaps better.

'Dalha,' I said when I had finished listening to the tape recording, 'I want you to tell me what you know about the artist who made these dream monologues. He doesn't even sign his works.'

From across the front section of the art gallery Dalha spoke to me in a strange, somewhat flustered voice. 'Well, why should you be surprised that he doesn't sign his name to his works – that's how artists are these days. All over the place they are signing their works only with some idiotic symbol or a piece of chewing gum or just leaving them unsigned altogether. Why should you care what his name is? Why should I?'

'Because,' I answered, 'perhaps I can persuade him to allow me to buy his works instead of sitting on the floor of your art gallery and renting these performances on my lunch break.'

'So you want to cut me out entirely,' Dalha shouted back in her old voice. 'I am his dealer, I tell you, and anything he has to sell you will buy *through me*.'

'I don't know why you're getting so upset,' I said, standing up from the floor. 'I'm willing to give you a percentage. All I ask is that you arrange something between myself and the artist.'

Dalha sat down in a chair next to the curtained doorway separating the front and back sections of the art gallery. She pulled her emerald shawl around herself and said, 'Even if I wished to arrange something I could not do it. I have no idea what his name is myself. A few nights ago he walked up to me on the street while I was waiting for a cab to take me home.'

'What does he look like?' I had to ask at that moment.

'It was late at night and I was drunk,' Dalha replied, somehow evasively it seemed to me.

'Was he a younger man, an older man?'

'An older man, yes. Not very tall, with bushy white hair like a professor of some kind. And he said that he wanted to have an artwork of his delivered to my gallery. I explained to him my usual terms as best I could, since I was so drunk. He agreed and then walked off down the street. And that's not the best part of town to be walking around all by yourself. Well, the next day a package arrived with the tape-recording machine and so forth. There were also some instructions which explained that I should destroy each of the audiotapes before I leave the art gallery at the end of the day, and that a new tape would arrive the following day and each day thereafter. No return address is provided on these packages.'

'And did you destroy the bungalow house tape?' I asked.

'Of course,' said Dalha with some exasperation, but also with insistence. 'What do I care about some crazy artist's work or how he conducts his career? Besides, he guaranteed I would make some money on the deal, and here I am already with seventy-five dollars.'

'So why not sell me this dream monologue about the derelict factory? I won't say anything.'

Dalha was quiet for a moment, and then said, 'He told me that if I didn't destroy the tapes each day he would know about it and that he would do something. I've forgotten exactly what he said, I was so drunk that night.'

'But *how* could he know?' I asked, and in reply Dalha just stared at me in silence. 'All right, all right,' I said. 'But I still want you to make an arrangement. You have his money for the bungalow house tape and the tape about the derelict factory. If he's any kind of artist, he'll want to be paid. When he gets in touch with you, that's when you make the arrangement for me. I won't cheat you out of your percentage. I give you my *word* on that.'

'Whatever that's worth,' Dalha said bitterly.

But she did agree that she would try to arrange something between myself and the tape-recording artist. I left the art gallery immediately after these negotiations, before Dalha could have any second thoughts. That afternoon, while I was working in the Language and Literature department of the library, I could think about nothing but the derelict factory that was so enticingly pictured on the new audiotape. The bus that takes me to and from the library each day of the working week always passes such a structure, which stands isolated in the distance just as the artist described it in his dream monologue.

That night I slept badly, thrashing about in my bed, not quite asleep and not quite awake. At times I had the feeling there was someone else in my bedroom who was talking to me, but of course I could not deal with this perception in any realistic way, since I was half-asleep and half-awake, and thus, for all practical purposes, I was out my mind.

Around three o'clock in the morning the telephone rang. In the darkness I reached for my eyeglasses, which were on the nightstand next to the telephone, and noted the luminous face of my alarm clock. I cleared my throat and said hello. The voice on the other end was Dalha's.

'I talked to him,' she said.

'Where did you talk to him?' I asked. 'On the street?'

'No, no, not on the street,' she said, giggling a little. I think she must have been drunk. 'He called me on the telephone.'

'He called you on the telephone?' I repeated, imagining for a moment what it would be like to have the voice of that artist speak to me over the telephone and not merely on a recorded audiotape.

'Yes, he called me on the telephone.'

'What did he say?'

'Well, I could tell you if you would stop asking so many questions.'

'Tell me.'

'It was only a few minutes ago that he called. He said that he would meet you tomorrow at the library where you work.'

'You told him about me?' I asked, and then there was a long silence. 'Dalha?' I prompted.

'I told him that you wanted to buy his tape recordings. That's all.'

'Then how did he know that I worked at the library?'

'Ask him yourself. I have no idea. I've done my part.'

Then Dahla said good-bye and hung up before I could say good-bye back to her.

After talking to Dalha I found it impossible to sleep anymore that night, even if it was only a state of half-sleeping and half-waking. All I could think about was meeting the artist of the dream monologues. So I got myself ready to go to work, rushing as if I were late, and walked up to the corner of my street to wait for the bus.

It was very cold as I sat waiting in the bus shelter. There was a sliver of moon high in the blackness above, with several hours remaining before sunrise. Somehow I felt that I was waiting for the bus on the first day of a new school year, since after all the month was September, and I was so filled with both fear and excitement. When the bus finally arrived I saw that there were only a few other early risers headed for downtown. I took one of the back seats and stared out the window, my own face staring back at me in black reflection.

At the next shelter we approached I noticed that another lone bus rider was seated on the bench waiting to be picked up. His clothes were dark-colored (including a long, loose overcoat and hat), and he sat up very straight, his arms held close to his body and his hands resting on his lap. His head was slightly bowed, and I could not see the face beneath his hat. His physical attitude, I thought to myself as we approached the lighted bus shelter, was one of disciplined repose. I was surprised that he did not stand up as the bus came nearer to the shelter, and ultimately we passed him by. I wanted to say something to the driver of the bus but a strong feeling of both fear and excitement made me keep my silence.

The bus finally dropped me off in front of the library, and I ran up the tiered stairway that led to the main entrance. Through the thick glass doors I could see that only a few lights illuminated the spacious interior of the library. After rapping on the glass for a few moments I saw a figure dressed in a maintenance man's uniform appear in the shadowy distance inside the building. I rapped some more and the man slowly proceeded down the library's vaulted central hallway.

'Good morning, Henry,' I said as the door opened.

'Hello, sir,' he replied without standing aside to allow my entrance to the library. 'You know I'm not supposed to open these doors before it's time for them to be open.'

'I'm a little early, I realize, but I'm sure it will be all right to let me inside. I work here, after all.'

'I know you do, sir. But a few days ago I got talked to about these doors being open when they shouldn't be. It's because of the stolen property.'

'What property is that, Henry? Books?'

'No, sir. I think it was something from the media department. Maybe a video camera or a tape recorder. I don't know exactly.'

'Well, you have my word – just let me through the door and I'll go right upstairs to my desk. I've got a lot of work to do today.'

Henry eventually obliged my request, and I did as I told him I would do.

The library was a great building as a whole, but the Language and Literature department (second floor) was located in a relatively small area – narrow and long with a high ceiling and a row of tall, paned windows along one wall. The other walls were lined with books, and most of the floor space was devoted to long study tables. For the most part, though, the room in which I worked was fairly open from end to end. Two large archways led to other parts of the library, and a normal-sized doorway led to the stacks where most of the bibliographic holdings were stored, millions of volumes standing silent and out of sight along endless rows of shelves. In the pre-dawn darkness the true dimensions of the Language and Literature department were now obscure. Only the moon shining high in the blackness through those tall windows revealed to me the location of my desk, which was in the middle of the long narrow room.

I found my way over to my desk and switched on the small lamp that years ago I had brought from home. (Not that I required the added illumination as I worked at my desk at the library, but I did enjoy the bleakly old-fashioned appearance of this object.) For a moment I thought of the bungalow house where none of the lamps were equipped with lightbulbs and moonlight shone through the windows upon a carpet littered with vermin. Somehow I was unable to call up the special sensations and mental state that I associated with this dream monologue, even though my present situation of being alone in the Language and Literature department some hours before dawn was intensely dreamlike.

Not knowing what else to do, I sat down at my desk as if I were beginning my normal workday. It was then that I noticed a large envelope lying on top of my desk, although I could not recall its being there when I left the library the day before. The envelope looked old and faded under the dim light of the desk lamp. There was no writing on either side of the envelope, which was bulging slightly and had been sealed.

'Who's there?' a voice called out that barely sounded like my own. I had seen something out of the corner of my eye while examining the envelope at my desk. I cleared my throat. 'Henry?' I asked the darkness without looking up from my desk or turning to either side. No answer was offered in reply, but I could feel that someone else had joined me in the Language and Literature department of the library.

I slowly turned my head to the right and focused on the archway some distance across the room. At the center of this aperture, which led to another room where moonlight shone through tall, paned windows, stood a figure in silhouette. I could not see his face but immediately recognized the long, loose overcoat and hat. It was indeed the statue-like individual whom I had seen in the bus shelter as I rode to the library in the pre-dawn darkness. Now he was there to meet me that day in the library, as he had told Dalha he would do. At that moment it seemed beside the point to ask how he had gotten into the library or even to bother about introductions. I simply launched into a monologue that I had been constantly rehearsing since Dalha telephoned me earlier that morning.

'I've been wanting to meet you,' I started. 'Your dream monologues, which is what I call them, have impressed me very much. That is to say, your *artworks* are like nothing else I have ever experienced, either artistically or extra-artistically. It seems incredible to me how well you have expressed subject matter with which I myself am intimately familiar. Of course, I am not referring to the subject matter as such – the bungalow house and so on – except as it calls forth your underlying vision of things. When – in your tape-recorded monologues – your voice speaks such phrases as "infinite terror and dreariness" or "ceaseless negation of color and life," I believe that my response is exactly that which you intend for those who experience your artworks.'

I continued in this vein for a while longer, speaking to the silhouette of someone who betrayed no sign that he heard anything I said. At some point, however, my monologue veered off in a direction I had not intended it to take. Suddenly I began to say things that had nothing to do with what I had said before and that even contradicted my former statements.

'For as long as I can remember,' I said, continuing to speak to the figure standing in the archway, 'I have had an intense and highly aesthetic perception of what I call the *icy bleakness of things*. At the same time I have felt a great loneliness in this perception. This conjunction of feelings seems paradoxical, since such a perception, such a view of things, would seem to preclude the emotion of loneliness, or any sense of a *killing sadness*, as I think of it. All such heartbreaking sentiment, as usually considered, would seem to be on its knees before artworks such as yours, which so powerfully express what I have called the icy bleakness of things, submerging or devastating all sentiment in an atmosphere potent with desolate truths, permeated throughout with a visionary stagnation and lifelessness. Yet I must observe that the effect, as I now consider it, has been just the opposite. If it was your intent to evoke the icy bleakness of things with your dream monologues, then you have totally failed on both an artistic and an extra-artistic level. You have failed your art, you have failed yourself, and you have also failed me. If your artworks had really evoked the *true* bleakness of things, then I would not have felt this need to know who you are, this killing sadness that there was actually someone who experienced the same sensations and mental states as I did and who could share them with me in the form of tape-recorded dream monologues. Who are *you* that I should feel this need to go to work hours before the sun comes up, that I should feel this was something I had to do and that you were someone that I had to know? This behavior violates every principle by which I have lived for as long as I can remember. Who are you to cause me to violate these long-lived principles? I think it's all becoming clear to me now. Dalha put you up to this. You and Dalha are in a conspiracy against me and against my principles. Every day Dalha is on the telephone making all kinds of arrangements for profit, and she cannot stand the idea that all I do is sit there in peace, eating my lunch in her hideous art gallery. She feels that I'm cheating her somehow because she's not making a profit from me, because I never paid her to make an arrangement for me. Don't try to deny what I now know is true. But you could say something, in any case. Just a few words spoken with that voice of yours. Or at least let me see your face. And you could take off that ridiculous hat. It's like something Dalha would wear.'

By this time I was on my feet and walking (staggering, in fact) toward the figure that stood in the archway. All the while I was walking, or staggering, toward the figure I was also demanding that he answer my accusations. But as I walked forward between the long study tables toward the archway, the figure standing there receded backward into the darkness of the next room, where moonlight shone through tall, paned windows. The closer I came to him the farther he receded into the darkness. And he did not recede into the darkness by taking steps backward, as I was taking steps forward, but moved in some other way that even now I cannot specify, as though he were floating.

Just before the figure disappeared completely into the darkness he finally spoke to me. His voice was the same one that I had heard over those enormous headphones in Dalha's art gallery, except now there was no interference, no distortion in the words that it spoke. These words, which resounded in my brain as they resounded in the high-ceilinged rooms of the library, were such that I should have welcomed them, for they echoed my very own, deeply private principles. Yet I took no comfort in hearing another voice tell me that there was nowhere for me to go, nothing for me to do, and no one for me to know.

The next voice I heard was that of Henry, who shouted up the wide stone staircase from the ground floor of the library. 'Is everything all right, sir?' he asked. I composed myself and was able to answer that everything was all right. I asked him to turn the lights on for the second floor of the library. In a minute the lights were on, but by then the man in the hat and long, loose overcoat was gone.

When I confronted Dalha at her art gallery later that day, she was not in the least forthcoming with respect to my questions and accusations. 'You're crazy,' she screamed at me. 'I want nothing more to do with you.'

When I asked Dalha what she was talking about, she said, 'You really *don't* know, do you? You really are a crazy man. You don't remember that night you came up to me on the street while I was waiting for a cab to show up.'

When I told her I recalled doing nothing of the kind, she continued her anecdote of that night, along with an account of subsequent events. 'I'm standing there so drunk I can hardly understand what you're saying to me about some little game you are playing. Then you send me the tapes. Then you come in and pay to listen to the tapes, exactly as you said you would. Just in time I remember that I'm supposed to lie to you that the tapes are the work of a white-haired old man, when in fact you're the one who's making the tapes. I knew you were crazy, but this was the only money I ever made off you, even though day after day you come and eat your pathetic lunch in my gallery. When I saw you that night, I couldn't tell at first who it was walking up to me on the street. You did look different, and you were wearing that stupid hat. Soon enough, though, I can see that it's you. And you're pretending to be someone else, but not really pretending, I don't know. And then you tell me that I must destroy the tapes, and if I don't destroy them something will happen. Well, let me tell you, crazy man,' Dalha said, 'I did not destroy those tape recordings. I let all my friends hear them. We sat around getting drunk and laughing our heads off at your stupid *dream monologues*. Here, another one of your artworks arrived in the mail today,' she said while walking across the floor of the art gallery to the tape machine that was positioned on the small plastic table. 'Why don't you listen to it and pay me the money you promised. This looks like a good one,' she said, picking up the little card that bore the title of the work. '*The Bus Shelter*, it says. That should be very exciting for you – a bus shelter. Pay up!'

'Dalha,' I said in a laboriously calm voice, 'please listen to me. You have to make another arrangement. I need to have another meeting with the tape-recording artist. You're the only one who can arrange for this to happen. Dalha, I'm afraid for both of us if you don't agree to make this arrangement. I need to speak with him again.'

'Then why don't you just go talk into a mirror. There,' she said, pointing to the curtain that separated the front section from the back section of the art gallery. 'Go into the bathroom like you did the other day and talk to yourself in the mirror.'

'I didn't talk to myself in the bathroom, Dalha.'

'No? What were you doing then?'

'Dalha, you have to make the arrangement. You are the go-between. He will contact you if you agree to let him.'

'*Who* will contact me?'

This was a fair question for Dalha to ask, but it was also one that I could not answer. I told her that I would return to talk to her the next day, hoping she would have calmed down by then.

Unfortunately, I never saw Dalha again. That night she was found dead on the street. Presumably she had been waiting for a cab to take her home from a bar or a party or some other human gathering place where she had gotten very drunk. But it was not her drinking or her exhausting bohemian social life that killed Dalha. She had, in fact, choked to death while waiting for a cab very late at night. Her body was taken to a hospital for examination. There it was discovered that an object had been lodged inside her. Someone, it appeared, had violently thrust something down her throat. The object, as described in a newspaper article, was the 'small plastic arm of a toy doll.' Whether this doll's arm had been painted emerald green, or any other color, was not mentioned in the article. Surely the police searched through Dalha D. Fine Arts and found many more such objects arranged in a wire wastebasket, each of them painted different colors. No doubt they also found the exhibit of the dream monologues with its unsigned artworks and tape recorder stolen from the library. But they could never have made the connection between these tape-recorded artworks and the grotesque death of the gallery owner.

After that night I no longer felt the desperate need to possess the monologues, not even the final bus shelter tape, which I have never heard. I was now in possession of the original handwritten manuscripts from which the tape-recording artist had created his dream monologues and which he had left for me in a large envelope on my desk at the library. Even then he knew, as I did not know, that after our first meeting we would never meet again. The hand-writing on the manuscript pages is somewhat like my own, although the slant of the letters betrays a left-handed writer, whereas I am right-handed. Over and over I read the dream monologues about the bus shelter and the derelict factory and especially about the bungalow house, where the moon-light shines upon a carpet littered with the bodies of vermin. I try to experience the infinite terror and dreariness of a bungalow universe in the way I once did, but it is not the same as it once was. There is no comfort in it, even though the vision and the underlying principles are still the same. I know in a way I never knew before that there is nowhere for me to go, nothing for me to do, and no one for me to know. The voice in my head keeps reciting these old principles of mine. The voice is his voice, and the voice is also my voice. And there are other voices, voices I have never heard before, voices that seem to be either dead or dying in a great moonlit darkness. More than ever, some sort of new arrangement seems in order, some dramatic and unknown arrangement – anything to find release from this heartbreaking sadness I suffer every minute of the day (and night), this killing sadness that feels as if it will never leave me no matter where I go or what I do or whom I may ever know.

SEVERINI

I was the only one among a local circle of acquaintances and associates who had never met Severini. Unlike the rest of them I was not in the least moved to visit him along with the others at that isolated residence which had become known as 'Severini's Shack.' There was a question of my *deliberately* avoiding an encounter with this extraordinary individual, but even I myself had no idea whether or not this was true. My curiosity was just as developed as that of the rest of them, more so in fact. Yet some kind of scruple or special anxiety kept me away from what the others celebrated as the 'spectacle of Severini.'

Of course I could not escape a second-hand knowledge of their Severini visits. Each of these trips to that lonesome hovel some distance outside the city where I used to live was a great adventure, they reported, an excursion into the most obscure and idiosyncratic nightmares. The figure that presided over these salon-like gatherings was extremely unstable and inspired in his visitors a sense of lurid anticipation, an unfocused expectation that sometimes reached the pitch of lunacy. Afterward I would hear detailed accounts from one person or another of what had occurred during a particular evening within the confines of the notorious shack, which was situated at the edge of a wildly overgrown and swampy tract of land known as St Alban's Marsh, a place that some claimed had a sinister pertinence to Severini himself. Occasionally I would make notes of these accounts, indulging myself in a type of imaginative and also highly analytical record-keeping. For the most part, however, I simply absorbed all of these Severini anecdotes in a wholly natural and organic fashion, much as I assimilated so many things in the world around me, without any awareness – or even a possibility of awareness – that these things might be nourishing or noxious or purely neutral. From the beginning, I admit, it was my tendency to be highly receptive to whatever someone might have to say regarding Severini, his shack-like home, and the marshy landscape in which he had ensconced himself. Then, during private moments when I returned to the small apartment in which I resided during this period of my life, I would recreate in my imagination the phenomena that had been related to me in conversations held at diverse places and times. It was rare that I actively urged the others to elaborate on any specific aspect of their adventures with Severini, but several times I did betray myself when the subject arose of his past life before he set himself up in a marshland shack.

According to first-hand witnesses (that is, persons who had actually made the pilgrimage to that isolated and crumbling shack), Severini could be quite talkative about his personal history, particularly the motives and events that most directly culminated in his present life. Nevertheless, these persons also admitted that the 'marvelous hermit' (Severini) displayed a conspicuous disregard for common facts and for truths of a literal sort. Thus he was often given to speaking about himself by way of ambiguous parables and metaphors, not to mention outrageous anecdotes, the facts of which always seemed to cancel out one another, as well as outright lies which afterward he himself would sometimes expose as such. But much of the time – and in the opinion of some, *all* of the time – Severini's speech took the form of total nonsense, as though he were talking in his sleep. Despite these obstacles to both credibility and coherence, all of the individuals who spoke to me on the subject somehow conveyed to my mind a remarkably focused portrait of the hermit Severini, an amalgam of hearsay that attained the status of a potent legend.

This impression of a legendary Severini was no doubt bolstered by what certain persons described as 'Exhibits from the Imaginary Museum.' The entourage of visitors to the hermit's dilapidated shack was composed of more or less artistic persons, or at least individuals with artistic *leanings*, and their exposure to Severini proved a powerful inspiration that resulted in numerous artworks in a variety of media and genres. There were sculptures, paintings and drawings, poems and short prose pieces, musical compositions sometimes accompanied by lyrics, conceptual works that existed only in schematic or anecdotal form, and even an architectural plan for a 'ruined temple on a jungle island somewhere in the region of the Philippines.' While on the surface these productions appeared to have their basis in a multitude of dubious sources, each of them claimed the most literalistic origins in Severini's own words, his *sleeptalking*, as they called it. Indeed, I myself could perceive a definite unity among these artworks and their integral relationship to the same unique figure of inspiration that was Severini himself, although I had never met this fantastical person and had no desire to do so. Nevertheless, these so-called 'exhibits' helped me to recreate in my imagination not only those much-discussed visits to that shack in the marsh country but also the personal history of its lone inhabitant.

As I now think about them – that is, recreate them in my imagination – these Severini-based artworks, however varied in their genres and techniques, brought to the surface a few features that were always the same and were always treated in the same way. I was startled when I first began to recognize these common features, because somehow they closely replicated a number of peculiar images and concepts that I myself had already experienced in moments of imaginative daydreaming and especially during episodes of delirium brought on by physical disease or excessive psychic turmoil.

A central element of such episodes was the sense of a place possessing qualities that were redolent, on the one hand, of a tropical landscape, and, on the other hand, of a common sewer. The aspect of a common sewer emerged in the feeling of an enclosed but also vastly extensive space, a network of coiling passages that spanned incredible distances in an underworld of misty darkness. As for the quality of a tropical landscape, this shared much of the same kind of darkly oozing ferment as the sewer aspect, with the added impression of the most exotic forms of life spawning on every side, things multiplying and also incessantly *mutating* like a time-lapse film of spreading fungus or multi-colored slime molds totally unrestricted in their form and expansion. While I experienced the most intense visions of this place, this tropical sewer, as it recreated itself in my delirious imagination year after year, I was always outside it at some great remove, not caught within as if I were having a nightmare. But still I maintained an awareness (as in a nightmare) that something had *happened* in this place, some unknown event had transpired that had left these images behind it like a trail of slime. And then a certain *feeling* came over me and a certain *concept* came to my mind.

It was this feeling and its companion concept that so vividly arose within my being when the others began telling me about their strange visits to the Severini place and showing me the various artworks that this strange individual had inspired them to create. One by one I viewed paintings or sculptures in some artist's studio, or heard music being performed in a club that was frequented by the Severini crowd, or read literary works that were being passed around – and each time the sense of that tropical sewer was revived in me, although not with the same intensity as the delirious episodes I experienced while suffering from a physical disease or during periods of excessive psychic turmoil. The titles of these works alone might have been enough to provoke the particular feeling and the concept that were produced by my delirious episodes. The concept to which I have been referring may be stated in various ways, but it usually occurred to my mind as a simple phrase (or fragment), almost a chant that overwhelmed me with vile and haunting suggestions far beyond its mere words, which are as follows: *the nightmare of the organism*. The vile and haunting suggestions underlying (or inspired by) this conceptual phrase were, as I have said, called up by the titles of those Severini-based artworks, those Exhibits from the Imaginary Museum. While I have difficulty recalling the type of work to which each title was attached – whether a painting or a sculpture, a poem or a performance piece – I am still able to cite a number of the titles themselves. One of them that easily emerges in recollection is the following: *No Face Among Us*. Here is another: *Defiled and Delivered*. And now many more of them are coming to my mind: *The Way of the Lost, On Viscous and Sacred Ground* (a.k.a. *The Tantric Doctors*), *In Earth and Excreta, The Black Spume of Existence, Integuments in Eruption*, and *The Descent into the Fungal*. All of these titles, as my artistic acquaintances and associates informed me, were taken from selected phrases (or fragments) spoken by Severini during his numerous episodes of *sleeptalking*.

Every time I heard one of these titles and saw the particular artwork that it named, I was always reminded of that tropical sewer of my delirious episodes. I would also feel myself on the verge of realizing what it was that had happened in this place, some wonderful or disastrous event that was intimately related to the conceptual phrase which I have given as *the nightmare of the organism*. Yet these artworks and their titles allowed me only a remote sense of some vile and haunting revelation. And it was simply not possible for the others to illuminate this matter fully, given that their knowledge of Severini's past history was exclusively derived from his own nonsensical or questionable assertions. As nearly as they were willing to speculate, it appeared that this deranged and all-but-incognito person known as Severini was the willing subject of what was variously referred to as an 'esoteric procedure' or an 'illicit practice.' At this point in my discoveries about the strange Severini I found it difficult to inquire about the exact nature of this procedure, or practice, while at the same time pretending a lack of interest in actually meeting the resident of that ruined shack out in the marshland backroads some distance outside the city where I used to live. It did seem, however, that this practice or procedure, as nearly as anyone could speculate, was not a medical treatment of any known variety. Rather, they thought that the procedure (or practice) in question involved occult or mystical traditions that, in their most potent form, are able to exist inconspicuously in only a few remaining parts of the world. Of course, all of this speculation could have been a cover-up orchestrated by Severini or by his disciples – for that is what they had become – or by all of them together. In fact, for some time I had suspected that Severini's disciples, despite their parade of artworks and outlandish accounts of their visits to the marshland shack, were nevertheless concealing from me some vital element of their new experiences. There seemed to be some truth of which they had knowledge and I had not. Yet they also seemed to desire that, in due course, I might share with them this truth.

My suspicions of the others' deception derived from a source that was admittedly subjective. This was my imaginative recreation, as I sat in my apartment, of the spectacle of Severini as it was related to me by those who had participated in the visits to his residence in the marsh. In my mind I pictured them seated upon the floor of that small, unfurnished shack, the only illumination being the hectic light of candles that they brought with them and placed in a circle, at the center of which was the figure of Severini. This figure always spoke to them in his uniquely cryptic way, his sleeptalking voice fluctuating in its qualities and even seeming to emanate from places other than his own body, as though he were practicing a hyper-ventriloquism. Similarly, his body itself, as I was told and as I later imagined to myself in my apartment, appeared to react in concert with the fluctuations in his voice. These bodily changes, the others said, were sometimes subtle and some-times dramatic, but they were consistently ill-defined – not a matter of clear transformation as much as a *breakdown* of anatomical features and structures, the result being something twisted and tumorous like a living mound of diseased clay or mud, a heap of cancerous matter that slowly thrashed about in the candlelight which illuminated the old shack. These fluctuations in both Severini's voice and his body, the others explained to me, were not in any way under his own guidance but were a totally spontaneous phenomenon to which he submitted as the result of the esoteric procedure or illicit practice worked upon him in some unknown place (possibly 'in the region of the Philip-pines'). It was now his destiny, the others elaborated, to comply with whatever was demanded of his flesh by what could only be seen as utterly mindless and chaotic forces, and even his consciousness itself – they asserted – was as amorphous and mutable as his bodily form. Yet as they spoke to me about these particulars of Severini's condition, none of them conveyed any real sense of the nightmarish quality of the images and processes they were describing. Awestruck, yes; passionate, yes; somewhat demented, yes. But nightmarish – no. Even as I listened to their account of a given Severini meeting, I too failed to grasp fully their nightmarish qualities and aspects. They would say to me, referring to one of Severini's metamorphoses, 'The naked contours of his form writhed about like a pool of snakes, or twitched like a mass of newly hatched spiderlings.' Nevertheless, upon hearing statement after statement of this kind I sat relatively undisturbed, accepting without revulsion or outrage these revolting and outrageous remarks. Perhaps, I thought at the time, I was simply under the powerful spell of social decorum, which so often may explain otherwise incomprehensible feelings (or lack of feelings) and behaviors (or lack of behaviors). But once I was alone in my apartment, and began to imaginatively recreate what I had heard about the spectacle of Severini, I was overwhelmed by its nightmarish essence and several times lapsed into one of my delirious episodes with all of its terrible sensations of a tropical sewer and all the nightmares of exotic lifeforms breaking out everywhere like rampant pustules and suppurations. It was this discrepancy between my *public* response (or lack of response) to the purportedly objective data with which I was being inundated regarding the whole Severini business and my *private* response (or hyper-response) to this data that ultimately led me to suspect that I was being deceived, even if the deception was as much on my part as it was on the others'. Then I considered that I was not as much the victim of a deception as I was the subject of a *manipulation* – a process of seduction that would culminate in my entering as a full-fledged initiate into the Severini cult. In either case, it remained my conviction that some vital element had been withheld from me concerning the recluse of St Alban's Marsh until a propitious moment had arrived and I was prepared to confront the truth that was hitherto denied me, or that I was willfully denying to myself.

Finally, on a rainy afternoon, as I was working alone in my apartment (making Severini notes), the buzzer signaled that someone was downstairs. The voice over the intercom belonged to a woman named Carla, who was a sculptress and whom I barely knew. When I let her in my apartment she was wet from walking in the rain without a coat or umbrella, although her straight black hair and all-black clothes looked very much the same whether wet or dry. I offered her a towel but she refused, saying she 'kind of liked feeling soggy and sickish,' and we went on from there. The reason for her visit to my apartment, she revealed, was to invite me to the first 'collective showing' of the Exhibits from the Imaginary Museum. When I asked why I should be receiving this personal invitation in my apartment on a rainy afternoon, she said: 'Because the showing is going to be at *his place*, and you've never wanted to go there.' I said that I would think seriously about attending the showing and asked her if that was all she had to say. 'No,' she said as she dug into one of the pockets of her tight damp slacks. '*He* was really the one who wanted me to invite you to the exhibit. *We* never told him about you, but he said that he always felt someone was missing, and for some reason we assumed it was you.' After extracting a piece of paper that had been folded several times, she opened it up and held it before her eyes. 'I wrote down what he said,' she said while holding the limp and wrinkled note close to her face with both hands. Her eyes glanced up at me for a moment over the top edge of the unfolded page (her heavy mascara was running down her cheeks in black rivulets), and then she looked down to read the words Severini had told her to write. 'He says, "You and Severini" – he always calls himself Severini, as if that were someone else – "you and Severini are sympathetic . . ." something – I can hardly read this. It was dark when I wrote it down. Here we go: "You and Severini are *sympathetic organisms*."' She paused to push away a few strands of black, rain-soaked hair that had fallen across her face. She was smiling somewhat idiotically.

'Is that it?' I asked.

'Hold on, he wanted me to get it right. Just one more thing. He said, "Tell him that the way into the nightmare is the way out."' She folded the paper once again and crammed it back into the pocket of her black slacks. 'Does any of that mean anything to you?' she asked.

I said that it meant nothing at all to me. After promising that I would most seriously consider attending the exhibit at Severini's place, I let Carla out of my apartment and back into that rainy afternoon.

I should say that I had never spoken to either Carla or the others about my delirious episodes, with their sensations of a tropical sewer and the emergent concept of the 'nightmare of the organism.' I had never told anyone. I had thought that these episodes and the concept of the nightmare of the organism were strictly a private hell, even one that was unique. Until that rainy afternoon, I had considered it only a coincidence that the artworks inspired by Severini, as well as the titles of these works, served to call up the sensations and suggestions of my delirious episodes. Then I was sent a message by Severini, through Carla, that he and I were 'sympathetic organisms' and that 'the way into the nightmare is the way out.' For some time I had dreamed of being delivered from the suffering of my delirious episodes, and from all the suggestions and sensations that went along with them – the terrible vision that exposed all living things, including myself, as no more than a fungus or a collection of bacteria, a kind of monumental slime mold quivering across the landscape of this planet (and very likely others). Any deliverance from such a nightmare, I thought, would involve the most drastic (and esoteric) procedures, the most alien (and illicit) practices. And, ultimately, I never believed that this deliverance, or any other, was really possible. It was simply too good, or too evil, to be true – at least this is how it seemed to my mind. Yet all it took was a few words from Severini, as they reached me through Carla, and I began to dream of all kinds of possibilities. In a moment everything had changed. I now became ready to take those steps toward deliverance; in fact, *not* to do so seemed intolerable to me. I absolutely had to find a way out of the nightmare, it seemed, whatever procedures or practices were involved. Severini had taken those steps – I was convinced of that – and I needed to know where they had led him.

As might be imagined, I had worked myself into quite a state even before the night of the showing of the Exhibits of the Imaginary Museum. But it was more than my frenzy of dreams and anticipation that affected my experiences that night and now affects my ability to relate what occurred at the tumble-down shack on the edge of St Alban's Marsh. My delirious episodes previous to that night were nothing (that is, they were the perfection of lucidity) when compared to the delirium that overtakes me every time I attempt to sort out what happened at the marshland shack, my thoughts disintegrating little by little until I pass into a kind of sleeptalking of my own. I saw things with my own eyes and other things with other eyes. And everywhere there were voices . . .

It was all weedy shadows and frogs croaking in the blackness as I walked along the narrow path that, according to the directions given to me, led to Severini's place. I left my car parked alongside the road where I saw the vehicles of the others. They had all arrived before me, although I was not in the least bit late for this scheduled artistic event. But they had always been anxious, I had long before noticed, whenever a Severini visit was planned, all that day fidgeting with some restless impulse until nightfall came and they could leave the city and go out to St Alban's Marsh.

I expected to see a light ahead as I walked along that narrow path, but all I heard were frogs croaking in the blackness. The full moon in a cloudless sky revealed to me where I should next step along the path leading to the shack at the edge of the marsh. But even before I reached the clearing where the old shack supposedly stood, my sense of everything around me began to change. A warm mist drifted in from either side of the path like a curtain closing in front of my eyes, and I felt something touch my mind with images and concepts that were from elsewhere. 'We are sympathetic organisms,' I heard from the mist. 'Draw closer.' But that narrow path seemed to have no end to it, like those passages in my delirious episodes which extended such great distances in the misty darkness of a tropical landscape, where on every side of me there were exotic forms of life spawning and seething without restraint. *I must go to that place*, I thought as if these were my own words and not the words of another voice altogether, a voice full of desperate intensity and confused aspirations. 'Calm yourself, Mr Severini, if you insist I still address you by that name. As your therapist I cannot advise you to pursue this route . . . chasing miracles, if that is what you *imagine* . . . this "temple," as you call it, is an escape from any authentic confrontation with . . .'

But he did find his way to freedom, although without properly being discharged from the institution, and he went to that place.

'*Documentes. Passportas!*' Looking around at those yellow-brown faces, you were finally there. You went to that jungle island, that tropical sewer, a great temple looming out of the misty darkness in your dreams. It rained in every town, the streets streaming like sewers. '*Disentaría*,' pronounced the attending physician. But he was not like any of the doctors whom you sought in that place. Amoebic dysentery – there it was, the nightmare continued, so many forms it could take. *The way into the nightmare is the way out*. And you were willing to follow that nightmare as far as you needed in order to find your way out, just as I was following that narrow path toward your shack on the edge of St Alban's Marsh to enter that same nightmare you had brought back with you. The Exhibits of the Imaginary Museum. Your shack was now a gallery of the nightmares you had inspired in the others with your sleeptalking and the *fluctuations* of your form, those outrageous miracles which had not outraged anyone. Only when I was alone in my apartment, imaginatively recreating what the others had told me, could I see those miracles as the nightmares they were. I knew this because of my delirious episodes, which none of the others had known. *They* were the sympathetic organisms, not I. I was antagonistic to you, not sympathetic. Because I would not go into the nightmare, as you had gone. The Temple of Tantric Medicine, this is what you dreamed you would find in that tropical sewer – a place where miracles might happen, where that sect of 'doctors' could minister with the most esoteric procedures and could carry out their illicit practices. But what did you find instead? '*Disentaría*,' pronounced the attending physician. Then a small group of those yellow-brown faces told you, told *us*, about that other temple which had no name. 'For the belly sickness,' they said. Amoebic dysentery, simply another version of the nightmare of the organism from which none of the doctors you had seen in the past could deliver you. 'How can the disease be cured of itself?' you asked them. 'My body – a tumor that was once delivered from the body of another tumor, a lump of disease that is always boiling with its own disease. And my mind – another disease, the disease of a disease. Everywhere my mind sees the disease of other minds and other bodies, these other organisms that are only other diseases, an absolute nightmare of the organism. Where are you taking me!' you screamed (we screamed) at the yellow-brown faces. 'Fix the belly sickness. We know, we know.' They chanted these words along the way, it seemed, as the town disappeared behind the trees and the vines, behind the giant flowers that smelled like rotting meat, and the fungus and muck of that tropical sewer. They knew the disease and the nightmare because they lived in that place where the organism flourished without restraint, its forms so varied and exotic, its fate inescapable. '*Disentaría*,' pronounced the attending physician. They knew the way through the stonework passages, the walls seeping with slime and soft with mold as they coiled toward the central chamber of the temple without a name. Inside the ruined heart of the temple there were candles burning everywhere; their flickering light revealed

239

an array of temple art and ornamentation. Intricate murals appeared along the walls, mingling with the slime and the mold of that tropical sewer. Sculptures of every size and all shapes projected out of the damp, viscous shadows. At the center of the chamber was a large circular altar, an enormous mandala composed of countless jewels, precious stones, or simply bits of glass that gleamed in the candle-light like a pool of multi-colored slime molds.

They laid your body upon the altar; they knew what to do with you (us) – the words to say, the songs to sing, and the esoteric procedures to follow. It was almost as if I could understand the things that they chanted in voices of tortured solemnity. *Deliver the self that knows the sickness from the self that does not know. There are two faces which must never confront each other. There is only one body which must struggle to contain them both.* And the phantom clutch of that sickness, that amoebic dysentery, seemed to reach me as I walked along that narrow path leading to Severini's shack at the edge of St Alban's Marsh. Inside the shack were all the Exhibits of the Imaginary Museum, the paintings lining the damp wood of the walls and the sculptures projecting out of the shadows cast by the candles which always lighted the single room of that ruined hovel. I had imaginatively recreated the interior of Severini's shack many times according to the accounts related to me by the others about this place and its incredible inhabitant. I imagined how you could forget yourself in such a place, how you could be delivered from the nightmares and delirious episodes that tortured you in other places, even becoming someone else (or something else) as you gave yourself up entirely to the fluctuations of the organism at the edge of St Alban's Marsh. You needed that marsh because it helped you to imaginatively recreate that tropical sewer (where you were taken *into* the nightmare), and you needed those artworks in order to make the crumbling shack into that temple (where you were supposed to find your way *out* of the nightmare). But most of all you needed them, the others, because they were sympathetic organisms. I, on the other hand, was now an antagonistic organism who wanted nothing more to do with your esoteric procedures and illicit practices. *Deliver the self that knows the sickness from the self that does not know. The two faces . . . the one body.* You wanted them to enter the nightmare, who did not even know the nightmare as *we* knew it. You needed them and their artworks to go into the nightmare of the organism to its *very end*, so that you could find your way out of the nightmare. But you could not go to the very end of the nightmare unless I was with you, I who was now an antagonistic organism without any hope that there was a way out of the nightmare. We were forever divided, one face from the other, struggling within the body – the organism – which we shared.

I never arrived at the shack that night; I never entered it. As I walked along that narrow path in the mist I became feverish. ('Amœbic dysentery,' pronounced the doctor whom I visited the following day.) The face of Severini appeared at the shack that night, not mine. It was always his face that the others saw on such nights when they came to visit. But I was not there with them; that is, my face was not there. His face was the one they saw as they sat among all the Exhibits from the Imaginary Museum. But it was my face which returned to the city; it was my body which I now fully possessed as an organism that belonged to my face alone. But the others never returned from the shack on the edge of St Alban's Marsh. I never saw them again after that night, because on that night he took them with him into the nightmare, with the candle flames flickering upon those artworks and the fluctuations of form which to the others appeared as a pool of twisting snakes or a mass of spiderlings newly hatched. He showed them the way into the nightmare, but he could not show them the way out. There is no way out of the nightmare once you have gone so far into its depths. That is where he is lost forever, he and the others he has taken with him.

But he did not take me into the marsh with him to exist as a fungus exists or as a foam of multi-colored slime mold exists. That is how I see it in my *new delirious episodes*. Only at these times when I suffer from a physical disease or excessive psychic turmoil do I see how he exists now, he and the others. Because I never looked directly into the pools of oozing life when I stopped at the shack on the edge of St Alban's Marsh. I was on my way out of the city the night I stopped, and I was only there long enough to douse the place in gasoline and set it ablaze. It burned with all the brilliance of the nightmares that were still exhibited inside, casting its illumination upon the marsh and leaving the most obscure image of what was back there – a vast and vague impression of that great black life from which we have all emerged and of which we are all made.

THE SHADOW, THE DARKNESS

It seemed that Grossvogel was charging us *entirely* too much money for what he was offering. Some of us – we were about a dozen in all – blamed ourselves and our own idiocy as soon as we arrived in that place which one neatly dressed old gentleman immediately dubbed the 'nucleus of nowhere.' This same gentleman, who a few days before had announced to several persons his abandonment of poetry due to the lack of what he considered proper appreciation of his innovative practice of the 'Hermetic lyric,' went on to say that such a place as the one in which we found ourselves was exactly what we should have expected, and probably what we idiots and failures deserved. We had no reason to expect anything more, he explained, than to end up in the dead town of Crampton, in a nowhere region of the country, of the world in fact, during a dull season of the year that was pinched between such a lavish and brilliant autumn and what promised to be an equally lavish and brilliant wintertime. We were trapped, he said, completely stranded for all practical purposes, in a region of the

country, and of the entire world, where all the manifestations of that bleak time of year, or rather its *absence* of
manifestations, were so evident in the landscape around us,
where everything was absolutely stripped to the bone, and
where the pathetic emptiness of forms in their unadorned
state was so brutally evident. When I pointed out that
Grossvogel's brochure for this excursion, which he deemed
a 'physical-metaphysical excursion,' did not strictly misrep-
resent our destination I received only evil looks from several
of the others at the table where we sat, as well as from the
nearby tables of the small, almost miniature diner in which
the whole group of us were now packed, filling it to capacity
with the presence of exotic out-of-towners who, when they
stopped bickering for a few moments, simply stared with a
killing silence out the windows at the empty streets and
broken-down buildings of the dead town of Crampton. The
town was further maligned as a 'drab abyss,' the speaker of
this phrase being a skeletal individual who always introduced himself as a 'defrocked academic.' This self-designation
would usually provoke a query addressed to him as to its
meaning, after which he would, in so many words, elaborate on how his failure to skew his thinking to the standards
of, as he termed it, the 'intellectual marketplace,' along with
his failure to conceal his unconventional studies and
methodologies, had resulted in his longtime inability to
secure a position within a reputable academic institution, or
within any sort of institution or place of business whatever.
Thus, in his mind, his failure was more or less his ultimate
distinction, and in this sense he was typical of those of us
who were seated at the few tables and upon stools along the
counter of that miniature diner, complaining that Grossvogel had charged us entirely too much money and to some
degree misrepresented, in his brochure, the whole value and
purpose of the excursion to the dead town of Crampton.

Taking my copy of Grossvogel's brochure from the back
pocket of my trousers, I unfolded its few pages and laid
them before the other three people who were seated at the

same table as I. Then I removed my fragile reading glasses from the pocket of the old cardigan I was wearing beneath my even older jacket in order to scrutinize these pages once again, confirming the suspicions I had had about their meaning.

'If you're looking for the fine print –' said the man seated to my left, a 'photographic portraitist' who often broke into a spate of coughing whenever he began to speak, as he did on this occasion.

'What I think my friend was going to say,' said the man seated on my right, 'was that we have been the victims of a subtle and intricate swindle. I say this on his behalf because this is the direction in which his mind works, am I right?'

'A *metaphysical swindle*,' confirmed the man on my left, who had ceased coughing for the moment.

'Indeed, a metaphysical swindle,' repeated the other man somewhat mockingly. 'I would never have imagined myself being taken in by such a thing, given my experience and special field of knowledge. But this, of course, was such a subtle and intricate operation.'

While I knew that the man on my right was the author of an unpublished philosophical treatise entitled *An Investigation into the Conspiracy against the Human Race*, I was not sure what he meant by the mention of his 'experience and special field of knowledge.' Before I could inquire about this issue, I was brashly interrupted by the woman seated across the table from me.

'Mr Reiner Grossvogel is a fraud, it's as simple as that,' she said loud enough for everyone in the diner to hear. 'I've been aware of his fraudulent character for some time, as you know. Even before his so-called "metamorphic experience," or whatever he calls it –'

'Metamorphic recovery,' I said by way of correction.

'Fine, his metamorphic recovery, whatever that's supposed to mean. Even before that time I could see that he was somebody who had all the makings of a fraud. He only required the proper conjunction of circumstances to bring this trait out in him. And then along came that supposedly near-fatal illness of his that he says led to that, I can barely say it, *metamorphic recovery*. After that he was able to realize all his unused talents for being the fraud he was always destined to be and always wanted to be. I joined in this farcical excursion, or whatever it is, only for the satisfaction of seeing everyone else find out what I always knew and always maintained about Reiner Grossvogel. You're all my witnesses,' she finished, her wrinkled and heavily made-up eyes scanning our faces, and those of the others in the diner, for the affirmation she sought.

I knew this woman only by her professional name of Mrs Angela. Until recently she had operated what everyone among our circle referred to as a 'psychic coffeehouse' which, in addition to other goods and services, was known for its excellent pastries that she made herself, or at least claimed that she made, off the premises. Nevertheless, the business never seemed to prosper either on the strength of its psychic readings, which were performed by several persons in Mrs Angela's employ, or on the strength of its excellent pastries and somewhat overpriced coffee. It was Mrs Angela who first complained about the quality of both the service and the modest fare being offered to us in the Crampton diner. Not long after we arrived that afternoon and immediately packed ourselves into what seemed to be the town's only active place of business, Mrs Angela called out to the young woman whose lonely task it was to cater to our group. 'This coffee is incredibly bitter,' she shouted at the girl, who was dressed in what appeared to be a brand-new white uniform. 'And these donuts are stale, every one of them. What kind of place is this? I think this whole town and everything in it is a fraud.'

When the girl came over to our table and stood before us I noticed that her uniform resembled that of a nurse more than it did an outfit worn by a waitress in a diner. Specifically it reminded me of the uniforms that I saw worn by the nurses at the hospital where Grossvogel was treated for, and ultimately recovered from, what appeared at the time to be a very serious illness. While Mrs Angela was berating the waitress over the quality of the coffee and donuts we had been served, which were included in the travel package that Grossvogel's brochure described as the 'ultimate physical-metaphysical excursion,' I was reviewing my memories of Grossvogel in that stark and conspicuously out-of-date hospital where he had been treated, however briefly, some two years preceding our visit to the dead town of Crampton. He had been admitted to this wretched facility through its emergency room, which was simply the rear entrance to what was not so much a hospital, properly speaking, but more a makeshift clinic set up in an old building located in the decayed neighborhood where Grossvogel and most of those who knew him were forced to live due to our limited financial means. I myself was the one who took him, in a taxi, to this emergency room and provided the woman at the admittance desk with all the pertinent information regarding Grossvogel, since he was in no condition to do so himself. Later I explained to a nurse – whom I could not help looking upon merely as an emergency-room attendant in a nurse's uniform, given that she seemed somehow lacking in medical expertise – that Grossvogel had collapsed at a local art gallery during a modest exhibit of his works. This was his first experience, I told the nurse, both as a publicly exhibited artist and as a victim of a sudden physical collapse. However, I did not mention that the art gallery to which I referred might have been more accurately depicted as an empty storefront that now and then was cleaned up and used for exhibitions or artistic performances of various types. Grossvogel had been complaining throughout the evening of abdominal pains, I informed the nurse, and then repeated to an emergency-room physician, who also struck me as another medical attendant rather than as a legitimate doctor of medicine. The reason these abdominal pains had increased throughout that evening, I speculated to both the nurse and the doctor, was perhaps Grossvogel's increasing sense of anxiety at seeing his works exhibited for the first time, since he had always been notoriously insecure about his talents as an artist and, in my opinion, had good reason to be. On the other hand there might possibly have been a serious organic condition involved, I allowed when speaking with the nurse and later with the doctor. In any case, Grossvogel had finally collapsed on the floor of the art gallery and had been unable to do anything but groan somewhat pitifully and, to be honest, somewhat irritatingly since that time.

After listening to my account of Grossvogel's collapse, the doctor instructed the artist to lie down upon a gurney that stood at the end of a badly lighted hallway, while both the doctor and the nurse walked off in the opposite direction. I stood close by Grossvogel during the time that he lay upon this gurney in the shadows of that makeshift clinic. It was the middle of the night by then, and Grossvogel's moaning had abated somewhat, only to be replaced by what I understood at that time as a series of delirious utterances. In the course of this rhetorical delirium, the artist mentioned several times something that he called the 'pervasive shadow.' I told him that it was merely the poor illumination of the hallway, my own words sounding somewhat delirious to me due to the fatigue brought on by the events of that night, both at the art gallery and in the emergency room of that tawdry hospital. Afterward I just stood there listening to Grossvogel murmur at intervals, no longer responding to his delirious and increasingly elaborate utterances about the 'pervasive shadow that causes things to be what they would not be' or the 'all-moving darkness that makes things do what they would not do.'

After an hour or so of listening to Grossvogel, I noticed that the doctor and nurse were now standing close together at the other end of that dark hallway. They seemed to be conferring with each other for the longest time and every so often one or both of them would look in the direction where I was standing close by the prostrate and murmuring

Grossvogel. I wondered how long they were going to carry on with what seemed to me a medical charade, a clinical dumbshow, while the artist lay moaning and now more frequently murmuring on the subject of the shadow and the darkness. Perhaps I dozed off on my feet for a moment, because it seemed that from out of nowhere the nurse was suddenly at my side and the doctor was no longer anywhere in sight. The nurse's white uniform now appeared almost luminous in the dingy shadows of that hallway. 'You can go home now,' she said to me. 'Your friend is going to be admitted to the hospital.' She then pushed Grossvogel on his gurney toward the doors of an elevator at the end of the hallway. As soon as she reached these elevator doors they opened quickly and silently, pouring the brightest light into that dim hallway. When the doors were fully opened I could see the doctor standing inside. He pulled Grossvogel's stretcher into the brilliantly illuminated elevator while the nurse pushed the stretcher from behind. As soon as they were all inside, the elevator doors closed quickly and silently, and the hallway in which I was still standing seemed even darker and more dense with shadows than it had before.

The following day I visited Grossvogel at the hospital. He had been placed in a small private room in a distant corner of the institution's uppermost floor. As I walked toward this room, looking for the number I had been given at the information desk downstairs, it seemed to me that none of the other rooms on that floor had any patients occupying them. It was only when I found the number I sought that I looked inside and actually saw a bed that was occupied, conspicuously so, since Grossvogel was a rather large-bodied individual who took up the full length and breadth of an old and sagging mattress. He seemed quite giantlike lying on that undersized, institutional mattress in that small, windowless room. There was barely enough space for me to squeeze myself between the wall and the bedside of the artist, who seemed to be still in much the same delirious condition as he had been the night before. There was no sign of recognition on his part that I was in the same room, although we were so close that I was practically on top of him. Even after I spoke his name several times his teary gaze betrayed no notice of my presence. However, as I began to sidle away from his bedside I was startled when Grossvogel firmly grabbed my arm with his enormous left hand, which was the hand he used for painting and drawing the works of his which had been exhibited in the storefront art gallery the previous evening. 'Grossvogel,' I said expectantly, thinking that finally he was going to respond, if only to speak about the pervasive shadow (that causes things to be what they would not be) and the all-moving darkness (that causes things to do what they would not do). But a few seconds later his hand became limp and fell from my arm onto the very edge of the misshapen institutional mattress on which his body again lay still and unresponsive.

After some moments I made my way out of Grossvogel's private room and walked over to the nurse's station on the same floor of the hospital to inquire about the artist's medical condition. The sole nurse in attendance listened to my request and consulted a folder with the name Reiner Grossvogel typed in one of its upper corners. After studying me some time longer than she had studied the pages concerning the artist, and now hospital patient, she simply said, 'Your friend is being observed very closely.'

'Is that all you can tell me?' I asked.

'His tests haven't been returned. You might ask about them later.'

'Later today?'

'Yes, later today,' she said, taking Grossvogel's folder and walking away into another room. I heard the squeaking sound of a drawer in an old filing cabinet being opened and then suddenly being slammed shut again. For some reason I stood there waiting for the nurse to emerge from the room where she had taken Grossvogel's medical folder. Finally I gave up and returned home.

When I called the hospital later that day I was told that Grossvogel had been released. 'He's gone home?' I said, which was the only thing that occurred to me to say. 'We have no way of knowing where he's gone,' the woman who answered the phone replied just before hanging up on me. Nor did anyone else know where Grossvogel had gone, for he was not at his home, and no one among our circle had any knowledge of his whereabouts.

It was several weeks, perhaps more than a month, after Grossvogel's release from the hospital, and apparent disappearance, that several of us had gathered, purely by chance, at the storefront art gallery where the artist had collapsed during the opening night of his first exhibit. By this time even I had ceased to be concerned in any way with Grossvogel or the fact that he had without warning simply dropped out of sight. Certainly he was not the first to do so among our circle, all of whom were more or less unstable, sometimes dangerously volatile persons who might involve themselves in questionable activities for the sake of some artistic or intellectual vision, or simply out of pure desperation of spirit. I think that the only reason any of us mentioned Grossvogel's name as we drifted about the art gallery that afternoon was the fact that his works still remained on exhibit, and wherever we turned we were confronted by some painting or drawing of his which, in a pamphlet issued to accompany the show, I myself had written were 'manifestations of a singularly gifted artistic visionary,' when in fact they were without exception quite run-of-the-mill specimens of the sort of artistic nonsense that, for reasons unknown to all concerned, will occasionally gain a measure of success or even a high degree of prominence for their creator. 'What am I supposed to do with all this junk?' complained the woman who owned, or perhaps only rented, the storefront building that had been set up as an art gallery. I was about to say to her that I would take responsibility for removing Grossvogel's works from the gallery, and perhaps even store them somewhere for a time, when the skeletal person who always introduced himself as a defrocked academic interjected, suggesting to the agitated owner (or least operator) of the art gallery that she should send them to the hospital where Grossvogel had 'supposedly been treated' after his collapse. When I asked why he had used the word 'supposedly,' he replied, 'I've long believed that place to be a dubious institution, and I'm not the only one to hold this view.' I then asked if there was any credible basis for this belief of his, but he only crossed his skeletal arms and looked at me as if I had just insulted him in some way. 'Mrs Angela,' he said to a woman who was standing nearby, studying one of Grossvogel's paintings as if she were seriously considering it for purchase. At that time Mrs Angela's psychic coffeehouse had yet to prove itself a failed venture, and possibly she was thinking that Grossvogel's works, although inferior from an artistic standpoint, might in some way complement the ambience of her place of business, where patrons could sit at tables and receive advice from hired psychic counselors while also feasting on an array of excellent pastries.

'You should listen to what he says about that hospital,' Mrs Angela said to me without taking her eyes off that painting of Grossvogel's. 'I've had a strong feeling about that place for a long time. There is some aspect of it that is extremely devious.'

'*Dubious*,' corrected the defrocked academic.

'Yes,' answered Mrs Angela. 'It's not by any means someplace I'd like to wake up and find myself.'

'I wrote a poem about it,' said the neatly dressed gentleman who all this time had been marauding about the floor of the gallery, no doubt waiting for the most propitious moment to approach the woman who owned or rented the storefront building and persuade her to sponsor what he was forever touting as an 'evening of Hermetic readings,' which of course would prominently feature his own works. 'I once read that poem to you,' he said to the gallery owner.

'Yes, you read it to me,' she replied with barely any vocal inflection.

'I wrote it after being treated in the emergency room of that place very late one night,' explained the poet.

'What were you treated for?' I asked him.

'Oh, nothing serious. I went home a few hours later. I was never admitted as a patient, I'm glad to say. It was, and I quote from my poem on the subject, the "nucleus of the abysmal."'

'That's fine to say that,' I said. 'But could we possibly speak in more explicit terms?'

However, before I could draw out a response from the self-styled writer of Hermetic lyrics, the door of the art gallery was suddenly pushed open with a conspicuous force that all of us inside instantly recognized. A moment later we saw standing before us the large-bodied figure of Reiner Grossvogel. Physically he appeared to be, for the most part, much the same person I recalled prior to his collapse on the floor of the art gallery not more than a few feet from where I was now standing, bearing none of the traits of that moaning, delirious creature whom I had taken in a taxi to the hospital for emergency treatment. Nevertheless, there did seem to be something different about him, a subtle but thorough change in the way he looked upon what lay before him: whereas the gaze of the artist had once been characteristically downcast or nervously averted, his eyes now seemed completely direct in their focus and filled with a calm purpose.

'I'm taking away all of this,' he said, gesturing broadly but quite gently toward the artworks of his that filled the gallery, none of which had been sold either on the opening night of his show or during the subsequent period of his disappearance. 'I would appreciate your assistance, if you will give it,' he added as he began taking down paintings and drawings from along the walls.

The rest of us joined him in this endeavor without question or comment, and laden with artworks both large and small we followed him out of the gallery toward a battered pick-up truck parked at the curb in front. Grossvogel casually hurled his works into the back of the rented, or possibly borrowed, truck (since the artist had never been known to possess any kind of vehicle before that day), exhibiting no concern for the damage that might be incurred on what he had once considered the best examples of his artistic output to date. There was a moment's hesitation on the part of Mrs Angela, who was perhaps still considering how one or more of these works would look in her place of business, but ultimately she too began carrying Grossvogel's works out of the gallery and hurling them into the back of the truck where they piled up like refuse, until the gallery's walls and floor space were entirely cleared and the place looked like any other disused storefront. Grossvogel then got into the truck while the rest us stood in wondering silence outside the emptied art gallery. Putting his head out the open window of the rented or borrowed truck, he called to the woman who ran the gallery. She walked over to the driver's side of the truck and exchanged a few words with the artist before he started the engine of the vehicle and drove off. Returning to where we had remained standing on the sidewalk, she announced to us that, a few weeks hence, there would be a second exhibit of Grossvogel's work at the gallery.

This, then, was the message that was passed among the circle of persons with whom I was associated at the time: that Grossvogel, after physically collapsing from an undisclosed ailment or attack at the first, highly unsuccessful exhibit of his works, was now going to present a second exhibit after summarily cleaning out the art gallery of those rather worthless paintings and drawings of his already displayed to the public and hauling them away in the back of a pick-up truck.

Grossvogel's new exhibit was unusually well advertised by the woman who owned the art gallery and who stood to gain financially from the sale of what, in a phrase used in the promotional copy for the event, were somewhat awkwardly called 'radical and revisionary works by the celebrated artistic visionary Reiner Grossvogel.' Nevertheless, due to the circumstances surrounding both the artist's previous and upcoming exhibits, the whole thing almost immediately devolved into a fog of delirious and sometimes lurid gossip and speculation. This development was wholly in keeping with the nature of those who comprised that circle of dubious, not to mention devious artistic and intellectual persons of which I had unexpectedly become a central figure. After all, it was I who had taken Grossvogel to the hospital following his collapse at the first exhibit of his works, and it was the hospital – already a subject of strange repute, as I discovered – that loomed so prominently within the delirious fog of gossip and speculation surrounding Grossvogel's upcoming exhibit. There was even talk of some special procedures and medications to which the artist had been exposed during his brief confinement at this institution that would account for his unexplained disappearance and subsequent re-emergence in order to perpetrate what many presumed would be a startling 'artistic vision.' No doubt it was this expectation, this desperate hope for something of brilliant novelty and lavishly colorful imagination – which in the minds of some overly excitable persons promised to exceed the domain of mere aesthetics, and even extend the bounds of artistic expression – that led to the acceptance among our circle of the unorthodox nature of Grossvogel's new exhibit, as well as accounting for the emotional letdown that followed for those of us in attendance that opening night.

And, in fact, what occurred at the gallery that night in no way resembled the sort of exhibit we were accustomed to attending: the floor of the gallery and the gallery's walls remained as bare as the day when Grossvogel appeared with a pick-up truck to cart off all his works from his old art show, while the new one, we soon discovered after arriving, was to take place in the small back room of the storefront building. Furthermore, we were charged a rather large fee in order to enter this small back room, which was illuminated by only a few lightbulbs of extremely low wattage dangling here and there from the ceiling. One of the lightbulbs was hung in a corner of the room directly above a small table which had a torn section of a bedsheet draped over it to conceal something that was bulging beneath it. Radiating out from this corner with its dim lightbulb and small table were several loosely arranged rows of folding chairs. These uncomfortable chairs were eventually occupied by those of us, about a dozen in all, who were willing to pay the large fee for what seemed to be an event more in the style of a primitive stageshow than anything resembling an art exhibit. I could hear Mrs Angela in one of the seats behind me saying over and over to those around her, 'What the hell is this?' Finally she leaned forward and said to me, 'What does Grossvogel think he's doing? I've heard that he's been medicated to the eyeballs ever since his stay in that hospital.' Yet the artist appeared lucid enough when a few moments later he made his way through the loosely arranged rows of folding chairs and stood beside the small table with the torn bedsheet draped over it and the low-watt lightbulb dangling above. In the confines of the art gallery's back room, the large-bodied Grossvogel seemed almost gigantic, just as he had when lying upon that institutional mattress in his private room at the hospital. Even his voice, which was usually quiet, even somewhat wispy, seemed to be enlarged when he began speaking to us.

'Thank you all for coming here tonight,' he began. 'This shouldn't take very long. I have only a few things to say to you and then something that I would like to show you. It's really no less than a miracle that I'm able to stand here and speak to you in this way. Not too long ago, as some of you may recall, I suffered a terrible attack in this very art gallery. I hope you won't mind if I tell you a few things about the nature of this attack and its consequences, things which I feel are essential to appreciating what I have to show you tonight.

'Well then, let me start by saying that, on one level, the attack I suffered in this art gallery during the opening night of an exhibit of my works was in the nature of a simple gastrointestinal upheaval, even if it was a quite severe episode of its type. For some time this gastrointestinal upheaval, the result of a disorder of my digestive system, had been making its progress within me. Over a period of many years this disorder had been progressively and insidiously developing, on one level, in the depths of my body and, on another level altogether, in the darkest aspect of my being. This period coincided with, and in fact was directly a consequence of, my involvement with the creation of artworks – my intense desire to make art, which is to say, my desire to *do* something and my desire to *be* something, that is, an artist. I was attempting during this period I speak of – and for that matter throughout my entire life – *to make something with my mind*, specifically to create works of art by the only possible means I believed were available to me, which was by using my mind, or by using my imagination or my *creative faculties*, some force or function of what people would call a soul or a spirit or simply a personal self. But when I found myself collapsed upon the floor of this art gallery, and later at the hospital, experiencing the most acute abdominal agony, I was overwhelmed by the realization that I had no mind or imagination that I could use, that there was nothing I could call a soul or self – those things were all nonsense and dreams. I realized, in my severe gastrointestinal distress, that the only thing that had any existence at all was this larger-than-average physical body of mine. And I realized that there was nothing for this body to *do* except to function in physical pain and that there was nothing for it to *be* except what it was – not an artist or creator of any kind but solely a mass of flesh, a system of tissues and bones and so forth, suffering the agonies of a disorder of its digestive system, and that anything that did not directly stem from these facts, especially producing works of art, was profoundly and utterly *false and unreal*. At the same time I also became aware of the force that was behind my intense desire to do something and to be something, particularly my desire to create utterly false and unreal works of art. In other words, I became aware of what in reality was *activating* my body. This realization was not made with my mind or imagination, and certainly it was not made through any such medium as my soul or self, all which are entirely nonsense and dreams. This realization of what was activating my body and its desires was made by the only means possible, this being by way of the human body itself and its organs of physical sensation. This is precisely how the world of non-human bodies has always functioned and functioned so much more successfully than the world of human bodies, which is forever obstructed by all the nonsense we fabricate about having minds and having souls or selves. The world of non-human bodies is activated directly in accord with the commands of that terrible force underlying all existence which issues only a few simple desires, none of which have to do with anything as nonsensical and dreamlike as creating works of art or of being an artist, of doing or being anything like these profoundly false and unreal things. Thus the world of non-human bodies never need suffer the pains of pursuing false and unreal desires, because such feelings have no relevance for those bodies and never arise within them.'

Before continuing with the introductory talk that comprised the first part of his art exhibit, or artistic stageshow, as I thought of it, Grossvogel paused and for a moment seemed to be surveying the faces of the small audience seated in the back room of the gallery. What he had expressed to us concerning his body and its digestive malfunctions was on the whole comprehensible enough, even if certain points he was articulating seemed at the time to be questionable and his overall discourse somewhat unengaging. Yet we put up with Grossvogel's words, I believe, because we had thought that they were leading us into another, possibly more engaging phase of his experience, which somehow we already sensed was not wholly alienated from our own, whether or not we identified with its peculiarly gastrointestinal nature. Therefore we remained silent, almost respectfully so, considering the unorthodox proceedings of that night, as Grossvogel continued with what he had to tell us before the moment came when he unveiled what he had brought to show us.

'It is all so very, very simple,' the artist continued. 'Our bodies are but one manifestation of the energy, the *activating force* that sets in motion all the objects, all the bodies of this world and enables them to exist as they do. This activating force is something like a shadow that is not on the outside of all the bodies of this world but is *inside* of everything and thoroughly pervades everything – an all-moving darkness that has no substance in itself but that moves all the objects of this world, including those objects which we call our bodies. While I was in the throes of my gastrointestinal episode at the hospital where I was treated I descended, so to speak, to that deep abyss of entity where I could feel how this shadow, this darkness was activating my body. I could also hear its movement, not only within my body but in everything around me, because the sound that it made was not the sound of my body – it was the sound of this shadow, this darkness, which is not like any other sound. Likewise I was able to detect the workings of this pervasive and all-moving force through the sense of smell and the sense of taste, as well as the sense of touch with which my body is equipped. Finally I opened my eyes, for throughout much of this agonizing ordeal of my digestive system my eyelids were clenched shut in pain. And when I opened my eyes I found that I could see how everything around me, including my own body, was activated from within by this pervasive shadow, this all-moving darkness. And nothing looked as I had always known it to look. Before that night I had never experienced the world purely by means of my organs of physical sensation, which are the direct point of contact with that deep abyss of entity that I am calling the shadow, the darkness. My false and unreal works as an artist were merely the evidence of what I concocted with my mind or my imagination, which are basically nonsensical and dream-like fabrications that only interfere with the workings of our senses. I believed that somehow these works of art reflected in some way the nature of my self or my soul, when in actuality they only reflected my deranged and useless desires to *do* something and to *be* something, which always means to do and to be something false and unreal. Like everything else, these desires had been activated by the same pervasive shadow, the all-moving darkness which, due to the self-annihilating agony of my gastrointestinal distress, I could now experience directly by means of my sense organs and without the interference of my imaginary mind or my imaginary self.

'I should confess that prior to my physical collapse at this very art gallery I had undergone a psychic collapse – a collapse of something false and unreal, of something nonsensical and dreamlike, it goes without saying, although it was all very genuine and real to me at the time. This collapse of my mind and my self was the result of how poorly my works of art were being received by those attending the opening night of my first exhibit, of how profoundly unsuccessful they were as artistic creations, miserably unsuccessful even in the sphere of false and unreal artistic creations. This unsuccessful exhibit demonstrated to me how thoroughly I had failed in my efforts to be an artist. Everyone at the exhibit could see how unsuccessful my artworks proved to be, and I could see everyone in the very act of witnessing my unmitigated failure as an artist. This was the psychic crisis which precipitated my physical crisis and the eventual collapse of my body into spasms of gastrointestinal torment. Once my mind and my personal sense of self had broken down, all that was left in operation were my organs of physical sensation, by means of which I was able for the first time to experience directly that deep abyss of entity that is the shadow, the darkness which had activated my intense desire to be a success at *doing* something and at *being* something, and thereby also activated my body as it moved within this world, just as all bodies are likewise activated. And what I experienced through direct sensory channels – the spectacle of the shadow inside of everything, the all-moving darkness – was so appalling that I was sure I would cease to exist. In some way, because of the manner in which my senses were now functioning, especially my visual sense, I did in fact cease to exist as I had existed before that night. Without the interference of my mind and my imagination, all that nonsensical dreaming about my soul and my self, I was forced to see things under the aspect of the shadow inside them, the darkness which activated them. And it was wholly appalling, more so than my words could possibly tell you.'

Nevertheless, Grossvogel went on to explain in detail to those of us who had paid the exorbitant price to see his stageshow exhibit the appalling way in which he was forced to see the world around him, including his own body in its gastrointestinal distress, and how convinced he was that this vision of things would soon be the cause of his death, despite the measures taken to save him during his hospital sojourn. It was Grossvogel's contention that his only hope of survival was for him to perish completely, in the sense that the person (or the mind or self) that had once been Grossvogel would actually cease to exist. This necessary condition for survival, he maintained, prompted his physical body to undergo a 'metamorphic recovery.' Within a matter of hours, Grossvogel told us, he no longer suffered from the symptoms of acute abdominal pains which had initiated his crisis, and furthermore he was now able to tolerate the way in which he was permanently forced to see things, as he put it, 'under the aspect of the shadow inside them, the darkness which activated them.' Since the person who had been Grossvogel had perished, as Grossvogel explained to us, the body of Grossvogel was able to continue as a *successful organism* untroubled by the imaginary torments that had once been inflicted upon him by his fabricated mind and his false and unreal self. As he put it in his own words, 'I am no longer *occupied* with myself or my mind.' What we in the audience now saw before us, he said, was Grossvogel's body speaking with Grossvogel's voice and using Grossvogel's neurological circuitry but without the interference of the 'imaginary character' known as Grossvogel: all of his words and actions, he said, now emanated directly from that same force which activates every one of us if we could only realize it in the way he had been compelled to do in order to keep his body alive. The artist emphasized in his own terribly calm way that in no sense had he chosen his unique course of recovery. No one would willingly choose such a thing, he contended. Everyone prefers to continue their existence as a mind and a self, no matter what pain it causes them, no matter how false and unreal they might be, than to face the quite obvious reality of being only a body set in motion by this mindless, soulless, and selfless force which he designated the shadow, the darkness. Nonetheless, Grossvogel disclosed to us, this was exactly the reality that he needed to admit into his system if his body was to continue its existence and to succeed as an organism. 'It was purely a matter of physical survival,' he said. 'Everybody should be able to understand that. Anyone would do the same.' Moreover, the famous metamorphic recovery in which Grossvogel the person died and Grossvogel the body survived was so successful, he informed his stageshow audience, that he immediately embarked upon a strenuous period of travel, mostly by means of inexpensive buslines that took him great distances across and around the entire country, so that he could look at various people and places while exercising his new faculty of being able to see the shadow that pervaded them, the all-moving darkness that activated them, since he was no longer subject to the misconceptions about the world that are created by the mind or imagination – those obstructing mechanisms which were now removed from his system – and nor did he mistakenly imagine anyone or anything to possess a soul or a self. And everywhere he went he witnessed the spectacle that had previously so appalled him to the point of becoming a life-threatening medical condition.

'I could now know the world directly through the senses of my body,' Grossvogel continued. 'And I saw with my body what I could never have seen with my mind or imagination during my career as a failed artist. Everywhere I travelled I saw how the pervasive shadow, the all-moving darkness, was *using our world*. Because this shadow, this darkness has nothing of its own, no way to exist except as an activating force or energy, whereas we have our bodies, we are *only* our bodies, whether they are organic bodies or non-organic bodies, human or non-human bodies, makes no difference – they are all simply bodies and nothing but bodies, with no component whatever of a mind or a self or a soul. Hence the shadow, the darkness *uses our world for what it needs to thrive upon*. It *has* nothing except its activating energy, while we *are* nothing except our bodies. This is why the shadow, the darkness causes things to be what they would not be and to do what they would not do. Because without the shadow inside them, the all-moving blackness activating them, they would be only what they are – heaps of matter lacking any impulse, any urge to flourish, to *succeed* in this world. This state of affairs should be called what it is – an absolute nightmare. That is exactly what I experienced in the hospital when I realized, due to my intense gastrointestinal suffering, that I had no mind or imagination, no soul or self – that these were nonsensical and dreamlike intermediaries fabricated to protect human beings from realizing what it is we really are: only a collection of bodies activated by the shadow, the darkness. Those among us who are successful organisms to any degree, including artists, are so only by virtue of the extent to which we function as bodies and by no means as minds or selves. This is exactly the manner in which I had failed so exceptionally, since I was profoundly convinced of the existence of my mind and my imagination, my soul and my self. My only hope lay in my ability to make a metamorphic recovery, to *accept in every way* the nightmarish order of things so that I could continue to exist as a successful organism even without the protective nonsense of the mind and the imagination, the protective dream of having any kind of soul or self. Otherwise I would have been annihilated by a fatally traumatic insanity brought on by the shock of this shattering realization. Therefore the person who was Grossvogel had to perish in that hospital – and good riddance – so that the body of Grossvogel could be free of its gastrointestinal crisis and go on to travel in all directions by various means of transportation, primarily the inexpensive transportation provided by interstate buslines, witnessing the spectacle of the shadow, the darkness using our world of bodies for what it needs to thrive upon. And after witnessing this spectacle it was inevitable that I should portray it in some form, not as an *artist who has failed* because he is using some nonsense called the mind or the imagination, but as a *body that has succeeded* in perceiving how everything in the world actually functions. That is what I have come to show you, to exhibit to you this evening.'

I, who had been lulled or agitated by Grossvogel's discourse as much as anyone in the audience, was for some reason surprised, and even apprehensive, when he suddenly ended his lecture or fantasy monologue or whatever I construed his words to be at the time. It seemed that he could have gone on speaking forever in the back room of that art gallery where low-watt lightbulbs hung down from the ceiling, one of them directly above the table that was covered with a torn section of bedsheet. And now Grossvogel was lifting one corner of the torn bedsheet to show us, at last, what he had created, not by using his mind or imagination, which he claimed no longer existed in him any more than did his soul or self, but by using only his body's organs of physical sensation. When he finally uncovered the piece completely and it was fully displayed in the dull glow of the lightbulb which hung directly above it, none of us demonstrated either a positive or negative reaction to it at first, possibly because our minds were so numbed by all the verbal build-up that had led to this moment of unveiling.

It appeared to be a sculpture of some kind. However, I found it initially impossible to give this object any generic designation, either artistic or non-artistic. It might have been anything. The surface of the piece was uniformly of a shining darkness, having a glossy sheen beneath which was spread a swirling murk of shades that almost seemed to be in motion, an effect which seemed quite credibly the result of some swaying of the lightbulb dangling above. There appeared to be a resemblance in its general outline to some kind of creature, perhaps a grossly distorted version of a scorpion or a crab, since it displayed more than a few clawlike extensions reaching out from a central, highly shapeless mass. But it also appeared to have elements poking upward, peaks or horns that jutted at roughly vertical angles and ended sometimes in a sharp point and sometimes in a soft, headlike bulge. Because Grossvogel had spoken so much about bodies, it was natural to see such forms, in some deranged fashion, as the basis of the object or as being incorporated into it somehow – a chaotic world of bodies of every kind, of shapes activated by the shadow inside them, the darkness that caused them to be what they would not be and to do what they would not do. And among these body-like shapes I recognized distinctly the large-bodied figure of the artist himself, although the significance of the fact that Grossvogel had *implanted* himself therein escaped me as I sat contemplating this modest exhibit.

Whatever Grossvogel's sculpture may have represented in its parts or as a whole, it contained more than a suggestion of that 'absolute nightmare' which the artist, so to speak, had elucidated during his lecture or fantasy monologue earlier that evening. Yet this quality of the piece, even for an audience that had more than a slight appreciation of nightmarish subjects and contours, was not enough to offset the high price we had been required to pay for the privilege of hearing about Grossvogel's gastrointestinal ordeal and self-proclaimed metamorphic recovery. Soon after the artist unveiled his work to us, each of our bodies rose out of those uncomfortable folding chairs and excuses for departing the premises were being spoken on all sides. Before making my own exit I noticed that inconspicuously displayed next to Grossvogel's sculpture was a small card upon which was printed the title of the piece. TSALAL NO. 1, it read. Later I learned something about the meaning of this term, which, in the way of words, both illuminated and concealed the nature of the thing that it named.

The matter of Grossvogel's sculpture – he subsequently put out a series of several hundred, each of them with the same title followed by a number that placed it in a sequence of artistic production – was discussed at length as we sat waiting in the diner situated on the main street of the dead town of Crampton. The gentleman seated to my left at one of the few tables in the diner reiterated his accusations against Grossvogel.

'First he subjected us to an artistic swindle,' said this person who was prone to sudden and protracted coughing spells, 'and now he has subjected us to a metaphysical swindle. It was unheard of, charging us such a price for that exhibition of his, and now charging us so outrageously once again for this "physical-metaphysical excursion." We've all been taken in by that –'

'That absolute fraud,' said Mrs Angela when the man on my left was unable to complete his statement because he had broken into another fit of coughing. 'I don't think he's even going to show up,' she continued. 'He induces us to come to this hole-in-the-wall town. He says that this is the place where we need to gather for this excursion of his. But he doesn't show his face anywhere around here. Where did he find this place, on one of those bus tours he was always talking about?'

It seemed that we had only ourselves and our own idiocy to blame for the situation we were in. Even though no one openly admitted it, the truth was that those of us who were present had been very much impressed with Grossvogel on the day when he entered the art gallery and had us assist him in throwing all of his works on exhibit into the back of a battered pick-up truck. None of us in our small circle of artists and intellectuals had ever done anything remotely like that or even dreamed of doing something so drastic and full of drama. From that day it became our unspoken conviction that Grossvogel was on to something and our disgraceful secret that we desired to attach ourselves to him in order to profit in some way by our association with him. At the same time, of course, we also resented Grossvogel's daring behavior and were perfectly ready to welcome another failure on his part, perhaps even another collapse on the floor of the gallery where he and his artworks had already once failed to everyone's thorough satisfaction. Such a confusion of motives was more than enough reason for us to pay the exorbitant fee that Grossvogel charged for his new exhibit, which we afterward dismissed in one way or another.

Following the show that night I stood on the sidewalk outside the art gallery, listening once again to Mrs Angela's implications regarding the true source of Grossvogel's metamorphic recovery and artistic inspiration. 'Mr Reiner Grossvogel has been medicated to the eyeballs ever since he came out of that hospital,' she said to me as if for the first time. 'I know one of the girls who works at the drugstore that fills his prescriptions. She's a very good customer of mine,' she added, her wrinkled and heavily made-up eyes flashing with self-satisfaction. Then she continued her scandalous revelations. 'I think you might know the kind of medications prescribed for someone with Grossvogel's medical condition, which really isn't a medical condition at all but a psychophysical disorder that I or any of the people who work for me could have told him about a long time ago. Grossvogel's brain has been swimming in all kinds of tranquilizers and anti-depressants for months now, and not only that. He's also been taking an anti-spasmodic compound for that condition of his that he's supposed to have recovered from by such miraculous means. I'm not surprised he doesn't think he has a mind or any kind of self, which is all just an act in any case.

'Anti-spasmodic,' Mrs Angela hissed at me as we stood on the sidewalk outside the art gallery following Grossvogel's exhibit. 'Do you know what that means?' she asked me and then quickly answered her own question. 'It means belladonna, a poisonous hallucinogenic. It means phenobarbital, a barbiturate. The girl from the drugstore told me all about it. He's been overdosing himself on all of these drugs, do you understand? That's why he's been seeing things in that peculiar way he would have us believe. It's not some shadow or whatever he says that's *activating* his body. I would know about something like that, now wouldn't I? I have a special gift that provides me with insight into things like that.'

But despite her gifts, along with her excellent pastries, Mrs Angela's psychic coffeehouse did not thrive as a business and ultimately went under altogether. On the other hand, Grossvogel's sculptures, which he produced at a prolific pace, were an incredible success, both among local buyers of artistic products and among art merchants and collectors across the country, even reaching an international market to some extent. Reiner Grossvogel was also celebrated in feature articles that appeared in major art magazines and non-artistic publications alike, although he was usually portrayed, in the words of one critic, as a 'one-man artistic and philosophical freakshow.' Nevertheless, Grossvogel was by any measure now functioning as a highly successful organism. And it was due to this success, which had never been approached by anyone else within our small circle of artists and intellectuals, that those of us who had abandoned Grossvogel upon hearing him lecture on his metamorphic recovery from a severe gastrointestinal disorder and viewing the first in his prodigious *Tsalal* series of sculptures now once again attached ourselves and our failed careers to him and his unarguably successful body without a mind or a self. Even Mrs Angela eventually became conversant with the 'realizations' that Grossvogel had first espoused in the back room of that storefront art gallery and now disseminated in what seemed an unending line of philosophical pamphlets, which became almost as sought after by collectors as his series of *Tsalal* sculptures. Thus, when Grossvogel issued a certain brochure among the small circle of artists and intellectuals which he had never abandoned even after he had achieved such amazing financial success and celebrity, a brochure announcing a 'physical-metaphysical excursion' to the dead town of Crampton, we were more than willing once more to pay the exorbitant price he was asking.

This was the brochure to which I referred the others seated at the table with me in the Crampton diner: the photographic portraitist who was subject to coughing jags on my left, the author of the unpublished philosophical treatise *An Investigation into the Conspiracy against the Human Race* on my right, and Mrs Angela directly across from me. The man on my left was still reiterating, with prolonged interruptions of his coughing (which I will here delete), the charge that Grossvogel had perpetrated a 'metaphysical swindle' with his high-priced 'physical-metaphysical excursion.'

'All of Grossvogel's talk about that business with the shadow and the blackness and the nightmare world he purportedly was seeing . . . and then where do we end up – in some godforsaken town that went out of business a long time ago, and in some part of the country where everything looks like an overexposed photograph. I have my camera with me ready to create portraits of faces that have looked upon Grossvogel's shadowy blackness, or whatever he was planning for us to do here. I've even thought of several very good titles and concepts for these photographic portraits which I imagine would have a good chance of being published together as a book, or at least a portfolio in a leading photography magazine. I thought that at the very least I might have taken back with me a series of photographic portraits of Grossvogel, with that huge face of his. I could have placed that with almost any of the better art magazines. But where is the celebrated Grossvogel? He said he would be here to meet us. He said we would find out everything about that shadow business, as I understood him. Furthermore, I have my head prepared for those absolute nightmares that Grossvogel prattled on about in his pamphlets and in that highly deceptive brochure of his.'

'This brochure,' I said during one of the man's more raucous intervals of hacking, 'makes no explicit promises about any of those things you've imagined to be contained there. It specifically announces that this is to be an excursion, and I quote, to a "*dead* town, a *finished* town, a *failed* town, a false and unreal setting that is the product of unsuccessful organisms and therefore a town that is exemplary of that extreme state of failure that may so distress human organic systems, particularly the gastrointestinal system, to the point of weakening its delusional and totally fabricated defenses – e.g. the mind, the self – and thus precipitating a crisis of nightmare realization involving ...," and I think we're all familiar with the shadow-and-darkness talk which follows. The point is, Grossvogel promises nothing in this brochure except an environment redolent of failure, a sort of hothouse for failed organisms. The rest of it is entirely born of your own imaginations ... and my own, I might add.'

'Well,' said Mrs Angela, pulling the brochure I had placed on the table toward her, 'did I imagine reading that, and *I* quote, "suitable dining accommodations will be provided"? Bitter coffee and stale donuts are not what I consider suitable. Grossvogel is now a rich man, as everybody knows, and this is the best he can do? Until the day I closed down my business for good, I served superlative coffee, not to mention superlative pastries, even if I now admit that I didn't make them myself. And my psychic readings, mine and those of all my people, were as breathtaking as they come. Meanwhile, the rich man and that waitress there are practically poisoning us with this bitter coffee and these incredibly stale, cut-rate donuts. What I could use at this moment is some of that anti-spasmodic medicine Grossvogel's been taking in such liberal doses for so long. And I'm sure he'll have plenty of it with him if he ever shows his face around here, which I doubt he will after making us sick with his suitable dining accommodations. If you will excuse me for a moment.'

As Mrs Angela made her way toward the lavatory on the other side of the diner, I noticed that there were already a few others lined up outside the single door labelled REST ROOM. I glanced around at those still seated at the few tables or upon the stools along the counter of the diner, and there seemed to be a number of persons who were holding their hands upon their stomachs, some of them tenderly massaging their abdominal region. I, too, was beginning to feel some intestinal discomfort which might have been attributable to the poor quality of the coffee and donuts we had been served by our waitress, who now appeared to be nowhere in sight. The man sitting on my left had also excused himself and made his way across the diner. Just as I was about to get up from the table and join him and the others who were lining up outside the rest room, the man seated on my right began telling me about his 'researches' and his 'speculations' which formed the basis for his unpublished philosophical treatise *An Investigation into the Conspiracy against the Human Race* and how these related to his 'intense suspicions' concerning Grossvogel.

'I should have known better than to have entered into this ... excursion,' the man said. 'But I felt I needed to know more about what was behind Grossvogel's story. I was intensely suspicious with respect to his assertions and claims about his metamorphic recovery and about so many other things. For instance, his assertion – his realization, as he calls it – that the mind and the imagination, the soul and the self, are all simply *nonsense and dreams*. And yet he contends that what he calls the shadow, the darkness – the *Tsalal*, as his artworks are entitled – is *not* nonsense and dreams, and that it uses our bodies, as he claims, *for what it needs to thrive upon*. Well, really, what is his basis for dismissing his mind and imagination and so forth, but embracing the reality of his Tsalal, which seems no less the product of some nonsensical dream?'

I found the man's suspicious interrogations to be a welcome distraction from the intestinal pressure now building up inside me. In response to his question I said that I could only reiterate Grossvogel's explanation that he was no longer experiencing things, that is, no longer *seeing* things with his supposedly illusory mind and self, but with his body, which as he further contended was activated, and entirely *occupied*, by the shadow that is the Tsalal. 'This isn't by any means the most preposterous revelation of its kind, at least in my experience,' I said in defense of Grossvogel.

'Nor is it in mine,' he said.

'Besides,' I continued, 'Grossvogel's curiously named sculptures, in my opinion, have a merit and interest apart from a strictly metaphysical context and foundation.'

'Do you know the significance of this word – Tsalal – that he uses as the sole title for all his artworks?'

'No, I'm afraid I have no notion of its origin or meaning,' I regretfully confessed. 'But I suppose you will enlighten me.'

'Enlightenment has nothing to do with this word, which is ancient Hebrew. It means "to become darkened . . . to become enshadowed," so to speak. This term has emerged not infrequently in the course of my researches for my treatise *An Investigation into the Conspiracy against the Human Race*. It occurs, of course, in numerous passages throughout the Old Testament – that potboiler of apocalypses both major and minor.'

'Maybe so,' I said. 'But I don't agree that Grossvogel's use of a term from Hebrew mythology necessarily calls into question the sincerity of his assertions, or even their validity, if you want to take it that far.'

'Yes, well, I seem not to be making myself clear to you. What I'm referring to emerged quite early in my researches and preliminary speculations for my *Investigation*. Briefly, I would simply say that it's not my intention to cast doubt on Grossvogel's Tsalal. My *Investigation* would prove me to be quite explicit and unequivocal on this phenomenon, although I would never employ the rather showy, and somewhat trivial approach that Grossvogel has taken, which to some extent could account for the fabulous success of his sculptures and pamphlets, on the one hand, and, on the other, the abysmal failure of my treatise, which will remain forever unpublished and unread. All that aside, my point is not that this Tsalal of Grossvogel's *isn't* in some way an actual phenomenon. I know only too well that the mind and the imagination, the soul and the self are not only the nonsensical dreams that Grossvogel makes them out to be. They are in fact no more than a cover-up – as false and unreal as the artwork Grossvogel was producing before his medical ordeal and recovery. Grossvogel was able to penetrate this fact by some extremely rare circumstance which no doubt had something to do with his medical ordeal.'

'His gastrointestinal disorder,' I said, feeling more and more the symptoms of this malady in my own body.

'Exactly. It's the precise mechanics of this experience of his that interested me enough to invest in his excursion. This is what remains so obscure. There is nothing obvious, if I may say, about his Tsalal or its mechanism, yet Grossvogel is making what to my mind are some fascinating claims and distinctions with such overwhelming certitude. But he *is* certainly mistaken, or possibly being devious, on one point at least. I say this because I know that he has not been entirely forthcoming about the hospital where he was treated. In the research pertaining to my *Investigation* I have looked into such places and how they operate. I know for a fact that the hospital where Grossvogel was treated is an extremely rotten institution, an absolutely rotten institution. Everything about it is a sham and a cover-up for the most gruesome goings-on, the true extent of which I'm not sure even those involved with such places realize. It's not a matter of any sort of depravity, so to speak, or of malign intent. There simply develops a sort of ... collusion, a rotten alliance on the part of certain people and places. They are in league with ... well, if only you could read my *Investigation* you would know the sort of nightmare that Grossvogel was faced with in that hospital, a place reeking of nightmares. Only in such a place could Grossvogel have confronted those nightmarish realizations he has discoursed upon in his countless pamphlets and portrayed in his series of Tsalal sculptures, which he says were not the product of his mind or imagination, or his soul or his self, but only the product of what he was seeing with his body and its organs of physical sensation – the shadow, the darkness. The mind and all that, the self and all that, are only a cover-up, only a fabrication, as Grossvogel says. They are that which cannot be seen with the body, which cannot be sensed by any organ of physical sensation. This is because they are actually non-existent cover-ups, masks, disguises for the thing that is activating our bodies in the way Grossvogel explained – activating them and using them for what it needs to thrive upon. They are the work, the artworks in fact, *of the Tsalal itself*. Oh, it's impossible to simply tell you. I wish you could read my *Investigation*. It would have explained everything, it would have revealed everything. But how could you read what was never written in the first place?'

'Never written?' I inquired. 'Why was it never written?'

'Why?' he said, pausing for a moment and grimacing in pain. 'The answer to that is exactly what Grossvogel has been preaching in both his pamphlets and his public appearances. His entire doctrine, if it can even be called that, if there could ever be such a thing in any sense whatever, is based on the non-existence, the imaginary nature of everything we believe ourselves to be. Despite his efforts to express what has happened to him, he must know very well that there are no words that are able to explain such a thing. Words are a total obfuscation of the most basic fact of existence, the very conspiracy against the human race that my treatise might have illuminated. Grossvogel has experienced the essence of this conspiracy first-hand, or at least has claimed to have experienced it. Words are simply a cover-up for this conspiracy. They are the ultimate means for the cover-up, the ultimate artwork of the shadow, the darkness – its ultimate artistic cover-up. Because of the existence of words, we think that there exists a mind, that some kind of soul or self exists. This is just another of the infinite layers of the cover-up. There is no mind that could have written *An Investigation into the Conspiracy against the Human Race* – no mind that could write such a book and no mind that could read such a book. There is no one at all who can say anything about this most basic fact of existence, no one who can betray this reality. And there is no one to whom it could ever be conveyed.'

'That all seems impossible to comprehend,' I objected.

'It just might be, if only there actually were anything to comprehend, or anyone to comprehend it. But there are no such beings.'

'If that's the case,' I said, wincing with abdominal discomfort, 'then who is having this conversation?'

'Who indeed?' he answered. 'Nevertheless, I would like to continue speaking. Even if this is only nonsense and dreams, I feel the need to perpetuate it all. Especially at this moment, when this pain is taking over my mind and my self. Pretty soon none of this will make any difference. No,' he said in a dead voice. 'It doesn't matter now.'

I noticed that he had been staring out the front window of the diner for some time, gazing at the town. Some of the others in the diner were doing the same, dumbstruck at what they saw and agonized, as I was, by the means by which they were seeing it. The vacant scene of the town's empty streets and the desolate season that had presided over the surrounding landscape, that place we had complained was absent of any manifestations of interest when we first arrived there, was undergoing a visible metamorphosis to the eyes of many of us, as though an eclipse were occurring. But what we were now seeing was not a darkness descending from far skies but a shadow which was arising from within the dead town around us, as if a torrent of black blood had begun roaring through its pale body. I realized that I had suddenly and unknowingly joined in the forefront of those who were affected by the changes taking place, even though I literally had no *idea* what was happening, no knowledge that came to my mind, which had ceased to function in the way it had only moments before, leaving my body in a dumb state of agony, its organs of sensation registering the gruesome spectacle of things around me: other bodies eclipsed by the shadow swirling inside their skins, some of them still speaking as though they were persons who possessed a mind and a self, imaginary entities still complaining in human words about the pain they were only beginning to realize, crying out for remedies as they entered the 'nucleus of the abysmal,' and still seeing with their minds even up to the very moment when their minds abandoned them entirely, dissipating like a mirage, able to say only how everything appeared to their minds, how the shapes of the town outside the windows of the diner were turning all crooked and crabbed, reaching out toward them as if with claws and rising up like strange peaks and horns into the sky, no longer pale and gray but swirling with the pervasive shadow, the all-moving darkness that they could finally see so perfectly because now they were seeing with their bodies, only with their bodies pitched into a great black pain. And one voice called out – a voice that both moaned and coughed – that there was a face outside, a 'face across the entire sky,' it said. The sky and town were now both so dark that perhaps only someone preoccupied with the photographic portraiture of the human face could have seen such a thing among that world of churning shadows outside the windows of the diner. Soon after that the words all but ceased, because bodies in true pain do not speak. The very last words I remember were those of a woman who screamed for someone to take her to a hospital. And this was a request which, in the strangest way, had been anticipated by the one who had induced us into making this 'physical-metaphysical excursion' and whose body had already mastered what our bodies were only beginning to learn – the nightmare of a body that is being used and that knows what is using it, making things be what they would not be and do what they would not do. I sensed the presence of a young woman who had worn a uniform as white as gauze. She had returned. And there were others like her who moved among us, and who knew how to minister to our pains in order to effect our metamorphic recovery. We did not need to be brought to their hospital, since the hospital and all its rottenness had been brought to us.

And as much as I would like to say everything that happened to us in the town of Crampton (whose deadness and desolation seem an illusion of paradise after having its hidden life revealed to our eyes) – as much as I would like to say how it was that we were conveyed from that region of the country, that nucleus of nowhere, and returned to our distant homes – as much as I would like to say precisely what assistance and treatments we might have received that delivered us from that place and the pain we experienced there, I cannot say anything about it at all. Because when one is saved from such agony, the most difficult thing in the world is to question the means of salvation: the body does not know or care what takes away its pain and is incapable of questioning these things. For that is what we have become, or what we have all but become – bodies without the illusion of minds or imaginations, bodies without the distractions of souls or selves. None of us among our circle questioned this fact, although we have never spoken of it since our ... recovery. Nor have we spoken of the absence of Grossvogel from our circle, which does not exist in the way it once did, that is to say, as an assemblage of artists and intellectuals. We became the recipients of what someone designated the 'legacy of Grossvogel,' which was more than a metaphorical expression, since the artist had in fact bequeathed to each of us, on the condition of his 'death or disappearance for a stipulated period of time,' a share in the considerable earnings he had amassed from the sales of his works.

But this strictly monetary inheritance was only the beginning of the success that all of us from that abolished circle of artists and intellectuals began to experience, the seed from which we began to grow out of our existence as failed minds and selves into our new lives as highly successful organisms, each in our own field of endeavor. Of course we could not have failed, even if we tried, in attaining whatever end we pursued, since everything we have experienced and created was a phenomenon of the shadow, the darkness which reached outward and reached upward from inside us to claw and poke its way to the heights of a mountainous pile of human and non-human bodies. These are all we have and all we are; these are what is used and thrived upon. I can feel my own body being used and cultivated, the desires and impulses that are pulling it to succeed, that are *tugging* it toward every kind of success. There is no means by which I could ever oppose these desires and impulses, now that I exist solely as a body which seeks only its efficient perpetuation so that it may be thrived upon by what needs it. There is no possibility of my resisting what needs to thrive upon us, no possibility of betraying it in any way. Even if this little account of mine, this little chronicle seems to disclose secrets that might undermine the nightmarish order of things, it does nothing but support and promulgate that order. Nothing can resist or betray this nightmare because nothing exists that might *do* anything, that might *be* anything that could realize a success in that way. The very idea of such a thing is only nonsense and dreams.

There could never be anything written about the 'conspiracy against the human race' because the phenomenon of a conspiracy requires a multiplicity of agents, a division of sides, one of which is undermining the other in some way and the other having an existence that is able to be undermined. But there is no such multiplicity or division, no undermining or resistance or betrayal on either side. What exists is only this *pulling*, this *tugging* upon all of the bodies of this world. But these bodies have a collective existence only in a taxonomic or perhaps a topographical sense and in no way constitute a collective entity, an agency that might be the object of a conspiracy. And a collective entity called the human race cannot exist where there is only a collection of non-entities, of bodies which are themselves only provisional and will be lost one by one, the whole collection of them always approaching nonsense, always dissolving into dreams. There can be no conspiracy in a void, or rather in a black abyss. There can only be this tugging of all these bodies toward that ultimate success which it seems my large-bodied friend realized when he was finally used to the fullest extent, and his body used up, *entirely consumed* by what needed it to thrive.

'There is only one true and final success for the shadow that makes things what they would not be,' Grossvogel proclaimed in the very last of his pamphlets. 'There is only one true and final success for the all-moving blackness that makes things do what they would not do,' he wrote. And these were the very last lines of that last pamphlet. Grossvogel could not explain himself or anything else beyond these inconclusive statements. He had run out of the words that (to quote someone who shall remain as nameless as only a member of the human race can be) are the ultimate artwork of the shadow, the darkness – its ultimate artistic cover-up. Just as he could not resist it as his body was pulled toward that ultimate success, he could not betray it with his words.

It was during the winter following the Crampton excursion that I began fully to see where these last words of Grossvogel were leading. Late one night I stood gazing from a window as the first snow of the season began to fall and become increasingly prolific throughout each dark hour that I observed its progress with my organs of physical sensation. By that time I could see what was inside the falling flakes of snow, just as I could see what was inside all other things, activating them with its force. And what I saw was a black snow falling from a black sky. There was nothing recognizable in that sky – certainly no familiar visage spread out across the night and implanted into it. There was only this blackness above and this blackness below. There was only this consuming, proliferating blackness whose only true and final success was in merely perpetuating itself as successfully as it could in a world where nothing exists that could ever hope to be anything else except what it needs to thrive upon ... until everything is entirely consumed and there is only one thing remaining in all existence and it is an infinite body of blackness activating itself and thriving upon itself with eternal success in the deepest abyss of entity. Grossvogel could not resist or betray it, even if it was an absolute nightmare, the ultimate physical-metaphysical nightmare. He ceased to be a person so that he could remain a successful organism. 'Anyone would do the same,' he said.

And no matter what I say I cannot resist or betray it. No one could do so because there is no one here. There is only this body, this shadow, this darkness.